VISANTHE RISING

First Edition

3 5 7 9 10 8 6 4 2

Saint John's, Antigua
West Indies

ISBN: 979-8-9868910-6-4

Visit the author's website at
https://lmsanguinette.wordpress.com

DEDICATION

To those who've given fate the middle finger and decided
to choose their own path.

VISANTHE RISING

L. M. SANGUINETTE

CONTENTS

YOZORA
OSIIR
MID
CAMP SAAR
ARALDIN FIELDS
RED DESERT

HAIZEA
ILISO
OLE ISLE
SOLIA
IDUNE

INTRODUCTION

THE RULES OF VISANTHE ARE SIMPLE:

1. You either have powers or you don't. There is no way to obtain powers other than through divination, as these powers are a blessing from the divine itself. These powers provide manipulation abilities over the six elements: Earth, Fire, Water, Air, Light, and Blood.

2. The deity, Iturri, is a mischievous being who should be prayed to and feared, and has more often than not been known to provide chaos over protection. Though only a concept in most lands, a long-lost reason for the methods and monotonies of Visanthian life (and its turmoil), much like Fate, Iturri should not be tempted—or trusted.

3. Currency of goods and services is made through coin; currency of promises is made through blood— and nothing good is traded in blood.

4. Visanthian life is lived in accordance with the law of equilibrium (though many have forgotten it). As much good as there is in the world, so too shall there be bad, pain and pleasure, success and suffering. For, even though there too may be light, remember, there is darkness in all of us.

5. In the end, we are all only the stories we tell ourselves, and not even those are entirely true.

PROLOGUE

GENERAL ISAAC TUGGED AT THE IRON CHAINS binding his wrists and ankles to the stone wall behind him. The cold of the granite soothed the welts on his back from the lashing he'd gotten for his dissidence. The dark of the night and the cool mountain air that filtered through a grate in the ceiling came as a blessing. He knew the soldiers who had beaten him had sympathised with his plight, but they couldn't disobey their orders, lest they find themselves in a similar position.

There were dark places in the Harri Territories. This was one of them. More than a prison, it was a torture camp. One that had been out of use for decades. But, considering the recent change of rule, he knew it wouldn't be long before more bodies lined these walls.

General Isaac had lost track of the days since his capture. The routine of his punishment—lashings during the day, nightmares through the night—caused them all to blend into one, though the biting cold would not see him alive much longer if his situation did not improve soon.

On occasion, someone would sneak in to apply salve to his wounds and spoon-feed him a tepid soup. But this was no great mercy. Merely postponement. Someone, it seemed, wanted him alive, but for what purpose, he knew not.

Tonight, however, brought variance to the routine. The sound of heavier footsteps echoed through the cavernous halls beyond his cell. General Isaac raised his head, curious as to who the new, incautious visitor might be. As expected, a different figure strode confidently into the dungeon, the torch in his hand burning a sickly green to match the emotions he provoked. A sinister grin curled on his face as he admired the torture written across General Isaac's bare skin.

"I must say, Isaac, there is a small part of me that pities the sorry sight you have become," said Councilman Dhoot.

General Isaac kept his mouth shut as he glared defiantly at his superior. The newly appointed councilman had taken too quickly to his position, in his opinion. His eyes lacked their previously characteristic dark circles now that he was in a position to sleep in more luxurious quarters, with people to wait on him hand and foot.

Councilman Dhoot let out a hissing laugh as he contemplated General Isaac in the shifting green firelight. "Not in the mood to talk, I see. Perhaps the guards were not hard enough on you. I thought that the sight of your own blood on the floor beneath you might have had an effect. Clearly, the rope was too soft. Maybe a stoning is in order…"

Still, General Isaac said nothing. He was not going to fall for the goading, knowing all too well that it would only mean additional punishment.

Councilman Dhoot sighed. "I tire of you, Isaac. A boulder would offer better conversation. And here, I thought I might make you an offer at escape from this dungeon…"

"I will not help you in your tyrannical quest for power—if that's what you're asking."

"You mistake my motives. I was offering you a chance at glory. I see promise in you, Isaac, but if I am to allow you a place in my new regime, you will need to learn to take orders."

"There is nothing glorious about what you are doing," General Isaac said, attempting to keep the rage building within from shining through his tone.

"Bringing fruitful lands under our domain to offer better lives to our people is not glorious?"

"You only plan to enrich yourself. The impoverished of our lands will see none of it. And that says nothing of the casualties the Ur will surely face."

Councilman Dhoot raised an eyebrow, his brow bone highlighted by the glow of the flames. "And here, it sounds as if you are more indebted to a people not your own. Tsk, tsk, tsk. More reason you should be hanged… but I am yet merciful."

"You can't believe me to be so dense…" General Isaac scoffed through laboured breaths. "You're keeping me alive to use as a scapegoat in the event that your plans do not pan out as expected."

"Well…" Councilman Dhoot brandished another wicked grin, licking his pointed incisors as though priding himself on the perfection of his plan. "It seems that blockish head of yours is filled with something other than your pathetic ideas of justice after all. Little good it will do you. I do not intend to let you out of this cell unless otherwise necessary. Either you will be tried and hanged, or your corpse will rot here indefinitely."

Councilman Dhoot turned confidently on his heels, leaving General Isaac just as he'd found him—or so he might have thought. Fire burned in the green of his eyes. Hope flowed through him once more. No more did his captor hide in the shadows. Now there was a face to attribute to the suffering.

General Isaac waited until the echo of the councilman's footfall faded into nothingness. Only then did he unhitch a laboured breath. He smiled into the darkness.

So… I was right all along…

General Isaac bit down on the laugh forming in his throat. The councilman was just as dense as he'd imagined. His ego had somehow landed itself in the clouds since the promotion. This, General Isaac knew, he could use to his advantage.

Above him, what little moonlight filtered through previously had faded. Clouds blotted out the rest of the lights in the sky. General Isaac cast his gaze upwards, the hairs on his neck and arms rising with a further drop in temperature. His smile widened. The sweet scent of rain quickly followed, along with a rhythmic clap of thunder.

It seems Iturri is on my side, after all, he thought.

The soldiers who had chained him to the dungeon walls had forgotten to chain his feet. An oversight on their part that General Isaac had been waiting to exploit, but not before finding out who was behind the troubles of his land. The incompetent councilman had ousted himself. Under the guise of the storm, Iturri was allowing him to work unheard and unseen. This was the only chance he was going to get at an escape.

He would not waste it.

* * *

An invitation arrived unceremoniously on the doorsteps of each of the ruling houses of Visanthe. This invitation was not only unexpected but very much unwelcome by all. The messengers alone struck fear in the hearts of all those who witnessed them. Even the skies seemed to take a turn for the worse with the arrival of the strange roll of parchment.

Shadows swept through the streets, following the path from each nation's gate to its palace. Upon arrival, the shadows pulled themselves together into eerie, person-like forms—featureless save for beady, red eyes. These figures waited patiently, hands outstretched, holding a single piece of dusty, rolled parchment. They stood through shifts in weather and climates, unmoved and unaffected by the world around them. Not even the various palace guards, with their exceptional training and prowess, could shake the stance of these creatures.

Queen Noor regarded the outstretched hand of the shadow before her with narrowed eyes. Initially thinking it was a living creature, she'd tried freezing its internal organs, but there were none to be found. The shadow was nothing more than a dust shifting in the breeze. Her guards had attempted slashing through it as well, but the figure's body simply dissipated at the point of impact before reforming unscathed. She quickly realised there would be little use in any further attacks on it. Instead, she ordered away her guards and the stragglers of her court and sat a small distance away from it, arms interlaced over her chest, staring into the glowing red of its eyes in challenge.

Various hours passed by, unnoticed and void of action, save for the growing potential for trouble. Queen Noor anticipated dangerous whisperings throughout her kingdom of the arrival of such a creature on their shores, but there was little that could be done to quell the anxieties of her people after the shadow's audacious entrance. Both she and it remained unfazed by the slow traversal of the sun across the sky. Her own shadow followed the shifting light, creeping up to the edges of the intruder in tune with the setting sun.

Still, she waited.

The moon climbed higher and higher into the sky. She could feel the strength of it in the swelling tides around her—strength she would need in the event that this shadow came prepared for a fight. The shadow remained still, statuesque, hand outstretched, holding the roll of parchment. Once night finally descended, and the rest of the shifting shadows of daylight disappeared, Queen Noor rose from her seat.

She drew closer to it, never once breaking eye contact with the creature. Slowly but surely, she reached out for the scroll. Her hand closed gently around the parchment which, unlike the shadow, was entirely stiff and tangible. Noticing the release of the scroll, the eyes of the shadow disappeared. Startled, Queen Noor took a sudden step backwards as the shadow, having now completed its task, dissipated into nothing.

* * *

"I have told you once before, Bismuth, and I will say it again. I will not be king," he said as he stared at the shadowy creature and its outstretched hand.

This same conversation had haunted their interactions ever since the funeral, always in the background, lingering like a sour aftertaste on his tongue. But the appearance of the creature brought the topic front and centre. From his bed in the hospital wing, he'd seen its ominous arrival, watching as the clouds darkened and parted as its shadowy dust swept through the streets of Haizea before pulling itself into the singular, almost human form.

Bismuth shook his head in dismay and stepped towards the shadow. He made a show of attempting to take the roll of parchment from its hand, but the dust comprising the creature flooded over the scroll, making it just as intangible as the creature itself.

"It watches you and you alone," Bismuth said, turning back to him with a frown. "Ever since its arrival, its eyes have been on you, as if knowing—"

"I have sworn to our late king, to Iturri even, that I shall not be king. Have someone else handle this situation," he said, holding firm to the oath sworn to the friend he'd accidentally killed in his youth to never take up the bloodied throne.

"We have had all our guards attempt to vanquish the creature. All with the same results as I." Finally, noticing reason would not sway him, Bismuth signalled for him to step towards the creature and attempt to take the scroll himself.

He let out a heavy sigh, relenting to the old guard's prodding. He hobbled towards it, still lending part of his weight to a cane given to him in his recovery. The beast of a man who had scorched his back with lightning had left him with significant damage to his internals. He was doing his best to keep up his strength, but his nerves still had a ways to go before he would be back in fighting condition. Part of him wondered why he had survived at all, and he knew better than to attribute his continued life to Bismuth's healings alone. Such an attack should have left no room for healing, let alone survival. But he, like Bismuth, had begun to believe in what, for him, was the worst possible outcome—divine intervention.

Brass came face to face with the creature, staring into the glow of its beady red eyes, and finding a part of himself knowing what was about to happen. Before the shadow vanished into thin air, before his fingers closed around the scroll, before he'd even raised his hand…

Staring into the creature's eyes, he knew already what the outcome would be.

Thunder rolled through the sea of clouds above them as a gentle shower began to fall. For him, the rain had always been a symbol of renewal, revival, of better times ahead. But this rain, gentle as it was, felt heavy as it seeped through his robes. A new beginning waited on the horizon, tangling itself with the scent of water on weathered stone, but a soft voice in the back of his mind wondered if it wasn't the beginning of the end.

Brass turned back to Bismuth, scroll in hand, unable to hide the frown that had settled on his face. They exchanged a single, knowing glance; their suspicions having been confirmed at that moment.

"It seems, my king," said Bismuth, "the choice is no longer yours. Iturri has chosen for you."

CHAPTER 1

THE FORGOTTEN GATE

SAVARA LANDED ON THE FOREIGN GROUNDS with an uneasy thud, tumbling instantly to the floor. No matter how many times she travelled by dust, the unsettling sensation of her mind arriving before her body always sent her crumpling to the floor on arrival. It was a sensation she doubted she'd ever shake, and one she'd prefer not to get used to.

Beneath her, grasses had swallowed the remnants of an old stone path. Savara noted the sound of waves crashing against cliffs somewhere behind them. The sky above was an indiscriminate grey, a colour that could've signalled dusk or dawn in monotoned photographs, but which here meant something different entirely. Life was at a standstill. They'd jumped to a land ruled only by the elements, or so it seemed.

She stared up at the moss-covered ruins of a stone gate that looked older than time itself and furrowed her brow.

"Where are we?" she asked once her stomach settled. Her voice barely carried on the savage breeze that carved a path between them and endeavoured to keep her down.

"Welcome to the Arima lands, Queen of the Damned," Alexei replied as he cracked his neck and replaced the stray tendrils of greasy black hair that had freed themselves from their gelled casing. He reached a hand out for her to hold and pull herself up. She eyed it cautiously, remembering the lightning trapped just beneath the black leather.

"That isn't funny," she said as a scowl formed on her face.

"I wasn't trying to be," he replied.

She took hold of the slick, leather glove, hoisting herself off the ground with his help, and dusted herself off. "You're not as charming as you think you are," she added.

"Again, I wasn't trying to be. Get moving. We have a lot of ground to cover."

"Why didn't we just jump to wherever the Prince of Shadows is?"

"You think it's a good idea to drop in on a man who keeps death as a playmate?" he teased, but fear contoured his voice. Savara pursed her lips in reply. "Besides, no one can jump anywhere near the palace. I don't know if it's because of the cage or if the dust just won't take you that far, but if you want to get to this palace, you walk." He took no further pains in waiting for her to understand. He started off in the direction of the jagged mountain range ahead of them, walking slowly enough for her to catch up when she was ready.

Savara wandered over to the source of the crashing waves first—a sheer cliff that gave way to a fierce and deadly ocean. The mist on her skin wasn't welcoming like the salty spray she'd grown up around. This one was cold and cruel, and she knew the ocean it came from was no different. The froth on the breaking waves stretched far beyond her field of vision, past a field of grey clouds that lurked but never neared.

Staring off into the distance, Savara was reminded of the map she'd once seen of Visanthe in Griffin's tent. She hadn't realised it then but the entirety of the Arima lands were marked by whorls of cloud, rather than by depictions of the land itself. Anyone without knowledge of these lands would've simply written off the clouded patch at the top of the map to be a cartographer's design choice instead of something which served a purpose.

Not only a purpose but a warning, she thought.

When she first discovered the existence of the sixth nation, Savara had wrongly assumed that the lack of a drawing came from fear. No one had dared near the lands of the Blood Daemons, hence why none would have ever gotten close enough to depict the actual landmass. Now, she wondered if they had been barred entry by these storm clouds. Both seemed to be valid reasons, and Savara knew the truth lay somewhere in the middle.

A chill rushed over her shoulders as the next wave broke, the splash reaching high above her head and falling away with an unfriendly roar. It was time to go. Right now, nothing mattered beyond the whorl of clouds. Her future was waiting at the end of the swallowed-up cobblestone path—whatever that future was.

Savara sprinted after Alexei, who leaned up against one of the strange rocks that lined the trail. Upon closer inspection, she realised it bore an eerie resemblance to a dated tombstone.

"Don't get too caught up yet, there's a lot more sightseeing to do, and I can assure you that's nothing compared to what awaits," he said.

"I'm not the biggest fan of dead things…"

A wicked smirk graced his face. "Afraid, princess?"

The sound of the word from his lips sent shivers down her spine and, unlike when Amon said it, they weren't the good kind. "That's none of your business…"

"I have a feeling you'll settle as soon as we get there."

"You make it sound as though we were standing in a paradise rather than a forgotten wilderness," she called over the wind. The hairs on her arms stood on end the nearer she got to him. It wasn't long before she realised that the sensation came from further along the path. Something strong waiting out of sight, beckoning her the way her uncle's library once had in the home that she'd begun to forget.

"Any land would suffer if its spirit were caged. Any creature, too, for that matter."

"Caged?" It was the second time he'd used that word, but Savara had yet to see something that bore the resemblance to a cage.

"This was once the most beautiful of the six nations, or so legends say. Only two people alive today might be able to confirm that. You can ask about it when we get there. Now, stop asking questions and walk up."

"I want to know what you mean by cage."

"Princess, I told you, I was only hired to deliver you to him, and I don't do anything for free."

"What will it take?"

Alexei halted his stride abruptly. "For what?" he asked, turning back to her with a raised brow as intrigue laced his voice.

"For you to explain."

"Nothing you can yet offer."

Savara gulped, tentatively preparing herself to agree to yet another one of those deals Griffin had made explicitly clear not to make. "Try me."

"Hmm…" His burning blue eyes traced up and down her person in contemplation. "There might be something."

The sharp hiss of his voice made the hairs on the back of her neck stand up. "Go on…"

Alexei drew himself in close, intimately so. She smelled the lingering hit of spiced tobacco on his breath as he bent down to whisper in her ear. "I want your life."

Savara shoved him away and rubbed at the goosebumps on her arm. "Not a chance."

Alexei chuckled in a way that should've been disarming but only made her question him more. "Hear me out," he began. From within his coat, he drew a knife. Compared to the one Amon brandished, this one was nothing special. A simple blade with a leatherbound hilt, one she imagined protected the blade from the currents in his fingers. "I want to strike a deal. A soulbond. You cannot kill me; I cannot kill you. Entangle our lives from this moment onwards."

"The last soulbond I made almost killed me."

"The last soulbond you made was struck with a man whose intent was never to keep you alive. The intent behind the bond is almost as important, if not more so, than the bond itself. His bond was made to death, and a bond like that is poisonous to the soul. What he realised too late was that the poison flowed both ways."

The explanation resonated deep within her soul, but that didn't stop the concerns she had from bubbling up. Alexei had proven himself yet one of the most dangerous people in Visanthe and potentially the most unhinged. Would his intent be any less toxic to the both of them?

"What would make our bond any different?" she asked, trying to make sense of his reasoning.

"I am asking for life. I am asking that you bind your soul to the mutual inability to kill one another in exchange for your explanations."

Savara furrowed her brow. "Why?"

"I believe I am being more than generous with my offer. I have even considered your own protection. I wouldn't be able to kill you."

"Yes, but I've learned that people here find loopholes in everything."

"That may be true, but not in this case. No loopholes, no side deals," he clarified. "For your sake as much as mine."

"Hmm…" Savara bit her lip. As much as she hated to admit it, as terrible as he was, Alexei was the only person who ever told her the truth when asked, with no qualms or complaints. She knew he wasn't hiding anything from her, but she didn't trust his motives that much either. And the price he charged was steep, much steeper than she'd imagined.

"Besides, if anyone should fear losing their life after all they've done, it's me."

Savara contemplated his words with a frown. If he'd intended for them to ease her worries, he'd failed miserably. Still, there was some solace to be found in the fact that he couldn't kill her. Eventually, she relented. "Why my life?"

Alexei grinned. "Because, Queen of the Damned—"

"Stop saying that," she hissed.

"Your life is intertwined with spirit itself. If anyone could make a deal with death and come out of it unscathed, it would be you."

She raised an eyebrow. "Are you saying it has never been done?"

He leaned up against another curious tombstone-shaped rock and crossed his arms over his torso, taking too many pains to avoid her gaze. He picked at specks of dust on his gloves, trying to seem casual about the situation, as if he'd asked something as simple as to borrow a pen rather than entangle their souls. "I'm saying it hasn't been successfully tried."

"And what would happen if it didn't work? If we weren't successful?"

"Let's try not to think of that."

Savara let out an angry huff. The human part of her wanted to run, from the deal, from him, from these strange, stagnant lands… It trembled at the thought of binding her entire existence to another—especially him. But the thing inside her that felt connected somehow to the promise of blood and bonds prodded at her in a voice not entirely her own. It asked that she do it, that she agree. Considering it had been the only thing to save her from Big Tog, Savara knew she should follow its guidance. She hoped it knew something she didn't.

"Fine," she relented.

Alexei's charade of nonchalance faded just as quickly as it had appeared. He cast his gaze towards her as a sly grin reappeared at his mouth. He twirled the dagger between his leatherbound fingers as he pushed off the wall, stalking towards her until he was but inches from her face. "Lift your hair," he whispered as his shocking blue eyes burned their way into the back of her mind.

"Why?" Savara asked, leaning her head away from him in her discomfort.

"In a practical sense, it's better that the bond is hidden. In a personal sense, I'm not going to leave you something you'll wake up to every morning and hate."

"How thoughtful," Savara grumbled as she exposed her ear beneath the waves of dark hair.

"It's class, princess," Alexei replied as he carved a thin line down the outer side of his left ear before moving on to hers. His touch was gentle, delicate, as he slid the blade down the fleshy part of her outer ear. It was a lover's touch, but he was no lover. Neither lover nor saint, though, to his credit, he'd never pretended to be, either.

Savara felt the warm blood trickle down her neck and onto her collarbone. Remembering just how much ears bleed, she wondered if he didn't choose to carve at them out of some gruesome desire to see pools of blood.

"Don't heal it. Repeat after me," he began. "I, Princess Savara, Harbinger of Death…"

Savara's intestines bunched themselves together. She hadn't liked the title when she'd first heard it from the Prince of Shadows, and she didn't like hearing it now, especially not coming from his voice. "I, Savara, Harbinger of Death…"

"Bind my soul, under the eyes of Iturri, to Alexei, son of Najma and Ivoire, and in doing so ensure my soul be not the cause of his death, nor his soul the cause of mine, in spite of pain or penalty. By my hand or power, he shall not die, nor I by his."

"Pain or penalty?"

"Safety clause, it's for your benefit as much as it is mine."

"Fine." Savara repeated the phrase he'd given her as he stripped off one of his gloves. The lightning danced over his fingers as it had in the Palace of Winds. He gathered it into a small charge in the middle of his palms. As she finished, he let it strike the blade, burning their collected blood on the edges of the knife.

At first, nothing happened. Then, a soft voice somewhere in the back of her mind sounded.

Do you accept? it said. When she didn't instantly respond, it repeated the question, the words growing in strength as though being fuelled by the morbid deal. *Do you accept?*

"Yes," she replied aloud. Suddenly, Savara felt a sharp pain where he'd made the slit before noting a heaviness gathering along the side of her ear. She brought her fingers up to meet the familiar sensation of crystals sprouting from flesh. Alexei mirrored her movement. She could see a trail of rubies along the side of his ear and knew she bore a matching set.

"How do we know if it…" but before she could get the full sentence out, he turned his hand on her and fired a streak of lightning directly at her chest. Her skin recoiled, tightening as though it were being seared. The force of the blow sent her clattering to the ground. Her eyes closed softly under the fading light wary skies.

CHAPTER 2

INCLINATIONS OF INTIMACY

"YOU'LL HAVE TO TELL HIM AT SOME POINT," Lucy chided. Her bouncy white curls were tied back, revealing sparkling blue eyes fraught with the concern reserved only for friends in deep trouble. "He has a right to know."

Storm lifted her head from the wash pail briefly and wiped her lips. The colour had almost entirely drained from her face, the contrast heightened by the vibrance of her red locks. "Not now," she groaned. "I can't tell him now. Not in the middle of this."

Storm had a hard time keeping anything down these days, least of all her fears. For some reason, being in this weakened state caused her mind to do strange things. Whisperings of her past crept back in. Feelings of not being enough plagued her. This time, however, they were not in her father's voice, but in a child's.

The ship had been docked for the last few days since they'd arrived in Yozora. She had no good explanation—or rather excuse—for the nausea. Except for the truth. Thankfully, the boys were oblivious, or else concerned with other matters. They hadn't spared more than a passing thought to her occasional sickness.

But Lucy was no fool. She'd pieced it together almost instantly.

"He's not as dense as you think he is. At some point, he'll figure it out," Lucy replied as she stroked Storm's back through the next wave.

Lucy was right, of course. Storm knew Sebas wouldn't believe the "seasickness" ruse forever. But how could she tell him now, when their happiness had only just begun?

"Simon is making me tonics."

"The brother? Does he know?" Lucy prodded.

"I think he suspected it after I told him his strongest seasickness tonic was useless," Storm admitted, a guilty blush creeping into her cheeks. "Since then, he altered the formula…"

Lucy raised a brow. "It still doesn't seem to be working…"

"Trust me, it is," Storm replied before another wave of nausea ripped through her.

"You should at least tell Griffin. He'd never put you out there if—"

"No!" Storm barked, regretting the raised tone of her voice almost instantly in case someone came running. She leaned back against the wall, closing her eyes as she rested her head against the old wood. She inhaled deeply, allowing the salty scent of the sea to fill her nose and occupy her thoughts, in place of the sharp taste of acid in her mouth. "No..." she whispered in her next exhale, "Griffin can't know. You guys need me out there."

"Anika, we'll be fine. You can't jeopardise your future."

"Lucy..." She opened her eyes, hoping their silver glow shone with the same ferocity that she felt in her heart. "He. Needs. Me." Each word, punctuated with the depth of her concern, highlighted the fear only an emotion as strong as love could bring. There would be no swaying her. She needed Lucy to understand this above all else. She would not let him go into battle without her. She never had, not since the day they met, and she never would, not 'til the day they set the ashes of her burned corpse to the winds.

Lucy shook her head as she sighed, the many spangly metals adorning her person clinking with the movement. "At some point, someone is going to notice."

"That some point is still a ways away," Storm replied, glancing momentarily down at her stomach. There were still no visible signs of her ailment. She still had time to pretend it was just a passing thing.

"Let's hope we make it 'til then..." concluded Lucy.

Storm knew her friend had already chosen the flight side of her basal instincts and she would never judge her for her choices. But whether good or bad, Storm had spent too much of her childhood cowering to go back. She had a fighter's spirit and would continue to fight—extenuating circumstances be damned.

She pressed her hands against the wall and made to stand, struggling against the crippling nausea, all the while convincing herself she would make it 'til then. Resolve burned in the pit of her stomach.

Lucy must have seen a sliver of it in her eyes, acknowledging her strength with a singular nod. Together, they strode onto the deck, a prodding silence lingering between them. Neither wished to continue the conversation about eventualities that were still a war away. Eventually was a time so far off in the future that it seemed like a luxury to think of—one not yet afforded to them.

In the meantime, the present was pounding at her door— and her internals. A fight was brewing that they could not lose, for it would cost them more than their lives. It would cost the world. They would all make it, Storm tried to convince herself, but the reality of the situation made such outcomes seem tentative at best. All she had left was hope, something which, before Sebas, had only ever been a fancy word for nothing.

And so, they would all make it, she hoped. They had to…

CHAPTER 3

FOREIGN ISLES

FOR A SECOND, THERE WAS NOTHING. Empty space where there should've been a world, a life, or even something more. But instead, there was nothing. It was a void. Not nearly as terrifying as she'd imagined it to be, nor as exciting as she might have hoped.

It was a void, and nothing more.

Savara pulled herself together as best she could, feeling as though pieces of her soul had been set adrift, carried off by horsemen in opposing directions, leaving behind only a base. A shell. A hole to be filled. It was a sensation that might have even felt liberating to some but, in her current state of consciousness, was concerning at best.

The act of grounding herself was slow and cumbersome. Despite the natural urge to breathe, no air left her lips, no pull came from her lungs. Similarly, the unconscious habit of blinking disappeared along with it. She was simply there, existing—if one could call it such. A sensation of want bubbled from deep within the remnants of her soul. It searched for something to latch on to. Something that would anchor it to whatever had come before and whatever would come next.

A want to know, to truly feel. Not just to imagine.

A tree appeared first, floating at a distance time could not comprehend. At the thought of it, feet she could not feel beneath her carried whatever form she now held towards it. At least it was a start. Then, hands appeared before her, or at least the vaguest inclination of them, glowing within this void. They moved on her command, though—similarly to the feet—she could not sense them. They were mostly hers, but in truth, she didn't quite feel herself at all. As she contemplated them, the tree drew nearer. Whether it was the result of her walking or its own movements she could not say, but sure enough, it soon came within reach.

The time-marked trunk of the tree glowed before her, traced by grooves and knots that could've been words to knowing eyes. Hers, she knew, were not. The marks wove around the tree trunk in streams, carving paths through the bark. She followed these grooves from the base of its roots to the tips of its branches, finding the entirety of the tree both within her grasp and all the while untouchable.

What is this? Savara thought, finding the words amplified through the void.

It was then she realised that this place, wherever it was— whatever it was—didn't play by the rules of the five senses.

It wasn't the world she'd left behind, nor was it a new one entirely. It felt like a place between worlds rather than a destination. A gap in space, one no map could place.

Suddenly, her eyes caught on a figure lingering beyond the ethereal glow of the tree. Unlike the tree, or her hands, this figure had a clear, crisp outline. The rest of it was shadow, darker than the blackness of the void. It watched her—a face with no eyes, no mouth, no nose. It was a figure, nothing more than the outline of a person of indiscriminate gender.

And it watched her, intently.

"Hello?" Savara called out to it, hoping her acknowledgement would ease the eerie sensation drifting in the void around her.

The figure stalked out from behind the tree, tilting its head as if in contemplation. After a moment, its voice rang out through the void. "You shouldn't be here."

"What?" she asked.

"It's not your time," came the reply. The voice had a depth and timelessness to it that belonged to no world, much like the creature itself.

Before she knew it, the figure snapped its fingers. Everything shifted once more. This strange new world, and its curious inhabitant, vanished before her eyes. And then, so did she.

* * *

Savara woke with a sharp pain in her chest to find Alexei hovering over her, a look of concern plastered across his face. She blinked, noticing how he strained against a relieved smile that wanted to grow at his lips. When she blinked again, the smile was gone. Savara wondered whether she'd imagined it. This was Alexei, after all. She doubted whether he could feel those emotions at all.

"What happened!?" she screamed.

"You *almost* died."

"You almost killed me!"

"Yes, but not quite. It should've killed you, yet here you are, alive and well and mostly unharmed. Hence, *almost-death*."

"You're a psychopath," Savara hissed as she pushed herself to stand.

She scanned the length of her person. To her great surprise, he was right. There were no lingering ill effects to speak of, save for a burn mark she knew she'd be able to heal on her own. The things she'd seen in her state of limbo had also faded from memory. If he were to be believed, she'd somehow cheated death, but something in the mortal part of her said that cheating death was not something to be celebrated.

On the contrary, it felt more dangerous than anything.

"How is this possible?" she asked, staring down at the scorched part of her dress and the burn peeking through.

Savara tapped the singed skin, wincing at the pain beneath her fingers. She covered the burn with her hand and allowed the same healing energy from her powers to stitch it back together as she listened to Alexei's warped explanation.

"It isn't entirely possible. In some way or another, we will have to face these deaths, just not now," he said, unfazed by the murder glinting in her eyes.

"Are you saying I'll have to get electrocuted at some point and die for real!?" she yelled. He was lucky she didn't believe in retribution—otherwise, she'd have forced the blood from his body and left him a shrivelled corpse.

"Maybe," he replied all too casually.

Irritation surged through her. Savara clenched a fist and let it fly towards his jaw, hoping the force of the blow would wipe the arrogance from his face…and leave a decent mark in the process.

"Why did you do it then?" she hissed, stroking at the pain blooming over her knuckles.

Alexei staggered backwards upon impact, having been caught off-guard by her outburst. He stroked the afflicted part of his jaw as he spoke. "To make sure it would work." He fixed his hair back into place and tugged at the leather on his gloves, trying to regain his composure. "If it makes you feel better, you can stab me."

Savara narrowed her eyes at him. If the lightning hadn't worked on her, she doubted a little steel would work on him. "I just might if I could be sure I'd find a corpse at the end of the blade," she growled, already regretting their bond.

"And they say *I'm* gruesome." A wild spark glinted in his eyes. Savara almost wondered if he hadn't had his own plans for her, had he not been hired by the Prince of Shadows.

Everything about Alexei scared her. Even now, she could picture his attacks on both Brass and Amon. He'd done so without so much as batting an eyelash. He was a creature without remorse, vain, arrogant, and as he so aptly put it, untethered. He was an eager match looking for the next forest to burn down.

Still, she needed him, for now, to get her safely to where she was going—although, after his little game, she realised the word *safely* seemed to come with liberties.

"Fine." Savara laced her arms over her chest and let out a resigned huff. "Does this bond mean we cannot die?"

"No," he replied. "Any number of things can still kill you. But, for now, I'm not one of them."

"For now?"

"Let it go, princess," he scoffed. Irritation rippled off him, though she could tell there was something almost like relief in the way he spoke. She knew, however, that pressing the issue would earn her another strike—now that they were sure it wouldn't kill her—but neither of them had the time to wait for her to dip off to…wherever that place was…and return. "Let's get going. We have a fair bit of ground to cover."

Alexei started down the path again without waiting to see her follow. A frigid wind whipped around him, dislodging his hair as he walked. His grand strides would not be deterred. Savara wondered why he was so eager to get her there. He looked like a man with an agenda—and not one entirely dependent on payment.

Savara turned back briefly to the cliff at the other end of the path, expecting to see only the whorl of clouds. As another wave broke high and splattered the cliffside, from inside the spray, she thought she spied a form, a figure like the one from her *almost-death*. It looked like little more than a shadow, but something about it gnawed at her bones. As the spray receded once more, the shadow disappeared with it, leaving a new sense of uncertainty in the pit of her stomach.

She cast a furtive glance around the rest of the barren landscape, fearing they were not as alone as Alexei had made it seem. Noticing how far he'd gotten, Savara scurried along the path, rushing to catch up with him. As much as she disliked him, if there was anything roaming around these abandoned lands, she knew she'd be safer with him than without—especially now that he could not kill her.

"Hold on a second!" she called, but Alexei made little effort to calm his stride. She scoffed, cursing him under her breath as she pursued him. "You promised to explain everything."

"And?" he asked, his voice no more than a whisper on the howling wind.

"You lied."

Alexei halted abruptly, body stiff as an icicle and shoulders tense at the insinuation.

Uh oh, she thought, wondering which nerve she'd hit with her comments but knowing there would be consequences. Savara stopped her chase, keeping a safe distance between them as she waited for his reaction.

"Do you want to repeat what you said?"

"You promised to explain…" she replied, her voice trailing off the closer he got.

Alexei stalked towards her, no amusement in his expression, closing her safety gap until his face hovered above hers. His eyes narrowed as they glared down at her at the end of his pointed nose. The tips of his hair raised, lifted by a static that seemed to come from a suppressed bolt of lightning. "Don't mock me, princess. I told you, I never lie," he growled. "Try asking something first before you get so testy."

"I—"

"Because," he continued, raising his chin higher, "if we are testing powers, between the two of us, I'm the only one who has studied. Are we clear?"

Pride glinted like knifepoints in his eyes as he gazed down at her. The sharpness of his cheek bones and the dimness of the starlight above them made him look more skeleton than man. Savara retreated a step and nodded. The annoyance in his glare was more than a warning. It was unhinged violence, waiting to be let loose. Even if he couldn't kill her, another jab at his pride would bring her suffering, and it wasn't worth picking a fight with a loose cannon like him.

"As crystal." She cleared her throat, ignoring the goosebumps that rose on her arms and neck.

Alexei stretched his gloved fingers at his sides as his eyes consumed her. "So… What questions do you have burning inside, princess?"

Savara swallowed hard at her fear. "What did you mean earlier when you said this land was caged?"

The feral side of him that she'd seen in the Palace of Winds had returned, looking for a way to toy with her as it had with Amon. "Careful, questions like that might wake monsters you can't even begin to imagine."

Savara knew she couldn't let his mind games get the best of her. If he wanted to play, it was time she learned to as well. "Wasn't it you who said I was Queen of the Damned? What would I care about monsters that couldn't hold a candle to me?"

A vicious smile broke across his face. He bowed his head, acknowledging her play as though he too had been waiting for their game.

"The rulers of Visanthe are bound to their lands and vice versa. They have the purest form of power that their land has to offer. I'm sure you've felt it—the wicked and wild energy that emanates from those whom Iturri has deemed worthy of a crown…" He reached a leather-gloved hand up to her cheek, stopping just shy of touch. He closed his hand into a fist, grasping at the air beside her flustered face before dropping it to his side. "They are a testament to the sheer force of the elements. Their powers run deeper than what a pathetic little ring could ever hope to offer…"

It was true. Savara had experienced such overwhelming ripples of power on multiple occasions, and from multiple sources—the king of Haizea and the beasts of his forests, Ori and his refuge in Idune, and of course, the Prince of Shadows himself. Their powers were almost suffocating in aura alone. And displays of them were akin to natural disasters.

Her own powers were something of the same nature—if she were to believe the stories. It hadn't occurred to her before, but perhaps the people around her sensed that wild and wicked energy from her presence as well. Perhaps that's why they had feared her…

And why so many still did.

"They claim it was punishment… For a misdeed committed well before our time. I doubt anyone alive today knows the true reason behind it…" Alexei continued, his voice lowering as though trying not to be overheard. "The people of these lands were exiled, and a hold was placed on the grounds themselves so that nothing born of this soil would ever leave… But nothing in this dark world is as simple as it seems. You can't just execute the keeper of souls, least of all without repercussions…"

The story of this world is one of repercussions, she thought as another wave of shivers descended through her body.

"This became a place outside of our realm. As did its leader. Though intangible, the bars of this cage were made to be unbreakable and everlasting. And to add insult to injury, they were made with the same powers they set out to restrict."

"But if this land was as inaccessible as you claimed, how are we here now?" Savara asked, her brow furrowing as she tried to follow the story. Not just them, she realised. Amon had gotten through somehow as well. There was something missing. Legend and hearsay alone were not enough to explain how the cage had fallen upon these lands, or how they had escaped its grasp.

"All I know is that, ever since you came into this world, things have been…unstable. Maybe Iturri is pulling strings in your favour," he said with a shrug. "It is, after all, a wicked puppet master with eternity on its hands if nothing else…" Alexei straightened his coat and cricked his neck. "Satisfied, Your Highness?"

"Not nearly…" she mumbled, but her words were masked by a sudden howling of the winds.

Channelled down by the mountainous rocks that lined the path, they curved between her and Alexei, as if they too had been listening in on the conversation and wished to take part. A stray bluster whipped the loose waves of hair into her eyes. Savara turned from him, facing instead the barren, stagnated landscape. As she batted the strands of hair from her eyes, she noticed the lands behind them looked different somehow. Nothing but her perception had changed, but the curious tale he'd spun had filtered its way into her vision. His words rang true, yet, something inside her made it clear that things were not quite as he'd described. Not quite as dead as he made them out to be.

At the end of the cliff, Savara spied the same shadow from before, mimicking its earlier contemplation of her. This time, it was visible regardless of the breaking waves. Though she still couldn't make out a face, its watchful gaze still burned on her skin.

She blinked, wondering if it wasn't a trick of the eye. The shadow didn't fade. She blinked again to confirm, but the creature held firm to its post on the cliffside. Its gaze fixed on her and her alone.

"Princess, we don't have time for your zoning out," Alexei said, breaking the trance-like connection between her and the shadow.

"Are you sure there are no other living creatures here?" she asked, ignoring his comment.

The question seemed to have caught him off-guard, a look of confusion plastered across his face. "Just us and the Prince of Shadows, and if we're being honest, I wouldn't quite classify him as alive…" He furrowed his brow, casting a glance between her and the cliffside. "Why do you ask?"

Savara made to speak when the words caught in her throat.

If he'd seen it, he would've reacted differently, she thought. *Maybe it's all in my head.*

"No reason… I just thought I saw something over by the cliff," she replied.

Alexei pursed his lips. "There's nothing there. Now, stop with the delays. You're on my time, remember? I have a life to get back to."

As Alexei's footsteps echoed down the path behind her, Savara remained rooted to the spot, her eyes drawn once more to the cliffside. Though she knew he grew further and further away, her feet refused to move. She couldn't tear her gaze away from the shadowy silhouette standing guard at the edge of the land. Nor could she shake the feeling that it was watching her. It radiated a sense of patience, as if only biding its time. As though it held some untold secret, waiting in all its omniscience to reveal it.

Despite Alexei's insistence of there being no other living creatures in this desolate place, Savara couldn't ignore the undeniable presence glaring at her from afar. Both ominous and mesmerising, it shone like a black knight through the misty white break of the waves beyond.

The wind whipped around her, carrying with it a sense of foreboding that carved its way beneath her skin.

Savara took a tentative step backwards, curiosity and apprehension flowing through her veins. There was something off about its presence here. She didn't know how she knew this, but something in her gut told her that this creature—whatever it was—was not born of these lands.

Nor did it belong here. She kept her eyes fixed on it, heartbeat ringing in her ears and fearing an attack. But the creature was still, not even shifting with the movement of breath. Savara took another step backwards—and another—allowing the figure to shrink as the distance between them grew.

The creature made no move to follow.

Soon, she relented to its stillness, knowing it was time to go, though its presence lingered in her mind like a haunting melody. Alexei was already a decent way down the path, and the biting cold had seeped its way through the fabric of her dress. Reluctantly, Savara tore her gaze away from the creature and ran after him. Her pulse quickened with each step, her mind racing with questions and uncertainties. What was this creature, and what did it want with her?

CHAPTER 4

FAMILIAL RIVALRIES

AS THE EMPTY SKY GREW DARKER and the sinister shadows of the barren lands began reaching out towards them, Savara felt an unmistakable twinge of fear creeping into her heart. It reminded her of Amon—or, better said, his absence. She used to find comfort in knowing his protection extended into the dark. Somehow, even worlds away, he had always found her. He had always come for her. But after what had happened between them, she doubted he would this time, nor did she want him to.

Things had changed, but her fears had not.

The loneliness ate at her now, highlighted by the howling winds and barren grounds. And then, of course, there were the thoughts of the strange creature at the edge of the cliffside. She knew better than to bother Alexei with such worries, considering how little compassion he'd shown her on every other occasion, but she needed something to keep her mind occupied. He'd pulled her away from the people she cared for most in the world with the promise of answers. She had no intention of letting him get away with only silence.

"What's your problem with him?" she asked, her mind having wandered to her time with Amon as a means of avoiding the darker thoughts.

"Who?" Alexei asked, his voice sounding almost affronted by her words.

"Amon. Back in the Zerua lands, you called him *cousin*," she began, remembering the scene with ease. Alexei had taken much pleasure in retrieving her from the Palace of Winds—and more specifically from him. But why?

"You can ask anything in the world, princess. Anything at all. And you ask about him?" Alexei grumbled in response. "What did he do to you?"

"Nothing," she hissed, but the sharpness of her tone must have intrigued him. He raised a curious brow as if meaning to pry. "It's not like I want to think about him," she added before he could comment. "I'd rather think of anything but him right now. He's a liar, a manipulator, a murderer…"

Savara clenched her fists. Amon was everything she'd said and more. He'd played her as well as any game. She'd fallen for his ruse without so much as a second thought. She'd even stood up for him when Brass had tried to warn her about his deceptions. But Brass had been right all along. If she ever saw Amon again, she'd use her powers on him in the way they were meant to be used.

As if sensing the back and forth in her head, Alexei let out a smirk, which only annoyed her further.

Savara took a steadying breath to regain her composure. "But..." she continued, "I'm curious as to why, if you are related, you took so much pleasure in leaving him there to die. Why is there such animosity between you two?"

The question seemed to remove the thought of taunting her from his mind, replacing it with something that looked a lot like bitterness. "Didn't your mother ever tell you not to meddle in familial rivalries?"

"No..." Her eyes darkened as she glared at him. "Probably one of the lessons she had pending before she died."

A shadow passed over his face, a fleeting moment of vulnerability that he quickly masked with his usual stoicism. "You're not missing out on much..." he replied tersely.

If Savara hadn't thought him heartless and cruel, she might have thought the words had left an unpleasant taste on his tongue. But Alexei wasn't capable of things like remorse or even sympathy. Was he?

"If you must know, Amon was annoyingly perfect. Destined for greatness," he said mockingly. "Loved by all from the minute he arrived in this world—well..." he paused, seemingly reconsidering his words. "Regardless, he never wanted for anything. His boredom and apathy at a life so many could only dream of was just...infuriating..." he trailed off. The last part sounded as though it had caught even him off guard, the words coming from a wound deep inside. "He was the chosen child. I was the monster that followed. The lesser being. Neglected, by everyone…except him…" He let a silence fall between them, echoing with unspoken resentment. The wounds of familial neglect, long suppressed but never truly healed, appeared in the lines of his face. "When my powers surfaced, there was no room for further doubt about my nature. A simple touch from me could send anyone to their grave. They all said it. Only a monster would harbour such abilities."

"Is that why you hate him?" Savara asked softly, careful not to trigger the layers of unhealed traumas she sensed lurking beneath his skin. "You resent the attention?"

"I'm not so ridiculous, princess. I don't need the attention of others…"

"That's not the impression you give off."

He glowered at her briefly before continuing. "He was my only friend, although it might have been out of some strange sense of familial duty. He kept me close enough, acknowledged me at very least. But then, he left. No warning, no explanation. Just gone." Alexei gazed around at the darkening winding path before them and whispered, "Only later did I find out why, but by then, we'd already made our beds."

"The Prince of Shadows?"

Alexei nodded curtly, cautious if there was something else in the darkness listening in. "Amon had promised never to abandon us… I doubt he would've done it for anyone else." A heavy sigh escaped him as he continued. "Since then, I vowed not to let anyone get too close again. I sought solace in transactions. The give-and-take. Contract and payment. No binding ties, no emotional investment." He straightened himself as he clarified his point, as though taking pride in his decisions. "And I have never regretted it. Not once. Not now, nor will I ever in some indeterminate future. Happy?"

Savara frowned as she contemplated him, the man she too had branded a monster, finding part of her own hurt and heartache resonating with his story. She saw, for the first time, the walls around him crack, giving her a glimpse into the inner turmoil that had paved the way to his becoming the man before her. Not so much monster as misguided. Cruel to a world that had shown him nothing but cruelty, and resentful of the abandonment shown to him by his only friend.

"I'm sorry..." she whispered.

"I didn't ask for your pity."

Before he could finish his sentence, Savara reached out and embraced him. Alexei stiffened in her arms, but Savara didn't let up.

"What are you doing?" he stuttered.

"You forget you can't kill me anymore," she replied, squeezing him tighter.

"Doesn't mean I accept unsolicited acts of sympathy either," he growled. "This is ridiculous, princess," he continued, but she maintained her speechless embrace. "I... Ugh..." Another moment passed between them before his muscles finally eased up. "Come on. You still have more questions to ask, and we aren't getting any closer to the palace." He patted her head awkwardly before shrugging her off.

"Fine," she said, biting down on her amusement. She knew there was a new bond forming between them. A bond not born of blood, but rather an understanding of their mutually traumatic circumstances. Misery truly did love company, it seemed. When she released him this time, she found his stride less aggressive and easier to follow. "You're right. I do have another question for you."

"Let's hear it."

"Tell me about the Prince of Shadows," she ventured, choosing her words carefully. "How did he become entwined with the Arima lands? Why is he trapped here?"

Alexei's eyes flickered with a mixture of caution and reluctance. "As far as I understand, he is a ferry to the souls, appointed by Iturri itself. For whatever he did centuries ago, he was stripped of the parts of him that allowed him to live in the realm that we do—his body, his heart—and also of the things that made him a king. His people. But as a ferry of souls, he alone could not fully die. He was inadvertently cursed to be little more than an apparition, roaming the lands he called his own, his powers preventing him from attaining that one respite we all have from life. Because Iturri had not chosen another to rule in his stead, life here ground to a halt. As a result of having a king who cannot die, the lands stagnated…"

"But that can't be true…" she interjected. "He appeared before me in Idune."

"There are rituals in Visanthe darker even than binding souls, Savara," he replied, his voice laced with warning. "Somehow, he attached himself to my idiot cousin's body, using it as a host until he was able to regain his own."

"How?"

Alexei shrugged. "The grounds of Idune are intimately

connected with the basal energies of the body. He could've used its soil to regain the body that was taken from him. Think of the soil as a vessel for his spirit."

"Which would make him a man made of clay?" She considered this, remembering the way the Prince of Shadows had appeared, rising from the sanctuary ground in a plume of dust. To add further weight to the idea, he hadn't bled when he'd made the soulbond with her. If he was a man made of clay and his body was all dust, then there might not have been any blood to bleed. The more she thought about it, the more she began to consider that the idea was not so fantastical after all.

"He's not whole. He exists in this liminal space, caught between worlds," Alexei added, confirming her line of thought. "That's why he needed Amon to collect the stones for him, so that he might regain the parts of himself that had been taken."

"A place between worlds?" she asked, her voice barely audible over the howling of the winds. Savara was reminded immediately of the place she'd visited after her encounter with death.

Alexei nodded, casting a furtive glance around them. "I've only heard stories. From what I understand, it's like a veil cast over our world. It's a world that isn't quite there enough to be a place of its own, but still real enough to affect ours."

Apprehension rippled in the air around him. Being here, in the land of spirits, seemed to amplify whatever torment lay within his mind. This nervous energy made it clear he had a personal connection to this world-between-worlds. Judging by the energy alone, this connection of his must have been something important. Something painful. But how deep did it run? And what did he mean when he said it still affected this world? Savara wondered why the mention of it alone would set him so on edge.

"But you have more to be worried about than such a place," he added, quickly regaining his composure. "You forget who we are walking towards…"

"You're the one leaving me here," she scoffed.

"A job is a job, princess. End of discussion."

But it wasn't.

Not for her.

She still didn't understand the intricacies of his wild mind, or how he knew of all these supposed secrets that the rest of the world had forgotten, or the reason she was being summoned.

"Why you?" she prodded. "Why not have his little *apprentice* bring me?" The word came out with greater bitterness than she'd intended. "Or why not fetch me himself?"

"I'm sure he would've loved to, but there were other things that needed taking care of… And my pathetic excuse for a familiar is no longer under his employ. Like I said back at the palace, most of his bonds should be broken now. He's only missing the final three stones: those of the Arima, the Izar, and the final stone which, as of yet, no one can even confirm exists."

It must, Savara thought to herself. Nothing the Prince of Shadows does is without reason, and he seems to be the only one with any real knowledge about this world. If one of his conditions with Amon was the finding of such a legendary object, it must, beyond any reasonable doubt, exist. But where?

As they continued down the path, her mind fell once again into thoughts of Amon. Images of his scars popped into her mind. He'd always been so secretive about his past and the traumas he'd faced. Savara almost believed she had seen a different side of him after the fight with Big Tog, at the death of the king. Amon had shown her vulnerability that she'd scarcely imagined of him. Because of this, she'd almost begun to trust him. She'd even started to fall for him.

It was true that being with him brought out an urge in her to better herself, to be stronger. To live, where she had scarcely felt alive before. Despite his many claims about being a monster, something about being with him felt like having a light through the darkness. When they were together, Savara never feared for anything. She knew that he was looking out for her. She had secretly come to depend upon the fact that he would always be there to get her out of even the toughest situations.

And then... She learned it was all a lie. That he was the cause of her suffering.

There had to have been some truth to it, though, came a small voice from within. Savara couldn't tell whether this voice had come from her head or her heart, but its words annoyed her—mostly because of how badly she wanted to believe them.

"The things he did... Were they because of his bonds? Or..."

"Are you trying to ask me, princess, whether I think he

wished to hurt you, or if it was entirely out of his control?" Alexei asked. Savara nodded. "What does it matter? The past cannot be changed. Your family is dead. The world you knew is gone. Whether he did it because of those bonds or not, does that excuse the hurt you feel?"

For someone as heartless and cruel as him, Alexei had a solid point. "No… It doesn't."

"But I will say this," Alexei added. "In all the time I've known him, he has never let a single person stand in the way of his goals. He has never once considered putting another's desires above his. There is no one whose ideals he has ever held in higher regard than his own."

"I can see—" she began, but Alexei interrupted her.

"Not until you."

Savara turned to him, a heavy frown setting in across her face. What new game was he playing? The back and forth of Alexei's descriptions of Amon was beginning to give her whiplash. One second, he wanted her to hate the very air in Amon's lungs, and in the next breath, he was singing his praises. Surely, he knew what he was doing by telling her that? Alexei had seen them in the throne room after the king's death, and he must have known something by the way he had taunted Amon throughout their encounter. That might have been familial rivalry, but this? This was something different. He owed her no mercies or mayhem, and as he'd made a point of repeating on numerous occasions, his actions—good or bad—were anything but free. They came at a price.

"Why are you telling me this?"

"So you don't forget who the real devil is, Savara.

Especially not while living under his roof..." he replied, pointing up at the darkened spires rising from the distance.

Another chill whipped across her shoulders. He'd done a good job so far of keeping her mind off the terror she associated with the Prince of Shadows, but nearing the castle, fear flooded through her body once more. Perhaps she'd made a mistake in coming with Alexei. In the heat of the moment, she chose who she'd thought was the lesser of two evils. Now, she realised the choice hadn't been between evils at all. She chose the lesser of two heartaches, and in so, played right into the devil's hand.

"The devil always demands his due..." She remembered Big Tog's warning, hearing it echo in his exact voice, as though he'd hissed it at her right then and there.

And now, the devil has you...

CHAPTER 5

THE PRINCE OF SHADOWS

THE STAGNANT AIR AROUND THE PALACE brought back memories of nightmares. Some stemmed from the horrors she'd witnessed in Idune—burning corpses, pools of blood, people possessed by shadows—while others came from a time before, one she had only recently begun to remember. If the priest she met in Idune was to be believed, this was only the beginning of her torment.

Savara stared up at the spires of the towers, fearing the way their daggerlike points glinted under the light of the moon. The charred stones along the path had given way to polished obsidian that crawled up the walls. The place was bathed in the strange glow of a sparkling stream of dust that weaved its way through the towers.

"What is that?" Savara asked, pointing up at the ethereal

light.

"Princess, I hate to ask after whatever demons lurk in your mind but, what are you seeing now?"

"The…" She looked back at him, his eyebrow raised in suspicion. *He can't see it*, she realised. Maybe it, like the shadow, had something to do with her *almost-death* or her powers. "Never mind. I thought I saw something."

"A word of caution, princess." Alexei leaned in closer to her and lowered his voice. "That which can be seen can be fought, but that which can't can still kill."

He must have seen through her lie. He knew there was something out there that he was incapable of seeing or wilfully chose to ignore. Either way, his warning gave her pause. It reminded her of the warning Brass had given her upon returning to Visanthe. Where there was knowing, there was fear, she realised, and even though Alexei tried harder to mask his own, not even he could hide from her powers.

"You sound scared…" she whispered.

The singular chuckle that escaped his lips hinted at apprehension. "You should be."

"Does that warning mean we are friends now?"

"Has it endeared you to me?" Alexei mocked. "I don't have friends, princess. But…" he began as he reached out and twirled a piece of her hair around one of his gloved fingers. He brought his lips to the outer edge of her ear and lowered his voice to nothing more than an intimate whisper. His breath was heavy against her neck as he spoke. "I know how hot and bothered you are about my dearest cousin. If you're looking for a last bit of mortal pleasure before your date with the devil, I'm happy to oblige."

Savara smacked him across the face as she pulled away. "You're sick," she hissed, knowing he had intended to get her blood boiling with that statement. He'd succeeded. She realised that if he had wanted to block the hit, he could have. He'd chosen not to.

Alexei licked the thin trail of blood from the side of his lips, unfazed by her outburst. "I'm mortal—as are you. Try to remember that," was his only reply.

"There's something wrong with you, Alexei."

At that, he smiled. "Keep up that rage. Such mortal emotions might just keep you sane."

Savara turned from him and headed cautiously towards the entrance. His words made their way into the nook in her mind that kept all the ominous warnings people had given her throughout her time in Visanthe, filed away for the eventual day such information would be needed. All of the other warnings had come to pass, so she knew it wasn't a matter of if, but rather when this one would too.

It wasn't long before Savara noticed she'd lost track of the sound of Alexei's footsteps. She turned back to find him planted firmly where she'd left him, waiting stoically for his pause to be acknowledged.

"Is something wrong?" she hissed.

"This is where I leave you," he replied.

"Are you afraid of the dark?"

"Not particularly."

"Then?"

"I'm not willing to give up the parts of me that are needed to continue."

Savara frowned, an icy sensation suddenly crawling

through her veins. "What do you mean?"

"My spirit holds no claim to these lands. Unlike you, I cannot pass through without sacrifice. Our time is up, princess," he replied as a grin curled on his face. "But don't fret; this isn't the last time we will be seeing each other. Our story isn't finished just yet. And who knows? Maybe, by the end of this tale, you won't be so averse to my previous offer. Maybe it'll be my name you call out for in the dark." He winked a feisty electric blue eye at her as he removed one of his leather gloves. With a flourish, he pointed a finger up towards the night sky, letting loose a bolt of lightning that ripped through the heavens with a thundering roar.

Startled, Savara clapped her hands over her ears until the echoing died. "What did you do that for!?" she yelled.

"To announce our arrival… And the end of my task."

Suddenly, a whorl of shadows streaked across the floor beneath her, reaching out towards him. Dust swirled at his feet, lifting off the ground in a vortex around him. Through the cloud, his eyes glowed, never once lifting from her, not until the last moment when the dust swallowed him whole. By the time it settled, Alexei was gone, sent outside the boundaries of these lands.

Once again, she stood alone.

Savara hated to admit that she missed having him around. She'd taken comfort in knowing there was someone standing beside her in case of danger—even a psychopath like him. But this was a task she knew she had to face alone. The first part of her life had been dictated to her, almost down to the smallest details. Now, she was taking her fate by the reins.

Feeling a sudden chill on her skin, her eyes floated up to

the towers once more, spying a figure on one of the balconies. Unlike the rest of these lands, this figure was teeming with life. His skin glowed against the dark backdrop of the palace. His burning red eyes shone the colour of the stones that no longer marred her cheek. She lifted her hand up to it to ensure they were truly gone. The tips of her fingers met only skin, but the threat lingered.

The Prince of Shadows looked on, contemplating the effect he had on her. His glance alone was a threat that sent shivers down her spine. Every nerve in her body urged her to turn back. Common sense would've fought hard against her entering the den of a lion like him, but she was on a mission, and considering how far she'd come, she couldn't find a reason to turn back now.

Before her, the ancient door lurched open. In the second it took for her eyes to bounce from the balcony to the door and back, the Prince of Shadows was gone. Worry settled into the pit of her stomach, but her decision was made—had been made long before this moment.

Savara took a deep breath, preparing herself for whatever waited beyond, and stepped inside. Ready or not, this was what she'd been looking for all along.

Something inside her smiled.

The air inside the palace tasted stale in her lungs. The stillness reminded her of a mausoleum, somewhere that once meant the world to lives that had long since been lost to time—a prison of age and mercy.

Tapestries hung heavy and untouched surrounded by darkened busts of nameless figures. Delicate, hand-painted tiles inlaid with gold symbols lined the floors, gleaming even through the darkness, as though they recognised the presence of new life and wished to claim it.

Something sharp and sinister lingered in the emptiness, dormant but not dead. A well of untapped power. Savara knew it would not stay that way for long.

As she waited, she stared up at the mystifying streams of gold and silver dust that slithered across the ceiling. Their twinkling reminded her of the orbs of light in Griffin's tent back in Camp Saar. The memory of the burnt down camp triggered a wave of sadness within her. Her chest grew heavy as she breathed, laden with the guilt of having played a part in all the anguish. She'd thought she'd gotten over it, but the shame was still there, lingering in the shadows of the many troubling events that had since occurred.

Unlike the orbs in Griffin's tent, however, this dust was not the result of someone's power. This dust had an energy surrounding it that felt darker somehow. Alluring in its glow and deadly in its temptation. It pulled out those harsher emotions she carried within, acting like a conscious entity all its own. More concerning still, her powers found a certain resonance with it. A connection. As though she were sensing a soul behind the particled façade.

But how could that be? she wondered, a wave of goosebumps rushing down her arms as she considered the parallel.

Whatever this dust was, it was alive.

Savara reached her hand up, extending her fingers out as if to touch it. A small stream slithered through the stagnant air to meet it, hovering in coils around her fingers, never quite touching the skin. The dust snaked its way around her hand, raising the hairs on her arms. Warmth flooded into her heart.

She could sense the dust trying to communicate with whatever was inside her, the way that the stone of the Arima had when she first saw it. Like with Arima stone, however, the message was lost on her.

"I didn't realise you were so far along in your journey," a sombre voice called from the other end of the room.

The glittering light of the dust danced across his ebony hair, highlighting the occasional strands of silver, the only sign that time—even in a minimal capacity—had any effect on him whatsoever. His tunic glistened like wet ink, catching the light in waves the colour of the darkest red wine, making the matching glow of his eyes even more prominent. As he walked towards her, the room was silent, as though he had such a command over his domain that not even sound escaped his grasp. The Prince of Shadows stopped before her, staring at the coil of dust around her wrist as he smiled.

"You look confused," he said, the gravity of his tone reminded her of the low hummings of earthquakes. His voice hinted at intrigue, but his eyes shone with a knowingness that made her bones tremble. "What troubles you?"

Savara swallowed hard on her innate fear of the man before her. She knew she needed to be strong in his presence. She had come so far already, fought against murderers and their bonds, shadows that hunted her like wild dogs, and tyrants who kidnapped her for their own gain. Yet, the man before her—his voice, his eyes, his essence—still haunted her nightmares.

"Can you see it? The dust?" she asked, fighting against the fear gnawing at her vocal cords.

His features were unreadable as he spoke. "Of course,

child."

"But Alexei—"

"He is not like us," he said, cutting her thought short. Though there was no threat in his tone, there was no kindness in it either. An air of superiority surrounded him, visible in the upward tilt of his chin as he spoke. "None of them are, you know this. And you and I both know that you did not come here to ask such trivial questions." He extended a hand towards her own, allowing the dust to slither from her wrist, forming into a ball in the palm of his hand before releasing it back into the air. "There will be time enough for explanations. I apologise for the trek but, as I was unable to collect you myself, I was forced to use that particular workaround."

"So, it's true then… you are not allowed to leave these lands."

The Prince of Shadows' eyes darkened. "It had been an impossibility for quite some time."

"Then, how did you appear in Idune? The day Ori…" she bit down on the words, refusing to finish the sentence. Savara was already on edge around him, she didn't wish to remind him of his darker deeds—just in case. In her mind, he was still an enigma. Between their brief encounters and the stories she'd heard of him from the others, the Prince of Shadows was more bogeyman than person. She hoped being here with him would help her piece together not only the threads of her own story, but potentially his as well.

"It is true, there was a curse placed on me, but one which I have since broken, with the help of our mutual friend. My spirit and body were torn apart, and as my spirit was tied to these lands, it could not leave. However, through the powers provided by certain relics—like the one tucked into your dress—I have slowly been able to regain parts of myself that were lost."

Savara pressed a hand to the part of her dress that held the stone of the Arima, one of the last ones she knew he required to complete whatever ritual he was carrying out. He knew it was there. He'd known the whole time. He probably sensed it the moment she set foot on these grounds.

The Prince of Shadows had proved himself an unbeatable opponent on multiple occasions. If he wanted the stone, Savara didn't doubt that he could take it from her with relative ease. But the man before her seemed to show little to no interest in the very thing she'd been told to keep from him for all this time. Had they been mistaken?

"Not to worry, child; I have no intention of taking the stone from you, nor do I mean to harm you. The curse is mostly broken, and I have other pressing matters that need my attention."

"You still haven't answered my question," Savara replied, her hand still clutching the ripples of fabric covering the stone.

"All in due time, Savara, my dear." With the snap of his fingers, the shadow of a young woman appeared before them and dropped into a curtsey.

Her features were muted and fading, like those of a desert mirage, as though she no longer belonged to this world, but wasn't quite in the one beyond either. She wore modest servant clothes, a loose skirt and bonnet over a neatly tied braid. Her eyes flickered briefly from Savara to the Prince of

Shadows and back again.

Savara bowed her head, acknowledging the girl's assistance.

"Communication between you two will be limited, but she will show you to your rooms," The Prince of Shadows announced, paying little mind to the girl's obvious concern for him. "I will see you in the morning for a light meal, over which we can discuss any pressing matters on your mind. For now, you must be tired. Please, make yourself at home. This is, after all…" he paused, holding back his initial thought. "Regardless, if you are in need of anything that would make you feel more comfortable, all you need to do is ask, and it will be provided." He clasped his hands behind his back and held his shoulders high. "Goodnight, Savara."

With that, the Prince of Shadows pressed a hand to his heart and bobbed his head before departing down one of the darkened halls. Where he disappeared to, she knew not, but once again, his stride was entirely silent.

Savara remained frozen in place, her eyes following him as far as the light would allow. She hadn't noticed the way her hand still clutched the fabric covering the stone, its cool surface a stark contrast to the heat of her palm. Their brief encounter had already left her with more questions, and something told her the night was far from over.

With a heavy sigh, Savara turned to the shadowy figure of the young woman who had materialised before her. The ghostly apparition seemed to flicker in and out of existence, her features blurred and indistinct. Despite the uncertainty surrounding her, the figure offered a silent gesture towards the hallway, indicating that she should follow.

Savara took one last look towards the darkened hall, down which the Prince of Shadows had disappeared, assuring he was truly gone before making any further moves. He was an enigma. One she'd believed she was prepared to face. But the tension coursing through her body told her she was picking a fight well out of her league… One that would end very badly.

CHAPTER 6

THE VOICES WHICH SPEAK OF LEGENDS

THE FADED FIGURE OF THE GIRL WAITED for Savara to acknowledge her again before starting down a different hall. Like the Prince of Shadows, she made no sound as she walked. Her modest skirt shifted with each step, the braid swinging in tune behind her. Having neither an echo nor a breath, Savara figured there was a good chance she couldn't make any sound at all.

Perhaps she had been chosen for the task for that very reason, as to not be capable of divulging unwanted secrets. Savara's heart sank, realising she might once again have to suffer alone at the mercy of her thoughts.

Since her arrival in Visanthe, being 'alone with her thoughts' was a place she'd actively tried to avoid. Nothing good had ever come of it. If she closed her eyes for more than a second, she saw the faces of all those she'd hurt…and some she'd unintentionally killed…plastered on the backs of her eyelids. Between the resurging memories from the time before her Divination, and the torturous ones from after her return, she figured it was a miracle she hadn't gone insane.

Yet… she almost heard the voice in her mind say. She shook her head, trying to shake the thought itself. There was too much at stake for her to lose her mind now. Savara knew she would have to make a conscious effort to distract herself; otherwise, she just might fall prey to such sinister whisperings.

Alexei's warning wriggled its way to the forefront of her mind. Everything around her—the dim, flickering lights of the halls, the sombre portraits, even the hollow songs of the dust above her head as it slithered across the ceiling—reminded her of the threat in his words.

To remind you who the real devil is, especially as you'll be living under his roof…

The warning had come from a psychopath. Someone she wouldn't have wanted to cross paths with even on the brightest of days, under the clearest of skies. It showed just how much fear surrounded the Prince of Shadows, even from someone who lined his pockets with the demon's coin. Still, the prince had not made a move against her—not yet. She wondered just what he might have in store for her.

As Savara glided through the palace halls behind her spectral guide, she noticed how the girl's form drifted in and out of view under the shifting dust. Particles of it clung to her as she moved, as though she belonged to wherever it came from. Savara tilted her head to gain a better view of the connection. The dust seemed to drip onto the girl as if magnetised to her form, but the girl seemed unbothered—ignorant even—as if she couldn't sense its presence.

The curiosity became too much to bear. There was no way Savara could wait until the following morning for all her questions to be answered.

"I'm sorry to ask but, who are you?" Savara asked, hoping the girl might be in more of a talking mood than her host.

The girl turned to face her. The dust peeled away from her as she did, retreating into the streams above them. She shook her head. The faded corners of her mouth turned down as she pointed to it.

"You can't speak..." Savara realised. The girl nodded. "Right... That figures."

Of course the Prince of Shadows would not have made it so easy for her. The girl must have sensed her disappointment; her eyes filled with an equal amount of sadness—as if she too had been looking for company. Neither seemed to wish to linger too long in the state of loneliness that hung between them. The girl resumed her stride and Savara followed close behind, ignoring the feeling of unease forming in the pit of her stomach.

The shadow-stained walls of the palace seemed to drink in what little light there was, casting the corridors into a perpetual gloom. Unlike the airy rooms of the Palace of Winds—where sunlight streamed in through the many open balconies—or the fiery warmth of the magma-lined walls of her own Argia palace, here, in the House of Spirits, there was only darkness...

Darkness and dust.

Savara felt a sense of isolation here, as if the palace itself were a tomb, its secrets buried deep within its labyrinthine corridors. And yet, despite the darkness and the decay, there was a strange beauty to this House of Spirits. The air hung heavy with a sense of foreboding, as if the very walls themselves whispered secrets of the past.

The shadows danced and flickered away from what little light was cast by the dust drifting overhead, twisting and contorting with each passing moment, as if there was life to be found within them. Captivated by their glow, Savara regarded them with apprehension. The way they shifted, irrespective of the flow of light, gave her pause.

Could they be alive? She wondered if they were the reason for the unsettled feeling in her stomach.

As she watched them slither across the floors, she was reminded of the ones that had attacked her in the forest outside the Argia palace. Her heartbeat quickened. Thankfully, these shadows were not after her. Not this time. They moved about the floor, making no effort to interfere with her as she traversed the halls with her guide. Yet, Savara could feel them watching her as well.

"Is there something else here with us?" Savara called to the girl in front of her.

Once more, the girl paused her stride. The faded glow of her eyes bounced from the shadows streaking across the hall to the glowing particles above them, almost as if to say more than one something was present. Watching. Waiting.

Savara took this as confirmation that there were other entities in this house she could not see. Entities with a will and a purpose she could not fathom. The Prince of Shadows, she reasoned, was somehow able to communicate with them, summon them into view like he had with the girl, and possibly even control them.

But there was more to it.

Fear burned in the girl's eyes. Though she couldn't use her voice, the warning glow in her eyes said enough. Savara knew she would have to proceed with caution during her time here. She didn't know how much these entities could interact with her, whether they were simply observers or if they were capable of more, but she would remain guarded either way.

"Why are these lands like this?" Savara asked, but this time, the girl ignored her. "I can see there is pain here," she continued. Still, she received no response. "I want to help." This time, the girl disappeared entirely. Savara halted her pace, circling about to try and find her. "Great..." she mumbled. She'd just lost her guide.

Suddenly, she noticed a flash of light from the opposite end of the hall. The girl had returned, standing at one of the junctions they'd previously passed. She gestured for Savara to follow her, pressing a ghostly finger to her lips as if to say *quietly*. Savara obeyed, taking greater care of the echo of her footfall on the worn tiled floors.

The girl led Savara through the cavernous halls of the palace, finally arriving at a grand foyer adorned on all sides by ash-stained glass windows. These weathered panels offered little in the way of clarity, but even still, revealed views of desolate mountains looming beyond. Squinting, Savara could see the contours of a still lake resting at the base of the mountain range. A lake like that should have been crawling with life. Anywhere else in Visanthe, it would have been. But not here.

Here, it was yet another reminder of the chokehold placed upon these lands.

A sense of melancholy washed over her as she regarded the world beyond the glass. In another time—a time untouched by shadow and regret—these lands could have rivalled the most breathtaking in all of Visanthe. Alexei had told her as much on their journey. The potential for beauty lay hidden, imprisoned behind the invisible chains of a curse she knew little of, but which permeated even the air she breathed. The same sentiment resonated within the palace walls—a place which, under different circumstances, could have been a marvel of architecture and grace, but instead stood as a monument to a forgotten past.

Silence and stagnancy reigned supreme.

Sadly, the tranquillity promised by such stillness was far from peaceful. It hung in the air like a prelude to an impending storm, swollen and expecting. The world beyond the glass was frozen, suspended in the grip of time. The same unease echoed through the hushed corridors of the palace, where each flickering shadow seemed to conceal secrets and dormant threats.

Savara couldn't escape the feeling that these lands were on the precipice of transformation—and that she was somehow intrinsically involved. The potential for life lingered, only masked by this stagnancy and sorrow. She couldn't help but wonder if breaking these invisible shackles would unleash a resurgence of life and purpose upon these lands once more, and if that was exactly what the Prince of Shadows sought in his bringing her here.

At the opposite end of the room stood a solitary, stained glass door from which both the shadows and the glowing dust recoiled. Savara drew closer to it, feeling a shift in the air around her as she did. The dense sorrow of the halls peeled away from her as she neared. She recognised the sensation that replaced it instantly. She'd felt it before in both the sacred gardens of the Harri and the Zerua.

Her skin prickled as she drew closer, captivated by the scene depicted in the crystal panels—a bubbling fountain, divided into two, each half a contrasting mirrored image of the other. The upper portion cascaded an ethereal white stream, while the lower counterpart mirrored the flow with a rippling current of shadows. The glowing dust and the shadows hovered around their corresponding light and dark halves like twin halos. A delicate dance of illumination and obscurity, each element refrained from direct contact with it, but was unmistakably tethered to the door's ethereal depiction.

Soon, harmonic whisperings began trickling into her ears. *Voices*, she realised. They started low and soft, spectral almost, drifting in and out in whispers like the girl's form. The longer she stood before the door, the louder the sound grew in her ears until she could discern words through the mumbled stream:

A tale of strife and ruin sung,
the key to life is yet undone
Trapped within forgotten cage,

quelled and silent and seeking age
A truth whose feathers unruffled yet,
a legend of which in stone is set
Where lessons fall on broken thrones,
and power bestowed to undead bones
And in justice commands its fight,
sought out in the darkest night
A reckoning for souls impure,
in separation finds not freedom's cure
But in unity lay true freedom's test,
where ageless quarrels seek out rest
In destruction of wrecked grounds,
finds the daemon sleeping sound
Whence borne one soul left untethered,
break thee the chains that bind forever
To chaos and order a balance find,
a mission placed on thee divine
Only when the end is nigh,
shall this twilight soul arise
Seven bonds thy keepers make,
seven stones must Iturri break
Six to broken lands bestowed,
a final one soul alone may hold
Lay in that which no blood may currency,
uniting stone borne to eternity
And so it is as once begun,
to splintered worlds a setting sun
A return to that from whence we came,

the land to which time gave no name
The world unkept that keeps them all,
and watches as the kingdoms fall
To rise and fall and rise again,
to revel in winter's bitter end
And summers going and springs begot,
for living as to a life forgot
Where dawn breaks on barren skin,
and once more whole the age begins.

"What is this place?" Savara whispered as she raised her hand to the glass. As before, the dust from the lighter half of the image fluttered around her fingertips. The shadows followed suit but, instead of the warm sensation she'd received from the dust, a biting cold accompanied them. Soon, both opposites were slithering down to her wrist. They moved in spiralling loops, creating a strange helix of sorts— still tethered to the door, but unmistakably tethered to her as well.

Savara pulled her wrist away softly, allowing the dust and shadows to slither back into their original positions rimming the door. She flexed her fingers, still feeling the warmth of the dust and the cold of the shadows in a helix pattern on her skin. The strange voices lingered only a little while longer before fading as well.

Slowly coming out of her trance, Savara turned to the girl for a response. Unable to voice her thoughts, the little girl simply made a show of interlacing her fingers.

Savara mimicked her, trying to comprehend.

"Together? An intersection?" she asked.

The girl nodded.

"For what? What does it connect?" she prodded, but before Savara could get another word out, the girl pressed a spectral finger to her lips. Her eyes flicked from the door to the ceiling.

The dust around them had gathered speed. Streams of it began to swell, growing fierce near the strange fountain depiction. The girl gestured for her to return the way they'd come—probably back to their original destination. The look in her eyes as she did spoke of urgency.

"Is something wrong?" Savara whispered, cautiously retreating from the door.

The girl replied with a gesture of yawning and stretching, the act made unsettling by the fear in her ghostly eyes.

Savara didn't prod further. Whatever that thing was that had spooked the girl before was waking up, and by the looks of things, they were exactly where they shouldn't be. She could sense it too. A low rumble through the floor beneath her feet, as if she were standing on the chest of a giant slowly waking from slumber. The hairs on the back of her neck stood in alert.

It was time to go.

Reluctantly, Savara tiptoed away from the door, careful not to disturb the flowing dust around her. The further she got from the fountain, the softer the rumbling sensation beneath her feet became. Her presence seemed to have an effect on…whatever it was. Savara looked down at her hands again and repeated the act of interlacing her fingers.

A joining point… But what does it join? And what does it have to do with me?

A vicious gale whipped around her seemingly from out of nowhere. Savara brushed her hair from her eyes and found the girl waiting for her at the end of the hall, angry and fearful.

"Alright, I'm coming," she said as she followed behind her spectral guide, weaving back through the halls they'd traversed prior to her strange encounter with the door.

Savara took note of all the nuanced decorations that distinguished each turn, hoping to retrace her steps at a later time. Something important lay behind that door, something that called to her in the same way the stones had. When everything settled down once more, she would make a point to seek it out—if it didn't seek her out first.

CHAPTER 7

FLASHBACKS

THROUGHOUT THE REST OF THEIR WALK, Savara kept silent, focusing on the various bits of out-of-date décor and the occasional spectral sconce that, when approached, would light itself as if by magic. The resulting light glowed the colour of the full moon. It flowed over endless streams of wax that dripped like tears down ash-stained walls. The girl kept up the pace, pausing only when she sensed Savara lingering, and admonishing her through silent signals to move on.

She couldn't help herself. More than once, they passed portraits of people with sad, doe-like eyes which—like hers—were flecked with specks of rainbow and gold. It came to the point where she began to wonder if there was more to the passing resemblance.

The first portrait, that of an elderly woman with hair pulled into a tight, silver bun and a tiara of black gems that bled down from her crown to her shoulders, bore little in the way of resemblance to her, except of course the eyes. The second—a mostly bald, rotund man with a neatly coiffed beard adorned with various clamps of gold—shared both her eyes and button nose. The next depicted an older woman who—if not for the noticeable age difference and slightly darker skin—could've been her twin. Her ebony braids were streaked with white and cascaded far down her torso. She was regal in the way Savara could only imagine, matched only by her late Uncle Hyrum.

The final portrait halted her in her tracks.

Even now, as she stared up at his likeness on the weathered canvas, she could see the effects of whatever curse held him in place. His hair had only greyed slightly since sitting for the artist's brush. His skin had neither wrinkled nor sallowed. The only changes came in the form of the suit he donned, having been dulled by the effects of time but looking no less elegant, and the eyes, having shifted from their clearly inherited rainbow flecks to the ruby tinge she'd grown accustomed to in person. The Prince of Shadows gazed out from beyond the confines of his frame, his appearance much less menacing in the portrait than in reality. The version of him in the frame glowed with pride and confidence, unmarked by the bitterness that adorned him of late. Life—or something like it—fluttered from within the brushstrokes, as it had with the portraits in Osiir. This time, however, a cold accompanied it. The air around the painting felt as though it were in mourning, the sensation washing over her the closer she got to it.

Savara had not considered the possibility before, but each portrait she passed added fuel to the flame of intuition growing inside her. The striking resemblance between herself and the woman in the previous painting alone was impossible to ignore. Now, staring up at the man whom she'd spent most of her time in Visanthe fearing, she considered whether he meant something more by his words to her earlier. Was it possible that his referring to them as 'we' meant more than just a similar strain of power? Perhaps, though she took little comfort in the thought, their likeness extended like roots from a sparse family tree.

Suddenly, the girl appeared before her, inserting herself between the painting and Savara. Her spectral form flickered in and out with the same urgency as before.

"Alright, I'm coming," Savara replied, falling in step behind her once more.

At the end of their route was a much less prominent set of double doors made of aged wood and featuring engravings of what looked to be fairy tales on each panel. They opened with an otherworldly creak as she neared, revealing a space fit for the princess that time had forgotten.

Moonlight cascaded through expansive floor-to-ceiling glass panels, painting the space in the monochrome glow of the night. The dated room whispered of neglect, as though time had cast its gentle veil over a childhood that was never truly hers. Against the wall to her right, a large canopy bed stood as a solemn sentinel, dressed in pristine linens as if waiting for a slumber that never came. The thin swathes of netting tied to each post hung like ghosts frozen in their hauntings.

Opposite the bed, a silent assembly of freshly pressed gowns lined a polished golden rack, the only semblance of change in the stagnant room having been recently placed for the arrival of its no-longer-child occupant. Their delicate fabrics, though immaculate, seemed to ache with a longing to be worn. Locked away in a dresser nearby, other outfits of equally regal quality had been stowed away, awash with purpose unfulfilled from a childhood that never was.

Somewhere in between sat an old chest, reminiscent of those coveted by pirates in her storybooks. Savara caught a glimpse of a plush arm belonging to some forgotten stuffed animal peeking out from the slightly exposed interior. Seeing it alone sent shivers down her arms, finding a certain resonance with the neglect of the toy. Feelings from her non-mortal life bubbled up from within—feelings of guilt, shame, loneliness. Savara wondered if she would've felt such things had she resided here instead.

The room had been staged to perfection. The expected occupant of this room would never have lacked anything. Toys, clothes, a space to grow and expand, a space to practise talents and foster interests, all of these lay before her. Each detail had been placed with the utmost care, their presence in the room alone was an act of love, but as she cast her gaze about the room, Savara noticed only a sadness that permeated the air around each of these lovingly placed touches. Unlike the room in Osiir, whose memories had been covered with ghostly sheets and whose trappings had been almost entirely removed, this room clung to the potential of life, as though awaiting a promise that time had taken. This room wanted to be used. It wanted her.

The door closed behind her with a heavy thud, startling her out of her contemplation and pushing her further into the room. Savara took a turn about it, running her fingers over the furniture that was meant for her in a different life. Despite the lack of use, the room had not been neglected. There was not a speck of dust to be found on any of the surfaces. The floors too hinted at careful upkeep and constant polish. Someone had clearly been confident of her return.

Opposite the bed, Savara spied a small archway leading to a grand washroom with a sunken bath already filled and rippling with steam, and various plants whose green leaves had greyed, suffering from the same state of half-life as the rest of the rooms in the palace. She decided that it might be a good idea to freshen up after the journey. A nice warm bath was also on the top of her list, as the last bit of water that had touched her skin was that of the cold rain of the Palace of Winds when she killed Big Tog. She hoped that a bath might wash away the memories of that moment that still clung readily to her skin.

Savara stripped off her dress, taking care to rest the stone that had been nestled between the fabric gently on top of the heap before she descended into the bath. The water lapped at her ankles as she waded in, allowing the warmth to creep slowly up her legs. The sensation provoked a soft sigh from her as she lowered herself in completely.

Hints of lavender oil from the bath wafted in the air, the scent growing stronger the more she disturbed the water. It helped to release some of the tension she had been carrying within her after the ordeal in Haizea and the fears she had harboured in coming to the Arima lands. Somebody had gone to a lot of trouble to make sure she felt as comfortable as possible.

As she sunk her head beneath the water, memories appeared in the dark of her closed eyelids. Savara saw her mother, a vision of white light standing before her, holding a beautiful white lily out towards her. Her mother was smiling at her, gesturing for her to take the plant, and a younger her's little hand reached out to grab it. In another, she was chasing after a slightly older boy through the maze of palatial balconies and foyers of her home in Osiir. He giggled as he hid behind corners, waiting to be found and chased.

This was the childhood she'd lived—the one she was beginning to remember fully.

The next one that appeared saw her standing on a balcony, looking out over the gardens of the palace, towards the distant seas. There was a longing in the memory, palpable in her heart despite the time that had passed since the event. A looming decision weighed on her chest beneath the water. The memory of the day her world changed lingered in her mind. Had she known of her own Divination story, she might have refused to go to the ceremony, though she was sure Iturri would've found her regardless.

Now, the stares, the lights, the rings, the frowns… All of these came back to her again with a new clarity. Now, she truly understood the shock that settled amongst the crowd, the fear in their eyes as she was deposited before the empty dais, and the tragic meaning behind it all. She was their end of days. The world as they knew it was about to change forever. Perhaps had her mother not shipped her off to the mortal world, things would have unfolded much sooner, but looking back on it all, she knew that there was nothing anyone could have done to change the outcome. Regardless of how much she wished for it to have all been coincidence and bad circumstance, she could no longer deny the thread of events that had led from her birth to that very moment.

Savara recalled a conversation she'd had with the strange entity in the palace at Osiir known to her only as *No One*, in which he'd mentioned the peculiarity of her circumstances, how she had been the first of her kind in a long time. She hadn't realised then what he'd meant but, having come as far as she had, Savara knew now that he'd spoken of her soul.

Before she surfaced, a final memory flashed before her eyes, one that had a noticeably darker undertone. This memory was shaded in the same muted tones of the palace in which she stayed and showed a visibly agitated young man pacing about a grand foyer. He wrung his hands nervously with each echoing step, looking as though he were awaiting judgement.

In this memory, the man was about the same age as he had been in the portrait that hung in the halls of the palace. As he skirted between the shadows and the tendrils of sunlight that filtered in through the glass windows, Savara caught glimpses of his innocence. The shifting light highlighted the striking resemblance between them. In his youth, this man was a vision of charm and elegance, burdened by whatever news he awaited.

Suddenly, another figure stepped into view. She was a petite thing, radiant like the moon. Glowing coils of white hair cascaded down her back, and a pair of doe-like sapphire eyes sat nestled in her youthful face. She strode up to him and rested a gentle hand on the hollow of his back, unable to comfortably reach his shoulder.

"You know, Adrius, that this is what's best for everyone. They are showing lenience."

"This is not lenience; this is a crime against nature."

"I am ashamed you see it that way. Do you not realise how many lives we will be saving?"

"Iturri is not a thing to be caged, Aurelia…"

Savara shot up from beneath the bath water gasping for breath. That last memory, the one that hadn't belonged to her, shook her to her core. Somehow, she'd tapped into something that went beyond her own past. Possibly the past of the palace itself. Around her, new life and vibrance had begun bleeding into the leaves of the plants in the washroom.

"This is insane," she whispered to herself as she ran her hands over her eyes.

Savara reached for the towel hanging nearby and began drying herself, all the while thinking of the strange memory and why it had appeared in her mind. The list of questions only continued to grow, but being here felt like she was finally on the verge of getting the answers she'd been seeking. She wrapped her hair in the towel and sauntered back into the bedroom, finding a plain nightgown waiting for her, laid out over turned-down sheets. She wondered where they had come from when she heard the Prince of Shadows' voice ringing in her mind.

All you need to do is ask, and it will be provided.

She hadn't asked aloud, but her intentions must have been heard. By whom? She knew not—and thought it best not to find out.

That night, she dreamt of weathered storms, rains over blazing fields, and a man with hair like starlight reaching out towards her. Yet another vivid dream that had her believing there was something deeper, something more to it than just imaginary fancy. Something about her being here felt like the end of a cycle—or the beginning of one. Savara knew she was on the precipice of clarity; all she had to do was leap. The sensation of purpose clung to her through the quiet hours before dawn, long after she found she could no longer maintain a restful slumber. Especially not when there was clarity to be found elsewhere in the palace.

CHAPTER 8

DOG FIGHTS

JASPER HAD SEEN MANY A DOG FIGHT on his little island, strays walking up to gated gardens to harass their imprisoned counterparts, some of which even ended up on the other side of the fence, where the real bloodbath would then ensue. The conversation panning out between Griffin and Amon had all the makings of such a fight, only, instead of deafening barks, their words were laced with cold fury. However, something told him the bloodbath would ensue all the same.

"You are not in any position to make demands, least of all concerning her," Griffin hissed as he slammed his fist against the old mahogany desk that, even in its density, looked ready to crumble under his force. "You forget that you are the reason she is there with him. This mess is entirely your fault, Amon."

Neither he nor Griffin had been pleased to see the very man they'd blamed for most of the problems, the faceless entity known previously to them as The Apprentice, appear at their doorstep. Less so, to find out just how much he'd done in driving Savara away from them and towards the feared Prince of Shadows. Griffin had neglected to tell him just how much history was shared between himself and Amon, but Jasper could tell by the brazen criticisms and harshness of his tone that there was something intimate about the pain in his objections. He found himself secretly thankful to not be on the receiving end of one of Griffin's lectures. The man at the opposite end of the room hadn't been quite so lucky.

Amon looked like the harsh, contrasting midnight to Griffin's midday glow. His jet-black hair dangled in loose waves around his sharp cheekbones, framing eyes full of knowing and mischief. Jasper noticed the way his striking, electric blue eyes had surveyed everything on the ship since his arrival as if he were studying it for a future test. Though Amon and Griffin had similar temperaments and that annoying trait of knowing more than they let on, Jasper sensed the difference in his energy the moment he set foot on the ship. Where Griffin was pragmatic and reliable, Amon had a wilder unpredictability and ambition about him that set Jasper's nerves on edge. Despite his striking appearance, Jasper figured he was the kind of person you only saw when he wanted to *be* seen, and by that time, it would be too late to save yourself.

The fact that he meant to be seen now boded badly for everyone.

Amon interlaced his arms over his chest. "Do you think I don't know that, Griffin? I've told you the part I played in all of this and why. What more do you want from me?"

"Clearly it hasn't made its way deep enough into that thick skull of yours."

"You're one to talk about thick skulls…" Amon mumbled just loud enough for him to hear.

Griffin ignored the remark entirely. "Why would you ever expect I'd let you take part in any decisions concerning her, or any of my friends for that matter?"

Amon narrowed his eyes, raising his chin slightly. "Because I am still the best shot you have at everything working out, and you know it."

"We don't need your help," Griffin growled.

"You'd leave her to face him alone, then?"

Arrogance laced his tone, but Jasper noted a hint of worry peeking through. It was a tone he himself had used on many occasions, unsure of why until now, until he saw it reflected at him through Amon's eyes. They both fell victim to the horrible trait of showing care through overprotectiveness, masking worry with criticism. Impressive and imposing as he was, Amon still had some very lowly human traits—something which unintentionally endeared Jasper to him, even if only slightly.

"Alone, no. Without you, absolutely," Griffin said coldly and without remorse.

"Griffin, you're being ridiculous, and you know it," Amon replied, tension curling at the edge of his voice. "I have intimate knowledge of his strengths and weaknesses and am the only one capable of getting in and out of that place unscathed. At very least, you need me."

Jasper leaned against the back wall, watching from a safe distance as the tension between them thickened. The room was too small for the energy spilling from them, and the large wooden table in the centre did not help. At points, he wondered if it might not be better to step in, but in this room, he was a mouse amidst lions. He wasn't a fool. He had no intention of squaring up against people who could slaughter him with the twitch of a finger. Besides, they had issues between them that needed resolving, and he figured it best to let them hash it out sooner rather than later. Judging by the growing flicker of annoyance in Griffin's eyes, the hashing out would come soon enough.

"None of that clears you of all the damage you've caused, Amon," chided Griffin. "If it weren't for the respect I have for our past friendship, you wouldn't be here at all."

"You're letting your personal feelings cloud your judgement, Griffin. It would be dangerous for you to go it alone," Amon said, his voice flirting with danger.

"You forget, Amon, just how dangerous *you* are," Griffin shot back.

"Be reasonable, Griffin. There's an entire world hidden from you with creatures that make me appear to be nothing more than a moth on the wall. If I'm the danger you're worried about, you're blinding yourself."

"I am being reasonable, Amon. You've meddled enough. I have no intention of trusting you again."

His words echoed in the stillness of the room, lingering like grief at a funeral. The air seemed to vibrate with the unspoken history that bound them. Tangled threads of their shared past loomed overhead, keeping pain and resentment trapped like flies in a spider's web, and steadfastly refusing to unravel.

Suddenly, Jasper noticed the full force of Amon's penetrating gaze on his skin. Those eyes of his rested on him, but there was no peace to be found in such a rest. Amon had the kind of eyes that spoke to the tunes of restrained power, wells of knowledge… and a history steeped in blood. They glowed the colour of violent electric storms as they took him in. This was the first time Amon had looked his way since the conversation began, but now, Jasper could feel himself being sized up. For what? He knew not.

Jasper hadn't thought it possible, but there existed someone even more stubborn and terrifyingly in the know than Griffin. Amon, like Lance, was another powerful friend from Griffin's past whose reappearance was cause for alarm. Worse still was his apparent involvement in their being here in the first place. As Jasper had gathered, Amon was the reason for Savara's uncle's death, but he'd also saved her from capture in the Harri Kingdom and protected her from Big Tog. Jasper couldn't yet discern what his motives were or where his allegiances lay, but something about the look in Amon's eyes spoke of truth and true suffering. That he too was looking out for Savara, in his own twisted way.

Jasper sighed and relented, pushing himself off the wall, accepting the invitation into the conversation he'd actively avoided for the past half hour. He'd successfully held his tongue throughout the back and forth, knowing that he would just get in the way of whatever quarrelling was needed for them to reconcile, but he could see that Griffin's stubbornness was getting the better of him. Plus, Jasper knew he would be the only one capable of discerning the truth of any story this man told regarding Savara. They may never have been lovers, but their friendship still rang true.

"I want to hear what he has to say," he chimed, wondering if he'd soon regret speaking, even as the words fell from his lips.

As expected, Griffin shot him an annoyed glance. "Jasper, you don't understand. He'll just end up manipulating the situation for his own benefit."

"You say that as if you were as transparent as crystal and acted with no ulterior motives ever. As far as I'm concerned, our goal is to get her back safe and sound. If he can help, even as a side effect of whatever his final goal may be, I'm willing to at least hear what he has to say."

"Insensitive," Amon growled.

"Don't come with that, I'm pleading your case," Jasper barked. "I'm not under the impression that I will ever know what the two of you are thinking, but if we can at least agree that we want the same thing, none of the rest should matter," he clarified. "If you two are ready to at least put aside the past for the moment, I'd like to hear what he has to say."

Griffin's unrelenting glare would've sent shivers down his spine only a month ago, but they'd changed a lot since then. Their constant companionship had blossomed into a deep-rooted friendship. On his part, this friendship was fed by an appreciation for what he knew of Griffin's journey and his care of those he held close. On Griffin's, Jasper could only imagine that it came from a mixture of admiration for his courage and unwavering loyalty to Sav, and pity for the effects the book had on his life. Regardless of motives, at this point, they'd learned to read the subtleties in each other's demeanour like the most studied of critics to a painting. Hence why Jasper knew he'd reached through to Griffin— even if it meant he'd pay for it later.

Besides, Jasper was no fool and he knew Amon wasn't either. Amon had clearly done more than enough on his own, and judging by Griffin's brief description of him, that's how he'd always done things.

So, why now? Jasper wondered. Why come to them if he was already so capable? There was an air of desperation about him, faint as it may have been, and in it, Jasper found he recognised the source of it all too readily... He decided to test his theory.

Ignoring Griffin, Jasper cleared his throat and addressed Amon directly. "Why do you feel so strongly about protecting her, considering you were the person who dragged her into this mess?"

"I..." Amon began before taking a long pause. His search for words seemed to quell Griffin's bloodlust, as if it were somewhat of an unusual occurrence. Knowing the kind of company that Griffin kept, Jasper could imagine just how shocking such a revelation might be.

"Have you come to waste our time?" Griffin replied, his gaze prodding as he began to lower his guard.

"I can't explain it..." Amon whispered, his voice softening. It was a rare token of vulnerability on his part which gave further weight to his story. "Before her, I couldn't see. My world was empty…dark. I might not have been alone, but there was a feeling I had of knowing there was something more out there for me. Then, she appeared, and it was like finding a singular star in the night sky. She just… glowed. I'd never experienced anything like it before, and nothing since, either."

"Amon, I've known you for too long to believe such a thing. You'd avoided visiting me in Osiir every year. There's no way you could've crossed paths."

"I avoided it because of her," he admitted. "We met before even you and I, Griffin, on one of those ridiculous alliance-building visits. I don't think I realised what it was back then. I was only a boy. Even still, I knew there was something about her that I'd never found in anyone else."

"That doesn't explain your actions," Jasper said.

"I know…" Amon ran his fingers nervously through his hair. "I was so inexperienced with such a connection that, instead of trying to understand it, I ran from it. I got as far away as I possibly could. I fell deeper into the darkness rather than walking towards that light. But now I see the truth. I know that no matter how far I run from it, I will never escape this feeling of longing, this feeling of being tied to someone in ways only souls can comprehend…" He sighed as he stared down at his feet. "It's a strange kind of torture I've never experienced before, but what I feel for her goes deeper than any words can explain."

As he raised his head again, Jasper caught a glimpse of the hope and longing he'd once admired in Savara's eyes shining through Amon's. They were mirrors of each other, somehow. And more so, for there was one thing underpinning it all. *Love*, he realised. Amon was hopelessly in love with her. Jasper knew then that he was telling the truth. It didn't excuse his actions or the atrocities he'd so readily committed for his own personal gain, but it did mean that, from hereon in, he was working in her best interest. And that was something they had in common.

"Alright," Jasper said.

"Alright?" Griffin replied. "A sob story is all it takes to turn you?"

"It's more than just a story, Griffin, and you know it."

Griffin dragged his hands down his face and scoffed. "Alright, alright. Fine. But know this, Amon: you step out of line, you get any of my friends hurt, intentionally or otherwise, our past aside, I will kill you," he said before storming out of the room.

The door slammed shut behind him. Jasper looked over at Amon, whose eyes had regained their distance and impassivity, and frowned.

"She means the world to me, too," Jasper said when he was sure Griffin was long gone. Amon said nothing as Jasper strolled around the table towards the door. "I know what must happen. I also know how much you want to stop it." Still, Amon was silent. Jasper reached for the door handle and gave it a tug. Before departing, he looked back at Amon, who remained cross-armed and unwavering in his stoicism. "I'm trusting you for her sake. Don't make me regret that decision." He hoped that he was making the right choice, but deep down, he knew that it was no choice at all. Without Amon, there would be no winning this war. Whether they liked him or not, whether they trusted him or not, he was their only chance at getting Savara back and defeating the Prince of Shadows.

"I don't plan on it," was Amon's only reply.

CHAPTER 9

THE EYES THAT WATCH THE HOUSE

THE DAWN'S RAYS SAUNTERED IN through the windows, but Savara had long since been awake. She'd remained in her bed, contemplating her situation and the strange shift in her dreams, knowing there was more to both than she'd previously thought. Even back in her uncle's house, terrorised out of any kind of peaceful slumber by the reoccurring nightmare, she'd known her dreams had meant something. That they were trying to send her a message. One she'd yet to decipher.

Despite the relative tranquillity of her latest dream, a similar sensation plagued her. Last night's dream held weight. A glimpse into future events, perhaps, or a longing in her soul. Regardless, the vision had left her flustered and wanting, having felt as real as the mattress beneath her. A feeling of closeness, of reunion, had followed her into the waking hours of the morning. What she had yet to figure out was the identity of the stranger in her dreams. There was something so familiar about him, and yet, ethereal to the point of being almost angelic. Savara certainly knew no one who lived up to that description. Still, the phantom touch of his hands lingered where his presence could not. As did a singularly spoken word which had never before filled her with such incomparable hope.

"Soon."

Savara had no idea what it referred to or who had said it, but she clung to its promise.

Soon.

When the rising sunlight became too much to ignore, Savara made her way from the bed to the washroom again to begin readying herself for the day. As she entered, she was immediately assaulted by crisp green leaves that seemed to have grown rampant overnight. They'd lost their muted hues, looking as though they'd somehow been brought back to life. She wiped the sleep from her eyes and gazed around properly, realising that the rest of the room had gained a vibrance that wasn't there the night before. She pursed her lips, wilfully deciding to ignore the feeling that she had something to do with it as she prepared for breakfast.

Soon…

When Savara returned to the bedroom, she found the bed made and a plain silver dress pressed and laid out for her. Plain in this sense was relative. Compared to the other gowns hanging on the rack, which were laced and embellished with all sorts of gems and precious metals, this one simply stood out for the quality of the fabric. She ran her fingers over the soft cloth, admiring the perfection of the stitching and the luxurious texture of the material. A smile crept across her face as she contemplated it, acclimatising herself to the idea of the impending change, and wondering what surprises waited for her beyond the door.

Savara stepped towards the mirror, surveying the way the dress hung on her petite frame. She pulled her hair to one side and began braiding it, her eyes hitching on different parts of her reflection. Little time had passed since her return, and yet, she was an entirely changed woman. Even the ease with which she stood before the mirror, dressed like the queen she was born to be, spoke of transformation. Like the little caterpillar who became a butterfly, when compared to the girl she was before all this, she was wholly unrecognizable.

"I am a queen," she told herself.

A Queen of Daemons… she heard Alexei's voice say in her mind.

She pursed her lips, unwilling to let the comment haunt her the way it had before.

The morning light filtered through the windowpanes, casting a gentle glow that highlighted the rainbow flecks in her eyes. She had never noticed how vividly they sparkled, as though a painter had dipped his brush into wildflower petals, stealing their colours and adding strokes of each into her irises.

A fleeting thought appeared. Maybe returning to the lands of her soul had intensified their brilliance. In the back of her mind, the portraits lining the hall continued to occupy her thoughts. The coloured eyes that had stared back at her whispered of shared history and untold tales. Their glow, a hint at connection echoed in the depths of her own gaze. This same gaze seemed to follow her, in a way that almost demanded she ask after the undeniable resemblance.

With hair braided and dress pressed down, she took one last look at the final product, an almost mirror image of the woman she'd seen in the portrait, save for the noticeable age difference. It was this image before her of overwhelming similarity that solidified her need for truth.

Savara had almost made it to the door when she noticed a prickle in her collarbone. She touched a hand to the afflicted area wondering what might have caused such a thing. On instinct, she turned back to the dresser, finding the Arima stone resting atop a small jewellery box.

It might be good to keep it on me, she thought as she made to retrieve it. Something had gone as far as to place it where she could not ignore it. *There must be a reason.* As she took hold of the stone, she felt that same overwhelming rush of power flooding through her body. The sensation both tethering and liberating. On a whim, she opened the jewellery box, hoping to find a casing or a locket of some sort in which to keep the stone. Of course, resting in the centre of the box—as if placed there by magic—she found one: a small gold chain with a pendant shaped like half a sun, into which she knew innately the stone would fit.

Ask, and it will be provided, she remembered again.

It was the final touch.

Savara slotted the stone into the pendant and locked the chain around her neck. The dizzying rush of power seemed to be lessened by the pendant—something for which Savara was grateful, for she would not have to strain as much against her own powers and their need to establish resonance with the stone. Now, having readied herself for the occasion, Savara let out a final sigh, knowing that as soon as she stepped outside of the confines of the room, she'd be at the mercy of the Prince of Shadows.

Entering the hall, Savara found herself surrounded by sconces that seemed to come alive as she approached, casting warm light along the corridor. Their gentle illumination served as an unspoken guide, leading her toward the dining hall. As she drew nearer, she noticed the lingering aroma of breakfast in the air, causing her stomach to grumble in anticipation.

The doors to the dining hall opened of their own accord, revealing yet another room trapped in the confines of time and bound by the promise of eventual use. Marble floors spread out to columned walls which framed vistas of stagnant gardens and distant valleys. Above, a beautiful golden chandelier hung, illuminated by streams of the same curious glowing dust. Beneath it, she found a modest table, set for what looked to be a small gathering, rather than just two people.

Sweet and savoury scents danced in the air, that of jams and honey drizzled over caramelised toasts alongside the unmistakable aroma of breakfast meats and eggs. She found a surprising deal of comfort in it. Soon, the tantalising scent of warm, spiced dark chocolate mingled its way into the festival of aromas as well. A large silver teapot in the centre looked like a promising source for such a smell. It stirred her appetite, waking up the rest of her senses and drawing her in closer to the feast. Savara felt her mouth begin to water. The spread almost made her forget why she had come in the first place.

Almost.

At the far end of the room, the Prince of Shadows materialised. Specks of dust slithered in from nowhere, collecting in the shape of his enigmatic person, similar to how he'd appeared in the gardens of Idune after being summoned by Amon. Without her notice, the thought of him sent shivers down her neck. Savara took an involuntary step backwards as the ethereal figure took form, his presence commanding attention. To her surprise, he gestured for her to approach and smoothly pulled out the chair at the table, inviting her to take her place.

"Good morning, child. How did you sleep?" His voice, deep and spiced with mystery, hinted at reassurance as he waited. The contrast between his foreboding presence and the courteous act of pulling out the chair created a disconcerting harmony, leaving Savara torn between wariness and reluctant acknowledgement.

"Fine," she replied curtly as she moved toward the waiting chair. Savara decided she wasn't going to reveal anything about herself, allowing the Prince of Shadows to fill the air between them with answers, rather than with more confusion.

Tentatively, Savara eased herself into the offered seat. The Prince of Shadows, an enigma in the shifting light, observed her intently. A loaded silence lingered between them, a delicate dance of trust and suspicion. It was a thing of unspoken questions and the promise of revelations.

"Good. I am pleased," the Prince of Shadows responded, his words carrying an undertone of satisfaction, though she knew better than to assume anything of him. "I hope breakfast is to your liking," he continued as he swept across the floors to his chair at the opposite end of the table. He gestured towards the array of plates that adorned its surface before settling into his own seat. "I was not sure what would please you most, so I prepared a variety of tastes for you."

Savara nodded curtly, unsure if this was an attempt at bribery, or something else entirely. Out of respect for his efforts, she filled her plate with a bit of everything. The assortment of dishes displayed a culinary diversity that spoke of meticulous preparation. The Prince of Shadows mirrored her actions, seemingly enjoying their silent communion. This strange breaking of bread however, left her more confused than she'd been when she'd arrived.

With her plate filled, Savara waited for the Prince of Shadows to take the first bite, worrying the food might have been poisoned. The Prince of Shadows smiled, as if having expected the hesitancy, and began his feast. He spared not even a glance in her direction as he enjoyed his meal in silence.

I suppose it's safe… she thought as she took up the fork.

A soft sigh of delight escaped her lips. The flavours danced on her tongue in a sort of symphony of tastes, so uniquely attuned to her preferences that it was startling. There were tastes she herself could barely place but that her soul remembered with fondness. With each bite, her curiosity grew, the need for answers nagging at her between each morsel.

The Prince of Shadows seemed to relish in the simple pleasure of their shared meal. His features fell into the soft acceptance of homeliness, despite sitting across someone who should be considered an enemy, given their opposing goals. Savara could not so easily cast aside her doubts regarding her enigmatic benefactor, yet she accepted the act of dining together for what it was. A recognition of their mutual humanity—or, at least, whatever humanity he had left. The silence between them was punctuated by the occasional touch of golden fork to bone-white porcelain, but he made no attempt to fill it. Not until after the chocolate was poured.

"You have a lot on your mind," the Prince of Shadows observed.

These first words caught her mid-morsel and unprepared. She choked down the eggs with an uncomfortable gulp and tapped the napkin to her lips, all the while considering her next words with care.

"You summoned me here," she said, unsure how best to voice her concern without incurring his wrath.

"You came," he replied.

"I am still not sure why," she admitted, unwilling to share the true depth of her apprehension, but knowing somehow that he was very much aware already.

"I promised to answer all your burning questions, and I am not one to so easily break my word," he replied, a disarming smile making its way across his face.

The ease with which he spoke sent shivers down her arms. To his credit, he spoke candidly and truthfully. He had never once minced words with her. Meticulously crafted his sentences? Yes. Minced words or outright lied? Never. Which made their conversation all the more troubling. He looked eager even to divulge his secrets. She felt as though she'd once again fallen into a trap, only this time, she'd have to find her way out alone. She could almost hear Amon's concerned voice now, berating her for not having stayed out of trouble.

You were the one who pushed me to this, she thought, wondering if he'd hear it through whatever channel remained between them.

The thought of Amon even now made her blood boil. The killer of her family in both this world and the one beyond. He'd cosied up to her for reasons she still could not fathom. Perhaps only to hurt her more. How stupid she'd been to let her guard down with him in what she'd thought were moments of intimacy and weakness. Never before had she played such a game—or been played in such a way. But then, hadn't that been his intent all along?

"Life is a game, princess. One great, big, meaningless game. And we, its sentenced players, are all losers from the moment we place our piece on the board. The sooner you learn that, the better…"

Thinking back on those words, a loving part of her wanted to believe he'd said them out of guilt, out of a personal suffering that she'd not been able to comprehend. But she was tired of making excuses for him. She'd use her time here wisely, use it to forget him, the way she should've done the day they'd first met. Yet, something inside her felt as though it were reaching out for him. Treacherous little human heart of hers, longing for the pain only love could cause.

Savara stared down at her plate, unable to meet his prodding gaze, though feeling the force of it on her skin like the heat of a torch. She searched her mind for those same burning questions that had kept her moving along on this journey, favouring their confusion over that of her heart. As if by magic, an unexpected one bubbled to the surface, crossing the threshold of her lips with an undeniable urgency.

"I noticed the portraits in the hall," she began, considering the topic only after the words had left her mouth. "Who are they?"

"My ancestors," he replied with ease, his tone resounding with pride. "The many lords and ladies of the House of Spirits, rulers of the Arima lands spanning centuries."

"Their eyes…"

"You've noticed," he acknowledged, an almost imperceptible glint of amusement flashing in his gaze. "A commonality, a trait passed down through the bloodline."

"Does that mean…"

"That you too are a descendant of the house of spirits? Why, yes," he affirmed. His voice was filled with a matter-of-factness that should've calmed her nerves but only set her more on edge. He seemed to take his revelation of a previously unknown and potentially dangerous part of her lineage with little more than indifference. Her world, on the other hand, had been irreparably shaken. Her soul rattled, awakened with a precarious curiosity.

The question she hadn't thought to ask anyone before hung in the air. Why did she have this connection to the spirits of not only this world but the one beyond? Why had she been the only one in centuries divined Arima? Why her?

And why now? The answer had been so simple all this time, practically staring her in the face. Only now, seated across from the current guardian of the House of Spirits, had she the strength to look truth in the eye.

"Who are you, really?" she asked, her voice steady despite the uncertainty swirling within her. A little voice from deep within her had already come up with an answer, and not one she especially liked. But she needed to hear it for herself. She needed it confirmed by the man before her. She needed the truth, the one so obvious it almost pained her to admit she'd overlooked it entirely.

CHAPTER 10

THE HOUSE OF SPIRITS

THE PRINCE OF SHADOWS PLACED HIS CUTLERY gently down on the table and snapped his fingers. The sound reverberated through the house, summoning a pair of flickering spirits to his side out of nowhere, as if they had been there the whole time. They, like her own guide, could not speak and would hear no command, but would clear the table regardless.

"I believe the time has come for the full tour of the palace," he said, not entirely ignoring her comment, but postponing his response for effect. He, like his apprentice, seemed to have a flair for the nonchalantly dramatic, a trait which irritated Savara more than anything.

In one swift movement, he stood, catching rays of the morning light on the hollows of his cheeks. Savara thought back to their previous encounter in Idune, comparing the man before her with the hazy image she had of him in her mind. In Idune, she remembered, his skin had a grainy, almost translucent texture to it, as if he were as ephemeral as the constant stream of dust above their heads. The skin of the man before her now was sharper. Crisp. No longer a product of ash alone. Something had changed since then. Something had filled in part of the hollowness. Savara wondered what part of it involved her presence before him and what part, much like the rest of his history, was tainted with blood.

"I need to know," she insisted, unwavering in her determination. She hadn't come this far or gone through this much pain to be left wanting. Her identity—which she now believed to be more intrinsically tied to his own—had been called into question by the hauntingly beautiful eyes of the portraits on the walls. She needed to know, for her own peace of mind, just how entangled were their spirits—how similar was their blood. Was he a long-lost ancestor? Or did his life give reason to her own?

"And you will," he replied cryptically, his beady red eyes burning with the promise of revelation locked on her with intent like a hunter to his prey. Again, Alexei's words crept into her mind.

"Don't forget who the real devil is, Savara. Especially not while living under his roof…"

The Prince of Shadows strode silently over towards the other end of the dining hall, waiting for her with a hand extended. Savara placed her napkin down on the table and made to stand. Before her, the trays of food had already begun to disappear, carried out by the two spectral servants whose bodies could no more remain in this world than the one beyond.

Savara followed hesitantly, fearing what might happen to her if she didn't.

The Prince of Shadows led her down the same halls she'd traversed with her guide the previous night, basking in the expectant silence that lingered between them. Soon, they rounded a corner to where the line of portraits sat, almost glowing under the light of the curious dust that coated the ceilings.

"These, as you now know, were the keepers of the House of Spirits," he began, gazing proudly over the portraits. His pride dropped as he contemplated the final one—his own— seemingly irritated at the youthful optimism shining through his younger self's eyes. His had changed, ruby-red eyes filled with a deception he tried to mask. Savara realised that the dust had begun to recoil from his portrait, prickling away from it the way he did, focusing instead on the others. "My ancestors. Gifted individuals. Invaluable to the success of Visanthe as a state of broken lands. An entire line of those who could commune with forces beyond the comprehension of this world. The very same forces that rule it."

"Iturri," she whispered.

"Correct," he said with a grin. "What do you know of Iturri, Savara?" The Prince of Shadows continued down the hall, retracing the steps of the girl from the previous night that had led to the strange door. The one surrounded by dust and shadow.

As she followed, Savara considered his question, piecing together the many strange stories with the ever-obscure reference to Iturri. She remembered the ceremonial Divination speech, which gave mention to the role of Iturri in choosing the form each child's powers took. During her own Divination, she recalled her innate fear and distrust of it. At the time, she hadn't quite understood why. It was the god Griffin and the others had prayed to on several occasions, the curse on her mother's lips. Unlike the others, for some reason, she'd had it in her mind that Iturri was a trickster, a mess-maker. Not a benevolent kind of god, but one of chaos.

Yet, even as she considered her previous opinions, the stories she'd heard of the so-called god didn't strike her as complete. If anyone were able to complete the picture of this entity in her head, she knew it was the man who was uniquely able to commune with the spirits.

"Iturri chooses the powers of divined children," she replied as they arrived at the door.

"It does so much more, my darling Savara…"

As the Prince of Shadows extended his hand towards the glowing dust, there was a palpable shift in the density of the air. It weighed heavily in her lungs, brimming with power and mischief. Savara took an unconscious step backwards, putting some distance between herself and the source of this sudden change.

The particles responded to his gesture as they had the day before, swirling and tangling around his outstretched fingers as if magnetised to his touch. He allowed the dust to slither around his wrist and up his arms, letting its gentle glow cast sinister shadows across his features. As it coiled around his body, Savara sensed his essence entangling with the mystical energy of the shimmering particles. With each passing moment, she could see a swelling in the strength of his spirit, a growing force coaxed out by the surrounding magic.

"Iturri is the source of all power," he continued. "It is the bond between worlds, the fabric of our very being. Iturri is what makes up order and chaos. Life and Death…"

His spirit and that of the dust became entangled, consuming the space in the room in a way only they two could sense. It was a reminder of the unfathomable depths of his power, a power that seemed to pulse and thrum with a life of its own. Finally, the dust made its way back down his person, pooling in the palm of his hand.

"Iturri is the universal harmony that connects all beings and all times," he concluded as he extended it out to her, gesturing for her to take hold.

Hesitantly, Savara obliged, feeling as though she were witnessing something sacred, something ancient and primal that transcended the boundaries of time and space.

As she stood there, allowing the dust to crawl into her hands, a powerful surge of energy burst through her veins. The sensation was stronger than that of the day before. It felt almost like an attack on her senses, as if a thousand voices whispered in her ears, their emotions swirling around her like a tempest. Fear, longing, sorrow, hope—all mingled together in a symphony of sensation that threatened to overwhelm her.

"Do you feel it?" he asked, studying her carefully. "Existence, in its purest form…"

It was chaos, unbridled chaos.

"It's too much," Savara replied, wincing at the burning sensation rushing over her skin. It felt as though the energy was consuming her, sucking the blood from her veins rather than instilling her with power as it had him.

"Relax. You were made for this."

"I can't—" She hardly heard her own voice above the noise in her mind.

"You can. Breathe…"

Savara took a deep breath, trying to regain her focus through the cacophony, but it was too much. The noise was overpowering. She wished to scream, but she doubted she'd hear even that. Before she could get out another word, she felt his shadows creeping over her, cloaking her in their cool darkness. Their gentle embrace softened the effects of the dust enough for her to come to her senses. Just enough for her to find herself again.

Suddenly, the thing inside her rattled to life.

The powers she'd once feared shook her body, looking to escape and mingle with the dust. A sharp chill ran down her spine as she switched her focus from the dust in her palm to the beady red eyes of the man before her. Under the effects of the connection to Iturri, she noticed her field of vision expand. She began to see things she'd never seen before. Things that weren't entirely there.

Echoes of figures shuffled through the halls around them, working diligently as they had in life. Overhead, the dust streamed vividly, flashing images between the grains. On the ground between them, shadows danced, their nature still a mystery to her. Some slithered across the floors like serpents.

Others curled around their prince, protruding out from his back in almost winglike tendrils. They clung to him, their source of power.

"What is this?" she asked, her voice barely audible over the ethereal cacophony of this new field of sense.

"This," he said with renewed pride, "is the matter of souls. The collective sensations of those who have crossed the threshold; passed beyond the veil of this world. It is the essence of life, of Iturri. It is not Iturri itself, but the only part of it that can reach us. It is the invisible bond that connects us all, a bond only seen by those with blessed eyes. It resides here, in the land of spirits, and is supposed to filter out into the rest of Visanthe…"

"How come I've never seen it before?" she asked, slowly relaxing into the strange new buzz of power coursing through her.

"Let us not play ignorance, my dear. You know as well as I that a blockage exists, a chokehold on these lands. It will not allow these streams to flow freely out into the greater world. As such, powers across the lands have diminished."

"Why?"

"Fear, mostly. Arrogance. A need for control…" he added bitterly.

"But why me?" she asked. "You told me before that I was the Harbinger of Death, that we were kindred spirits. I hadn't realised it then, but there's more to it than our powers being the same… Isn't there?"

The Prince of Shadows' smile widened, revealing rows of gleaming teeth that seemed to shine with an otherworldly light. "Because, my dear Savara," he replied, his voice tinged with reverence, "you are the conduit between worlds. The heir to the House of Spirits. And most importantly, you are my daughter."

Savara's breath caught in her throat as his words echoed through her mind. She'd known. Part of her had always known. Even as she'd spied the portraits from the previous night, she'd known. The resemblance was unmistakable. But to hear it confirmed aloud… Perhaps that was why the dark had always found its way to her. She was the daughter of the Prince of Shadows—the very man who had haunted her dreams and shaped her destiny since the day she was born. She was his legacy, truly cut from the same cloth.

"But how is that possible? You've been trapped here for…"

"775 years, yes," he acknowledged. "At least, that is what they'd wish you to believe. But remember, it is I who communes with the gods, the spirits, and the planes beyond this one. My powers are much greater than these simpletons could ever imagine. Nothing and no one is out of my reach…"

The way he said it sent a wave of shivers down her spine. Had he been the thing in the shadows? Traversing worlds to find her. The thing that watched over her in the darkness, the reason for her every nightmare…

Even as she considered this, Savara recalled the dream that had plagued her for so long in the other world—the fire, the destruction—and wondered how she could've missed eyes like his staring back at her. But his presence was one she'd never forgotten. A feeling she'd never shake. Her father, the Prince of Shadows, was a rip current waiting to sweep even the most well-designed ships, a volcano waiting to erupt, the slowly approaching hand of death in human form…

So, what was he waiting for?

"But that is a story for another day, my dear. Know this now. You are the final link in a chain that was established many years ago, and one more perfect than even I could have ever envisioned. You are a daughter of light and dark, a being of soul and soil… You are the Harbinger of Death, my dear. You were always meant to be a beautiful end."

He spoke with a sense of pride that made the shadows around him grow restless and hungry, as if they too felt the weight of his words. His speech resonated somewhere within the depths of her soul, forcing her to wonder once more whether she was simply a pawn in some grander game, or if she was a player in her own right—a force to be reckoned with, or simply the catalyst for an impending storm.

"This death you mention, how far will it reach?"

The Prince of Shadows fixed his eyes on hers. His gaze penetrated all the walls she'd built up to protect herself. In his eyes, she found all the nightmares from her childhood— empty rooms, menacing moans, shadowy figures—their red glow burned in the back of her mind as he spoke. Even the voice that came through sounded less like his own, tinged with the darkness surrounding him.

"There will be no corner left untouched."

"Why?"

"The world has sat, unchanged and caged, for far too long. I will no longer allow this rotting of my lands to continue."

Rotting of lands?

She turned the words over in her mind. Now, she was certain the voice behind them was not his own. There was something else residing within him, and unlike whatever lived in her, she could see that it drove him to drastic measures. Savara knew there was no way she could say no to him, especially not while sharing a roof.

The Prince of Shadows reached a gentle hand out to her, the way a father might have to guide his beloved child. Yet in that moment, she felt no love at all. "Will you help me?" he said, softening his tone to match his actions. "Will you step up to meet your destiny?"

Knowing she had little choice in the matter, and still looking for a way out of this situation, Savara nodded. Already she could see that her actions would have a ripple effect that would span the world over. If she could somehow find a way to control these ripples, maybe the catastrophe could be avoided.

"I will."

The Prince of Shadows smiled as he pushed open the door, letting a light brighter than any she'd ever known engulf them.

CHAPTER 11

CHILDHOOD TRAUMAS

YOU ARE NOTHING BUT A FAILURE…

His mother's voice plagued him even now. The memory of her was one he'd actively avoided for so long that he was surprised at how his heart raced. He took a deep breath, looking to dispel it from his thoughts as he sunk deeper into his meditation.

The contours of his mind faded, taking with it the thoughts, the dreams, the nightmares. With his eyes closed, he allowed himself to find that steady rhythm of breathing, using his heartbeat as a guide. For each breath, seven thumps. For each thump, a count. Soon he was lost in the trance, and for a brief moment, the quiet that blanketed him was peaceful. Until, even there, his mother's voice crept in.

Failure…

"Don't let her get to you," he told himself.

Outside, on the streets of Yozora, people were engaged in the trivialities of daily life. Fetching food, walking pets, enjoying drinks on some of the sidewalk bistros. They were wilfully unaware of the changes to come.

The sounds filtered up to the small window in the flat he'd kept for emergency escapes. No one else knew of it, not even the Prince of Shadows. He'd charmed it well enough so that no passersby would notice the narrow wooden door and iron fencing that barred his flat from the two beside it. They were meant to be as unassuming as possible, so much so that people would unconsciously look the other way as they neared.

This was his safe haven.

This was the only place that had ever been his and his alone. For the longest time, he'd found solace between these chipped, white, painting-less walls. No other soul had set foot upon the weathered wooden floorboards. Yet, somehow, his mother's voice had found its way in.

The sound of the kettle boiling on the little fire brought him back to the present.

Amon uncrossed his legs and made his way over to the kitchenette. He pulled a mismatched porcelain mug from the open shelving and added a mix of herbs to it, followed swiftly by the boiling water. He inhaled deeply, hoping the tea would calm his nerves.

Now that he'd regained most of his soul, he felt things on a deeper level. Deeper even than from before his bonds were made. It was as though he needed to lose those parts of himself to appreciate them fully, and in regaining them, he'd slowly begun to realise their significance.

All of this had been planned by some greater entity—at least, that's what the stars had said when he was finally ready to hear their message.

He turned his back to the sturdy granite countertop, leaning against it as he contemplated his reflection in the tea. His eyes glowed brighter than they ever had before, a change that had come from the breaking of his bonds. Sadly, he spied streaks of his mother's characteristically blinding white hair through his own onyx-coloured curls as well.

The stars were right, he was being primed. Cycles that had started many years ago were beginning to close. He felt them all around him, and he wondered how many others could as well. The air had grown hesitant. The days clung to each other, as if fearing their own ends. Death lingered in each of the shadows.

He blew at the curls of steam and took a sip.

Fate would not be outrun forever…

CHAPTER 12

EMBRACING THE SHADOWS

THE STRANGE SPRAWLING GARDEN before them looked nothing like the stagnant planes of the Arima lands on the other side of the door. The life that had bled from the mainland existed here, trapped behind that junction between worlds. The same fountain marked on its panels bubbled away in the distance. The shadows and dust that surrounded it mingled around them in a dance of sacred harmony, welcoming them to the place from which they seemed to originate.

Savara shivered as she crossed the threshold, anticipation coursing through her veins. She felt a resonance between her powers and the gardens. A sense of belonging. As though what she had been searching for, in Visanthe and beyond, was right here. That it had been all along.

Her powers prodded for escape from beneath her skin, prickling at the edges of her fingertips. They held no malice this time, simply a need to be used. She stared down at her palms, noticing the lavender light that had seeped out into the centre of them.

Since her fight with Big Tog in Haizea, she'd learned that these life-taking powers of hers were merely tools. Not inherently harmful. It was the motives behind their use that should be feared. And yet, being here, surrounded by a power much like her own, she felt there was more to them than death and destruction.

"Where are we?" she asked, her eyes falling on the glowing path that led to the fountain. "And why does it feel like…"

"Home?" said the Prince of Shadows.

Savara turned to find him standing beside her, arms crossed casually behind his back, looking as regal as he had in his portrait. Something about the air around them brought his features back to life. In this new setting, the red of his eyes glowed a softer, kinder hue, though she knew they burned with the same desire for destruction that they had only moments before. The shadows danced around him, surrounding his figure in a glistening black halo. He looked like a dark angel, captivating and terrifying.

"This is the only part of the Arima lands that remains untouched by the cage," he explained. "This is home."

Home. The last time Savara had heard that word used in reference to Visanthe was when Griffin had come to collect her from the human world. Prior to that, her life had been nothing but a missing childhood, a routine made for sleepy fishermen that left her restless, and of course, a string of nightmares and longings. In spite of all that, she played the part she'd been given, working hard to convince herself that her uncle's house on that small island was her home, even when something inside her vehemently denied it. When she made the jump to Visanthe, she somehow knew she was getting closer to whatever she expected home to feel like, but as she revisited the places from her childhood that should've felt like home, a sense of lack and longing still prevailed.

Something inside her had known back then. The same thing that knew now…

No other place had made her feel the way this one did because no other place could. It was a sense of need, felt on both ends. A girl who needed the place as much as the place needed the girl. A harmony found on levels that surpassed all forms of comprehension.

A home.

Her home.

Savara knew she belonged here. More so than any place she'd ever encountered. It was as if the world opened unto her as she stepped through the doorway. The warm air that caressed her skin felt like a welcome hug. The fountain bubbling away in the background sounded like a lullaby. Flowers around her bloomed in salute. And, if she listened hard enough, she could almost hear the sound of children laughing in the phantom wind.

The Prince of Shadows had been right all along.

Before she could speak, a creature appeared at her feet, startling her as it did. It was a large, winged panther, with two sharp fangs that looked like they could pierce steel. The low rumbling that came from it set her nerves on edge, but she soon realised the creature was not there for her. It stalked around her once, taking in her scent, before seating itself next to the Prince of Shadows and nudging him with its snout. The Prince of Shadows patted it lightly on the head.

He smiled, noticing her confusion. "This is one of few creatures that can traverse the bounds of each world. In time, you too might be able to perform a similar feat." The creature's purring grew louder, rumbling like the beginnings of a strong earthquake. "She has been my most loyal companion throughout these years of confinement."

Captivated by its glossy black wings and piercing eyes, Savara knelt down to meet the creature face-to-face. She felt that, somehow, she'd seen those very same eyes before. Not here. Not in Visanthe. Strangely enough, she recognised them as having watched her from the shadows of the home she'd left behind in the human world. They were eyes that lingered in nightmares and became fears in the shadows. But here, fear did not afflict her as it once had.

Perhaps she'd spent so long in the dark that she was immune to the trappings of fear. Or, perhaps, she was becoming something to be feared herself. Either way, the eyes staring back at her no longer terrified her as they once had. Rather, they themselves were haunted by a sense of knowing and melancholia. Haunting and hauntingly beautiful at the same time.

"She is beautiful," Savara replied.

She thanks you, Majesty, came a whisper from deep within the confines of her mind. Had Savara been anywhere else, she might have jumped at hearing the foreign voice. But after the experience she'd had with hearing the whispers of the dust and the stones, and with a variety of other creatures throughout Visanthe, Savara knew exactly where this voice had come from. Its owner sat before her, staring intently into her eyes.

"I can hear her," Savara said, a sense of wonder filling her heart at the realisation.

"That is only one part of your powers, my child. Are you ready to learn to use the rest?"

Savara felt the hairs beginning to rise down the lengths of her arms. Excitement took hold, a kind she'd never anticipated feeling—especially not with the man from her nightmares. "I am."

"Good." The Prince of Shadows ordered the creature away with a graceful sweep of his hand. It disappeared, leaving them alone in the garden of wonders. "There are three main aspects of your powers that you must master. The first you are already familiar with, but we are going to strengthen: the sensing of souls."

"Is that how I am able to hear animals?" she asked, eager to learn more about her newfound abilities.

The Prince of Shadows nodded. "Each soul has a unique way of communicating. Those like you and I are privy to these communications—if only we know how to listen."

Savara thought back to all the strange creatures whose voices she'd pretended not to hear and whose stories had once been only a figment of her imagination. At least, that's what she'd claimed for fear of sounding crazy to those without her gift. Even in the human world, there were times when such things had occurred. There, had she shared such a gift with anyone, she would've been sent to a mental institution. In Visanthe, however, she was almost a god among mortals.

"Does this gift work with invisible creatures as well?" she asked, indirectly wanting to ask about the one she'd seen by the cliffs when she'd first arrived in the Arima lands. Maybe if she could talk to it and find out what it wanted, she would understand how to get rid of it.

The Prince of Shadows raised his brows thoughtfully. "Invisible in what way?"

"I suppose like the dust in the palace. We can see it, but no one else can."

He looked at her sceptically. "Anything with a soul can be heard, though they may not all communicate with words like you and me. You already experienced this with the spectres of the house…" He paused. "Is there a reason for your question, my dear? Has something happened to you?"

"No," she lied. "It was just a question."

"Alright," he replied, his disbelief echoed in the words, but he didn't press the issue further.

Savara wondered if he could read the thoughts from her mind, if he could sense that, beyond the simple question about the extent of her powers, she was planning to use them against him. She needed to be more careful with her line of questioning. There was no telling what might result from him otherwise.

"How far do these gardens stretch?" she asked, hoping to transition to a safer topic.

The Prince of Shadows' eyes lightened with amusement. The surrounding shadows relaxed their fluttering, curling instead like kittens around his feet. His eyes rested on the expansive greenery ahead, contemplating it fondly.

"That, my child, is a better question for the feet than it is for the mouth, and certainly for much more curious feet than mine," he replied, gesturing for her to explore.

Savara smiled at him, noticing a newfound sense of endearment towards her mentor. She connected immediately with his appreciation for the natural world, but there was something more. Something welcoming in his manner. A warmth to him that didn't exist outside of this pocket of ethereal beauty. These gardens seemed to soothe his spirit, making him much more approachable than in the world beyond the doors. Here, he softened. Not only his person but the energy surrounding him.

Was there something in the garden that made his mood shift so drastically? Or was it simply the effect of the gardens themselves? The respite from the curse perhaps. Or maybe he was just an admirer of life. Regardless, it felt as though he was more whole here. More at ease. More connected to the heart she hadn't believed he possessed.

Savara took cue from him as she gazed in awe at the vibrant world around her, eager to traverse all the paths and explore every corner. But this excitement was quickly replaced by a resounding sense of concern.

The empty skies and ethereal whisperings of the garden reminded her of the one in Haizea. It wasn't hard to imagine why either, she realised. Brass had told her then that those gardens, those lands, were steeped in blood. The Zerua boasted the greatest connection to Iturri—aside from the Arima—owing to the excessive quantities of spilt blood. And though this garden and its beauty were not born of spilt blood necessarily, she could not ignore the intrinsic connection to the world beyond.

Life abounding here meant death somewhere else.

"Is it safe?" she asked hesitantly.

"Of course," he chuckled. "For you, my dear, this garden is your servant; as is the house beyond, as are the lands… The spirits respond to their kind, of which you are royalty. Anything that will make you happy and keep you safe is their duty, their pleasure."

"In that case," she began, excitement teeming within, "would you mind if I looked around?"

"Wander to your heart's content. These lands are yours as much as they are mine," he replied. "However, you shall have to do so alone. My time with you has come to an end for now. I am being called to other matters," he added, his tone taking on a more sombre note.

Slowly, tendrils of his shadows curled out towards her.

Savara recoiled, her past fears of them prompting the movement, when a tendril smoothed out her hair as if in reassurance. The move was almost father-like.

Kind in a way she did not imagine of him. And something he realised she did not expect.

The shadows retracted, returning to their halo-esque positions around his body. With a final nod, the Prince of Shadows disappeared, his form dissolving into nothingness, taking the shadows along with him.

CHAPTER 13

UNBROKEN RINGS

SEBASTIAN WATCHED OVER HER AS SHE SLEPT, still in awe of how someone so dangerous when awake could sleep so peacefully. She looked like a fallen angel, her vibrant red hair splayed out beneath her acting like a fiery halo. Only a few months back, he would've thought such a scene impossible. Yet here she was. Here they were. Together. Sebastian had no idea which god had smiled upon him so, to allow him such a blessing—to be here, with her—but he would thank them all, each and every one, until the day he died.

His eyes traced lovingly over the various scars across her tiny person. Storm was stronger than most people he knew. None of these scars had ever stopped her or broken her spirit. It was one of the things he'd most admired about her.

But that didn't take away the inherent guilt he felt at seeing all the pain she'd endured, the memory of it left to stain her skin for the rest of her days. She would never need his protection, but a selfish part of him wished that she would want his help the way he wanted to give it.

But that wasn't her nature.

Sebastian inched himself off the bed gently, careful not to disturb her sleep. They hadn't told the others about their budding relationship, but he knew they wouldn't be able to sneak around forever. If it were his decision alone, he wouldn't have minded the rest knowing, but Storm was afraid of it getting out. He didn't understand her reasons, but he knew that it had something to do with a past that still haunted her. He promised to keep it quiet for her sake. At this point, he knew he'd do anything for her.

They'd spent the night ravelled in each other. The years of tension that had built up, the barriers they'd placed between them, all of them crumbled the night they finally admitted their feelings. Since then, passing glances led to stolen moments—lust, passion, and something more had grown where before there were only insults and facades of hatred. These feelings were unlike any he had ever experienced before. From the moment they met, Sebastian knew his life was changed forever, but he'd never imagined, not in his wildest dreams, how wholly and completely he'd fall for her—or she him.

Storm shifted in her sleep. Her gentle smile turned. Her brows knitted together. Sebastian worried a nightmare was about to surface. He leaned in and pressed a kiss to her forehead, wishing to be able to stay longer, but knowing that the others would soon wake.

"Not yet..." she whispered suddenly, her brows still knitted, and eyes closed, but her soul stirred. Her hand reached out for his at the edge of the bed, and slowly she laced her fingers with his.

"It's almost light out," he whispered in reply.

Storm held tighter. "Not yet."

Sebastian rested his back against the headboard and allowed her to inch onto his chest. As she softened into him, he noticed a small tear escape her eyes. Perhaps he was protecting her, only not in the way he imagined. The demons on the ground were no match for her, but the ones in her mind put up a stronger fight.

"Not yet..." he repeated, whispering the words into her forehead before pressing another kiss to it.

Storm let out a soft sigh that almost sounded like the word *never*. When the morning light came, she'd probably deny it. But he'd heard it. Soft as it was, he'd heard it. Such a trivial word. *Never.* Said by anyone else, it would have been a word like any other. But from her, it sounded like the sweetest lullaby, a ray of hope through the darkest of nights. A prayer. One he'd answer. A promise he'd keep above all others.

Suddenly, a heavy knock came from outside the door.

Storm shot up in a frantic state. The grey of her irises pierced his heart as she stared at him, urging him to find a way out. Sebastian shrugged and scrambled for his clothes. He hadn't expected anyone to be up so soon, let alone to come knocking.

"Put on your clothes, lovebirds, this is important," murmured Lucy from the other side of the door.

Storm rolled her eyes and let out a little sigh of relief. "Move," she whispered. "I'll get the door." She slipped on a large tunic and slid gracefully across the floor.

Sebastian couldn't help but stare as she made her way to the door, falling even more in love with the way her hips swayed beneath the fabric and the strands of brilliant red hair stuck out around the crown of her head. Storm only opened the door a tad, but it was enough for Sebastian to catch a glimpse of Lucy's all-knowing smirk. She was the only person who knew of their secret, and they trusted her to keep it. Lucy was a fortress—and Storm's best friend.

When Storm turned back to him, any amusement that had graced her face prior to opening the door had gone. Now, worry lined the crease in her brow. She slid onto the edge of the bed beside him.

"What's wrong?" he asked, taking her shoulders in his hands and attempting to affectionately smooth out the knots in them.

Storm held out the open scroll that Lucy had given her. "We need to find Griffin," she replied.

Sebastian nodded, pressing a kiss to her worried brow before searching for his clothes. Storm was already on her feet and out the door before he'd managed to button his trousers, but he lingered a moment longer in the room, watching the door shut behind her. As he did, he contemplated the time they'd spent together and how, because of it, he'd begun to see life differently. It was a foolish thing to desire someone as much as he did her, but now that he'd had a true taste of her, of joy, of hope, of pleasure, he knew he would seek to keep it the rest of his life.

In truth, there was more to it than that. He had a secret. One he intended on sharing with her at some point, when he was sure that whatever was happening between them was not merely a fantasy concocted by his traumatised mind, or a practical joke of fate—or her more mischievous counterpart, Iturri, for that matter.

He reached a hand into the pocket of his trousers and fished out two matching solid gold rings, similar to the ones placed on children's fingers at Divination Day. One for him. One for her. Inside the bands was the engraving, 'For the bond not even Iturri can break.' He'd made them himself, taken an old chain passed down from his deceased parents and melted it with his fire. When the rings came out of the moulds, Sebastian swore he'd felt two warm hands on his back, as though his parents were standing behind him, approving of his decision.

Sebastian stared at them for a little while longer before replacing them in his pocket. There would eventually be a right time for him to share this secret with Storm, but not now. Now, they had other matters to attend to. Ones that involved stopping a world war and rescuing their friend from the shadows.

CHAPTER 14

SACRED HARMONIES

ALONE IN THE ENCHANTING GARDEN, Savara started down one of the paths leading away from the doors and the fountain. Unlike the skeletal frames of the trees lining the path to the House of Spirits, the trees lining this path were blossoming with fruits and flowers of all kinds. Plump, ripe pomegranates hung heavily from their branches, glowing the colour of red wine. Cherry blossoms smiled at her, setting their muted sweetness adrift on the breeze. Fields of white narcissus and lavender sprawled out on either side of the path, colouring this world in all the shades of a perfect strawberry moon.

The vibrance of this world and the peace it made her feel within were a sharp contrast to the lands beyond the doors. Outside, gloom and stagnancy reigned supreme. Inside, her spirits were as light as the flower petals. The garden alone seemed to put to rest her darker emotions—her fears, her anxieties—and allowed for others to surge. She felt stronger here, stronger even than she had when fighting for her life in the outside world.

As she walked, Savara began to consider this drastic shift in mood. Not even the Prince of Shadows had been immune to the garden's effect. He'd softened towards her, revealing a layer to him that made him seem like an entirely different person. The maniacal darkness that had surrounded him back in Idune had disappeared. Traces of it lingered in the red glow of his eyes, but being in the garden allowed whatever was buried beneath that darkness to come to light. She reasoned it must have been there all along, that a touch of benevolence existed in him as much as that feared touch of darkness existed in her.

Savara's feet carried her aimlessly along the winding path as her mind wandered to the various encounters with him, the Prince of Shadows—her father. Though he'd never outright harmed her, his voice had antagonised her dreams for almost a decade, his shadows had hungered for her blood. He was, in grand part, the architect of her ill-fated destiny. Yet, even he was not as transparent as she'd hoped.

I suppose no one really is, she thought to herself. *Not even the Devil himself…*

As she came upon another curve in the path, Savara wondered what role the burden of fear and anxiety played in the shift in his demeanour. Perhaps he too worried, feared for things beyond those doors. Perhaps the weight of those emotions affected him more than he cared to admit. It was hard to deny the fact that she too had been afflicted, only realising the true extent of her suffering here amongst the flowers, in the origin of dust and shadow, where such emotions existed no longer.

It was a curious thought, to be sure. One that lent itself to other questions, too. How was this world able to remove those heavier emotions? And what other magical properties did it possess?

Savara lost all track of time and place, too ravelled in her contemplation to notice that the flamboyantly coloured trees and flowers had grown sparce. The path curved, veering towards a small dark plaza, lined by rosebushes and willow trees. Savara looked around, curious as to how she'd arrived at it, for there had been nothing similar in sight. The energy surrounding it differed from the rest of the gardens. There was something beyond the rosebush guardians that seemed almost…sad.

Though her curiosity tugged at her, she had learned from her previous experience in an ethereal garden to steer clear of things that shifted their energies so abruptly. Savara turned, wishing to make her way back down another path when she found it blocked by the same large, winged panther.

"Oh…" she gasped.

The panther tilted its head, its glowing red eyes contemplating her.

Have I scared you? The voice appeared in her mind, as it had before.

Savara regained her composure and smiled. "No, I just thought I was alone is all."

Do you wish to be? the panther asked.

Savara's gaze bounced from the panther to the plaza and back, taking the creature's presence as a sign to keep moving. "No, please. I'd love the company."

The panther purred as it circled her legs, nudging her before starting back down the path. Savara took one last look at the entrance to the plaza. The sadness seeping through was even more palpable as she made to leave, as though it were reaching out for her. She felt it grasping at the space around her feet. A chill caressed her shoulders. Something important lay within, but she was not yet willing to enter on her own.

She turned, abandoning the space, but wholly unable to forget the energy.

As they passed a small, overgrown grotto, Savara noticed other fluttering spirits playing at the edges of the grass. They danced like butterflies among the flowers. Unlike the panther or the Prince of Shadows, these spirits flickered. Their forms dipped in and out of view like that of her guide in the palace.

Not quite there, not quite gone, the panther said, noticing her gaze.

"Pardon?" Savara asked.

You watch the spirits, the panther replied, inclining her head in the way of the butterfly-shaped creatures. *Not ready to pass on, not able to return.*

Savara regarded them fondly as she turned the panther's words over in her mind. She hadn't been able to ask about the purpose of the garden while she was with the Prince of Shadows, but his panther companion was, so far, the most forthcoming of spirits in the Arima lands.

"Where do they come from?" Savara asked, looking to see how much information she could get out of the panther.

Memories mostly, it replied.

The little spirits seemed to notice her lingering. They drifted over to her like stray soap bubbles in a wanton breeze. Their energies danced across her skin. Like the dust beyond the door, warmth emanated from them. She extended her hand out in offering, allowing one of the flickering butterflies to settle in the middle of her palm. Suddenly, flashes of a life that did not belong to her appeared in her mind, disappearing as the spirit left her palm.

"These are souls…" she said, concern riddling her voice.

The panther bobbed her head in confirmation. She lowered to rest at Savara's feet and began picking at her wings. *They are held here for safekeeping until their release.*

"You say that as if they were trapped…"

Bonds were made. Bonds will be broken, the panther replied cryptically. *Balance will be restored.*

"What bonds? And what kind of balance?" Savara asked as she furrowed her brow, her mind reeling from the new information. Alexei had told her of a curse, a cage, not a bond. And the balance?

The stone at her neck pulsed, sending an image into her mind of the door to the gardens. She considered the helix of shadows and dust, the warmth and chill, recalling their strange harmony. Her spectral guide in the palace had informed her that the door was a joining point. At first, she'd wondered if it didn't join Visanthe to the world she'd been exiled to. But, considering this new information, Savara realised this garden had to be something different, something more. If this was a holding ground for souls, and the only place not afflicted by the stagnation of the Arima lands, did that make it…a place outside of life itself?

Consider the elements. Each one has its balancing opposite—water has fire, earth has air, and light has shadow. This is what keeps the world functioning. When one is thrown from balance, the world decays. But no candle can burn forever, even the stars go out eventually…

The question crept up from her throat in the most painful of ways. "Is this…death?"

"Not quite…" came a sinister voice from behind. Savara turned to find the Prince of Shadows standing firmly in the middle of the path. He looked darker somehow than when they'd first arrived in the garden. Whatever business had taken him away had also stripped him of his previous joy. What was left was grim, solemn, and sobering. "But I believe it is time you learned the truth. Come, my child," he said as he extended his hand towards her.

Savara regarded him cautiously, unsure of how to react to his change in demeanour. She chose not to verbalise a reply but laced her arm tentatively in his. His skin was cold in the way of a corpse, and in his energy was a sensation akin to mourning. She allowed him to promenade her to other parts of the garden, all the while cautious of the malicious shadows curling behind them.

CHAPTER 15

THE TRUTH BEHIND THE MAGIC

JASPER FORCED OUT A BREATH, spinning the sword around his shoulder before pointing it at Griffin again.

"Careful, you're getting slower. I might nick you next time," he said, watching the crease form at Griffin's brow.

The two of them had been going at it for the better part of the morning. Even before the sun rose over their latest destination, the somewhat busy town of Yozora, they were already engaged in combat. Since dawn, they'd been shuffling across the sands of the abandoned cove near their temporary dockside lodgings. The cove acted as a training ground, suiting both the morning's exercises, and (thankfully) taking them far enough from the two men who had Griffin's temper teetering on a knife's edge.

Jasper had gotten much better with the blade since their encounter with the shadows in Idune. Recently he'd seen less of Storm for training, but Griffin had taken it upon himself to take over in her absence. Because of this, Jasper felt comfortable enough with his skills to know that he could hold his own in a true fight—something he knew would not be too far away, given the state of the world.

His body still ached, wracked with the limitations of the poisoned veins beneath his skin. The book in his quarters sat unhappily beneath his bed, demanding nourishment he did not plan on giving it unless any new developments appeared. But the damage had already been done. Jasper never let on the full extent of the pain he felt, finding a sense of pride in pushing through it, though he knew Griffin was not as ignorant as he would've liked to believe.

"Don't make ridiculous statements," Griffin growled as he wiped the single bead of sweat from his temple and raised his own blade to meet Jasper's.

Alright, play dumb, he thought, but the words out of his mouth were not so harsh. "Then, you're distracted."

"You say that like you don't already know my reasons," Griffin replied, lunging into another attack.

Beyond the confines of the cove, fishing boats were already making their way out to find the day's catch. Gulls circled the morning sky above them, chasing after their prey. The clang of steel on steel reverberated through the air, a sharp contrast to the softer sounds of the morning. As the cold waves rolled up peacefully onto the shore beside them, the two men continued their deadly dance.

A slash.

A parry.

Jasper swore under his breath.

A riposte.

A near miss.

Griffin wiped the sweat from his brow.

They lunged.

A bind.

They pressed against their blades, waiting for the other to relent.

Release.

Another stalemate.

Most of the morning had been taken up with these moves. Their dance left tight circles in the sand around the cove. At alternating times throughout the morning, the two men stripped off their outer layers as the training grew more intense and the sun's rays finally crossed into their hideout. These layers lay discarded on the scattered, moth-covered stones near one of the ancient limestone walls built for storm surges that separated the cove from the town above.

"Is that why we're sparring today?" Jasper asked, pausing to rinse the sweat and sand from his brow with the cold salt water.

Griffin used the time to remove his tunic and place it down neatly with the rest of his layers. As he'd turned, Jasper noticed the three streaking scars along his back that aligned with the ones on his chin. When they first met outside of Visanthe, Jasper had assumed that Griffin was some sort of militant or hired assassin. Those scars on his chin might have signalled knife blades in another world, but in this one, Jasper was still out of his depths. Any number of creatures could've left such marks, and now, seeing how they connected with the ones on his back, Jasper knew it had to have been something more terrible than a simple knife blade.

"You're smarter than that, Jasper," Griffin said, noticing Jasper's obvious gaze and leaning up against the retaining wall to hide the scars.

Jasper shrugged. He was no fool. He knew exactly what he was doing; getting under Griffin's skin, nudging him to admit the things that troubled him, rather than keeping them bottled up. "Humour me."

"You shouldn't irritate a sleeping beast."

"Learned that one the hard way, I see." Griffin made no comment towards the remark, only scowling in the way that he did when Jasper was reaching dangerous territory with his prodding. "The sleeping beast should've let me have at least another hour of sleep for myself before grumpily banging on my door."

"You need the training," Griffin replied bluntly.

"We both know there's more to it. So, speak, Griffin. Before it consumes you. You are of little use to anyone in your current state, and you know it."

"You're beginning to sound like Brass."

Jasper ran the salt water through his mess of curls and stretched out his back. The sun slowly crept onto his shoulders, nudging him to take off his tunic and allow the feeling of warmth to come over his recently perpetually-cold body. The blackened veins streaking across his skin gave him pause. Abandoned cove or not, they were still in public. Though low, the chance of a stranger passing by was not nothing. The off chance that someone did appear meant explanations that would only cause problems.

"Someone has to be the voice of reason in his absence…" he said instead, rolling up the sleeves of his tunic to his elbows.

Griffin pushed himself off the wall and began practising his stance as Jasper watched from the shallows. "Amon."

"What about him?"

"He was my best friend growing up."

"Didn't seem like it."

"It's been years."

"Again, not quite the friendly reunion I'd expect from best pals," Jasper prodded.

"He disappeared. Got up and left in the middle of the night." Griffin slashed violently through the air. "Without so much as saying goodbye…"

Looking as though he'd grown weary of the rigidity of the weapon, Griffin cast the blade aside and conjured streams of light around him. His power, Jasper remembered, was always his weapon of choice.

"We both came from parents who neglected us. Somehow, we managed to find solace in each other," Griffin explained, continuing his story. "I was sent by my father to Yozora to join the Royal Guard. His mother had sent him there to learn discipline, but he was never meant to be a soldier like me. I thought he was an arse initially. Prince in pauper clothing with no real need to learn the lessons we'd been sent to learn. But he was not what I expected. Amon was looking for an escape from his life just as much as I was mine. He and I became inseparable from then on…"

"But then?" Jasper asked, dabbing the water at the nape of his neck.

"We stumbled upon the Izar stone while playing around in the palace catacombs. We did what any curious kids would do, unaware of the effect that touching it had on us until later. I became able to read snippets of futures in the stars. I'd only held it for a few seconds. Amon…" Griffin paused as though trying to gather his thoughts. "It gave him something more. For a few nights he kept going back, convinced it was trying to tell him something… Then, one morning, he was gone. No explanation, no warning, nothing… Vanished."

Throughout the story, Jasper paid closer attention to the light circling Griffin than to his words, though he got enough of it to understand the scepticism surrounding Amon's return. Jasper had seen Griffin conjure many forms of light since their time together, but what happened next was something that he seldom expected. Visions appeared through the streams. They were fleeting things, like reflections in windowpanes. If he focused hard enough on them, he was able to discern objects, figures, places…

Memories, Jasper quickly realised. They were glimpses of life through a younger Griffin's eyes—moments of pain, moments of sorrow. It was as though each of them had been tied to the specific conjurings of light. Jasper had never seen such a thing before, or possibly never noticed—though he highly doubted that last part, considering there was little his trained eyes didn't notice.

"Griffin… Strange question," Jasper began, veering slightly from the therapeutic spilling of anxieties.

"From you?" Griffin replied. "Not surprised."

"How do you do it?" he asked, ignoring the jab. "You know, conjure the light like that?"

"I hate to break it to you, Jasper, but it isn't something you can learn," Griffin replied, pausing the flow of his movements to emphasize his disbelief.

"Not my question. What do you feel when you do it? Or what do you think of?"

Griffin dropped his hands and crossed his arms. The lights and the images within them faded as he did. "Where is this coming from?"

"I saw things this time… in your light."

"What sort of things?" Griffin growled. The blue of his eyes burned with curiosity.

"I saw ballrooms as if from the sidelines, trainings with other weapons, and…" Jasper didn't know how to mention the apparent punishments that seemed to glow through each of the streams. "…a man, a soldier, who looked a lot like you, but more…fierce."

Griffin narrowed his eyes at him. There was calculation buried within them, and just behind it, fear. "How did you see those?"

"I don't know, this is the first time…"

Suddenly, it dawned on him that it might be an unintended side effect of the book. Maybe its strange powers had somehow bled into him. Could he be so far off? If the book was capable of taking something from him—his life force—maybe he had taken something too.

"That's how you do it, isn't it? You think of moments that made you feel something strong and use them to create that energy." When Griffin made no move to respond, Jasper continued his rant. "Is that how the others do it too? Are all of your powers based on things like anger, shame, resentment... fear?"

Griffin stalked towards him and grabbed him by the shoulder. He came close, intrusively close, and whispered in Jasper's ear, as if afraid of the words he spoke. "Don't ever breathe a word of this to anyone."

The sudden shift startled him. Jasper gulped at the concern constricting his throat. "I won't," he replied.

"And I don't just mean my...methods," Griffin continued. "Don't ever let anyone know what you are capable of..."

As he pulled away, Jasper noticed the shift in Griffin's demeanour had bled into his eyes as well. He was planning something, as if this newfound revelation had given him a reason to hope. A boon from some higher power. Reverence and caution danced in his darkened gaze. And Jasper decided he wasn't having any of it.

"I can see that look in your eyes, Griffin," he warned. "I'm not like the others. I don't want to be another pawn in whatever scheme you're concocting."

"Get over yourself, Jasper. We all become pawns someday. I just hope to keep mine standing by the end of the game."

"And what kind of end, pray tell, do you envision?"

Griffin cast a furtive glance around the cove to ensure no one would hear his prediction. "This world will go down in smoke and shadow... The stars have said as much for years.

It's now up to us whether we are on the other side to rebuild it or not. Happy?"

"Not… really…"

"Yeah, well, that's what you get when you poke after the truth." Griffin made his way back up the sand bank to collect his clothes, again brandishing his trio of scars.

Jasper regarded them thoughtfully, wondering at all the pains that lay beneath Griffin's skin. Judging by the strength of Griffin's power, if what he reasoned was true, the suffering extended far beyond a few measly, unhealed marks.

If Visanthian power was somehow attached to strong emotions… Jasper's mind began to race. He considered all the times he'd witnessed great displays of power. Even Savara had not escaped the parallel. When she'd accidentally lashed out at him in the forest of Osiir she'd been afflicted with fear. It stood to reason that the darker the feeling—or in Griffin's case, the memory—the stronger the resulting power. *But was it only the darker feelings that provided such strength?*

"Could you do it with better ones?" Jasper asked, trying to piece together his thoughts.

The question had caught Griffin off-guard. "What?"

"Emotions," Jasper clarified. "Like happiness, hope, love?"

Griffin frowned, letting a silence fall between them briefly. "…If you had them… Maybe." He collected his things, turning his back on Jasper and the conversation.

The time for prodding had ended, and so had training. Jasper made his way back up the sand, lost in his thoughts. He bent down to retrieve his sword, still reeling from his discovery when Storm appeared.

"Griffin!" she called, urgency burning in her voice. Storm stood at the top of the moss-covered staircase that led to the town beyond the bastion, a grim expression plastered across her face. She clutched tight to a scroll in her hand, her eyes wide with worry as she raced down the stairs, narrowly avoiding slipping on the damp moss as she descended.

"What's wrong, Storm?" Griffin asked, his voice matching the urgency in hers.

"Is it Sav?" Jasper added.

Storm didn't reply. She handed Griffin the scroll, watching nervously as he scanned the contents.

"No, worse," Griffin said to Jasper, his brow furrowing at her reached the end of the note. "Divination Day."

"The day the children receive their powers?" Jasper glanced between them, trying to understand the concern. "Why is that a problem?"

Griffin and Storm exchanged a knowing glance, worry highlighting their eyes. "It is usually a celebration called forth by the same entity that gives out these powers."

"Iturri," said Jasper.

Griffin nodded. Before he could reply, Amon appeared at the top of the staircase.

"Griffin!" he called. Amon bypassed the stairs entirely, leaping gracefully onto the sand unharmed, as if gravity bent in his favour. "Why have I been hearing about Divination Day around town?" Amon looked upon each of their worried faces and frowned, his suspicions having been confirmed. His eyes fell suddenly on Jasper's arms, pupils widening as he regarded the blackened veins. "Where did you get those marks?" He looked as though his thoughts were racing beneath those waves of jet-black hair of his, trying to process what he was seeing. "What have you done?"

Jasper rolled down his sleeves in response. "Can someone explain what's happening? Why are you all so up in arms about Divination Day?"

"Because," Griffin began, stepping in to avoid further prodding. "There hasn't been one since Savara's. When she disappeared, so did the ceremonies."

"And now that she's back, this Iturri is calling for them again?" Jasper asked as he scrunched his brows together.

"No," Amon said, lowering his voice for the intimacy of the conversation. "Not Iturri. *Him.* The rulers of the lands are being summoned to Middle Isle for a Divination ceremony, but it's not about the children this time."

"I'm not following," Jasper said, his eyes bouncing between the three Visanthians whose thoughts and worries had all clearly aligned.

"What do you know, Amon?" Griffin asked, ignoring Jasper's comment.

"Middle Isle is where Iturri was bound," Amon replied, clarifying the gravity of the situation.

"Bound? But then…"

All of a sudden, the pieces of the puzzle fell into place. The whisperings of the book rushed to the forefront of his mind. The verses that had gnawed at him for the better part of the last month had told him as much, hadn't they? He was only now beginning to understand.

Trapped within forgotten cage, quelled and silent and seeking age…
Iturri had been bound. Trapped.
And so it is as once begun, to splintered worlds a setting sun…

A return to the place where it had all started. The place where Savara learned of her powers, where the magic of the lands was born. The place to which the last of the rulers of this time were being called for a final Divination Day.

Jasper found it harder now to not believe in the existence of fate. Nothing else, he reasoned, could've orchestrated a plan of this magnitude. One that spanned lifetimes. One that would leave nothing untouched when the world went down in flames.

This is what the book was talking about, he realised. *This is how it all ends…*

"He's going to free Iturri."

CHAPTER 16

GIVING AND TAKING

THE PRINCE OF SHADOWS LED HER BACK through the winding paths and out of the garden. The door closed heavily behind them, and Savara felt some of her happiness had stayed trapped behind it. They traversed the palace in silence, exiting unto the stagnant grounds she'd arrived at with Alexei. There was something eerily forlorn about the world around them that gnawed at her bones. Whether the previous gardens were or not, these lands certainly felt closer to what she'd imagined of death—and looked like it too.

They strode over to a grey flowerbed at the edge of the entrance to the palace. Before them stood a rosebush that looked like it had been encased in ash. The flowers themselves were in bloom but their colours were not the vivid, blood reds of the roses she'd known outside of the

Arima lands. Their petals were the colour of charcoal and as delicate as butterfly wings. Savara feared that a stray breath might make them disintegrate.

The Prince of Shadows regarded them fondly. "I have a soft spot for flowers. Alas, these gardens are not what they used to be. When I was a youth…" he said as a wave of sadness swept over his face. It was a gentle wave. The kind that washes up on the shore and leaves no wake.

If she hadn't paid any mind to the flowers, Savara might not have noticed the way they drooped further following his temperament. If her powers had remained dormant, she might have also been oblivious to the dip in the temperature of the phantom air around them, or the low ripples of melancholy reaching towards her.

But Savara had seen the shift in the flowers. She'd felt the cold caressing her shoulders. These were subtle yet unmistakable signs of something she'd once questioned but was now coming to know for certain: the Prince of Shadows was intrinsically tied to these lands. And not like a man chained to a post and left for dead. No. It was the kind of connection that ran far deeper than mere physical presence.

Savara finally understood what Alexei had tried to explain to her about the prince's entrapment. Unlike other rulers who merely wielded the power of their lands, the Prince of Shadows was the very essence of these lands incarnate. He was not chained to them; he *was* them. He'd removed the separation between his physical body and his connection to Iturri, to source itself. Without him, there would be no gardens, no palace… Without him, Savara suspected there would be no lands at all.

"Well, times have changed. Even if I have not," he concluded, allowing a melancholy smirk to escape his lips. Savara figured it was best not to prod into his past, even though she was now more curious than ever. She simply nodded, waiting for his mood to shift once more. "Close your eyes, my dear. Take a deep breath and allow yourself to feel around us. Use only your powers."

Savara obeyed without hesitation, her mind already attuned to the task at hand. In truth, she'd learned the basics of this 'lesson' from her time with Big Tog. The defunct leader of the Argia underworld had once mentored her in the use of her powers for his own personal vendetta. Savara hadn't fully grasped the significance of what he had taught her then, but now, standing in the presence of the Prince of Shadows, everything seemed to fall into place.

Back then, Big Tog claimed to have owed a debt to 'The Devil'. At the time, Savara hadn't realised to whom he'd referred. She'd merely hoped to free her friends from capture by exchanging her yet-untapped power. Big Tog had treated her with kindness in his lessons only as a means to an end. She had been his weapon of choice, sharpening her like the blade of a sword, only to turn on her when he realised the sword he held was no sword at all, but a knifepoint on both ends. A knife that ended him before he could do the same.

Death and destruction had wisened her up since then. The so-called 'Devil' stood before her, dressed in an elegantly casual suit, basking in the ethereal air of the stagnant lands to which his soul was bound, and teaching her—his apparent ward—to better use the powers the rest of the world considered evil.

Yet, neither he nor her powers seemed as devilish as the rest of the world had made them out to be. On the contrary, thanks to the conversation with his panther companion, she began to understand that they had a place in this world, and an important one at that.

"What do you feel?" he asked, his voice ripe with curiosity.

Savara deepened her focus on her powers, which had been eagerly waiting to be used ever since they'd entered the gardens. "There is a pulse... I can feel it radiating from everything. The ground. The stones. The palace. The flowers..."

Unlike what she'd experienced with the dust in the halls, this sensation felt more like ripples in a tidepool. With each movement, she felt the souls of the objects reverberating around her. If she listened closely, she could almost hear a low humming coming from each wave. As though she were standing in the centre of a great orchestra. The world around her came to life. It sang, playing ethereal harmonies she doubted she'd ever hear elsewhere.

Soon, darker melodies crept into the symphony. Low, ominous rumbling, like the heavy breath of a beast, invaded her senses. Savara opened her eyes, seeking out the source of the noise, unsurprised when her powers led her to the Prince of Shadows himself.

Savara hesitated momentarily before adding, "Even from you."

"You are a natural, my dear," he said, his eyes twinkling with amusement. "I would expect nothing less from someone of your divine birth. It is my blood after all that runs through your veins." The Prince of Shadows plucked a rose from the bush and twirled it between his fingers. He held it up towards the light in a contemplative manner, scanning it for something she couldn't see. "Sensing souls is a power of ours that requires nothing of us. It takes nothing from us to feel, just as it takes nothing from you to see. It is simply an additional mode of receiving from the world. However, the next lessons are not as gratuitous," he added as he handed it to her.

Savara clutched the dead rose in her hand. It was a sorry sight to be sure. The petals clung to the memory of life at the base of the dried stem. A wanton breeze might uproot them, but luckily, these stagnant lands held no breezes—wanton or otherwise.

The Prince of Shadows plucked another rose from the bush.

"The first lesson you must learn, my child, is that dead is dead. There is no bringing anything back from death. Once a soul has moved on, it cannot be brought back to this world."

"Are these flowers not dead?"

"Not quite. The way the petals hold the stem implies an inkling towards life. When that is the case, we can *effect change* on its circumstances," he said, placing special emphasis on those words to highlight the lesson.

The way those two benign words fell from his lips was anything but. "When you say, 'effect change', do you mean give it life again?"

"Renew its life, yes. Watch closely, my child, and do as I do." The Prince of Shadows pricked his finger on one of the rose's thorns, but because he was still not whole, no blood trickled from the wound. He gestured with his chin for her to do the same.

Hesitating only for a moment, Savara pressed her finger onto the dried, sharpened point of the thorn, wincing as it pierced her skin. Blood pooled at the surface of the wound, glowing bright and vivid against the sombre scenery around them.

"Now, just as you do with the soulbonds, will the life back into the rose," said the Prince of Shadows.

"What would I say? To create the binding," she clarified.

"Nothing at all. Souls do not speak in words like you and I. Souls only understand intent. Imagine what you would wish to see before you and will it through your blood."

Savara closed her eyes, picturing a vivid red rose between her fingers. She pictured the ones she'd so frequently played with in her uncle's garden. Back then, Ms. Short would have shooed her away on the basis that her childish hands would wreck the plants. She remembered the scent of the fresh blooms after the spring showers, the velvety feel of the petals, and the shocking vibrance of the colour.

By the time she was through picturing the scene in her head, she almost believed she'd returned to the garden of the old house she'd once called home. When she opened her eyes again, the same rose she'd envisioned rested, alive and well, between her fingers, as if she'd plucked it from her memory.

"Well done," said the Prince of Shadows. "You are a fast learner."

"How is this possible?" Savara asked, slowly becoming aware of a headache growing from within the depths of her skull. She blinked rapidly to try and dissuade it of its pressure but to no avail.

Something was wrong.

Savara was never someone who had been prone to headaches, let alone migraines. The suddenness of this one too concerned her.

"You will be feeling the effects of the transfer," he commented, noticing her change in expression. His lips fell into a thin line, as though he were displeased at her show of pain. "This was a lesson you had to learn in the most physical of senses. Energy can neither be created nor destroyed, but it can be transferred by certain souls, like you. It must come from somewhere. The intention you put into the rose was imbued with your own essence, and in willing it into the rose, you committed to the transfer."

"Does that mean I gave some of my life to the flower?" she asked incredulously. The Prince of Shadows nodded. "You should have told me!" she yelled, frightened at both the idea of what she'd done and the prince's disregard for the gravity of such an act.

Aside from the pursing of his lips, his emotions were entirely unreadable. Not even with her powers could she divine an inkling of what he was thinking let alone feeling.

"You must learn the consequences of meddling in the affairs of spirit," was his only reply.

Savara felt conned. Cheated out of something that was entirely her own and not meant to be lost. In the back of her mind, Savara heard Alexei's sarcastic voice saying, *everything comes at a price, Savara.* And for the first time since she'd met him, she wished she'd paid more attention to what he'd said.

"I didn't ask to meddle with spirit!"

"You have these powers for a reason, Savara. You must learn to use them in their entirety."

"You could have told me," she hissed.

"You needed to experience the loss."

"I've experienced enough loss—"

"I will not have you behaving like a child in these lessons, young lady."

His sudden sharpness caught her off guard.

This was the first time he'd addressed her as a father might his daughter, but something about it felt wrong. Neither of them had much practice with this particular type of relationship, but Savara didn't think it was the time or place for them to start. He had never asked for her to address him as a father—nor had she ever intended to. The man sparked more fear in her than respect, and she certainly wasn't looking to exchange any more familial sentiments with him.

If he realised her shock at his words, he made no show of it outwardly, preferring to continue with the lesson, but she was furious. Furious at his teaching methods and frightened of their implications.

"The world is in need of a champion, Savara, not a child," he added, tension contouring his words as he spoke. Despite the façade of stillness, the shadows behind him grew restless.

"I didn't ask to be a champion either," she countered, cautious of the mounting atmosphere of threat around him.

"You came to me, Savara," he said as he stalked towards her, danger perfuming his person. Her heart pounded viciously in her chest as he neared. "Let's not forget that key detail. You wished to know the truth of this world, of *your* world. You made that choice. Hard as it may have been, you made it, knowing it was the right one."

"This is not what I wanted," she whispered. "I didn't know—"

"What would be required of you?" he growled. "Everything comes at a price, Savara. Understanding is no different. As for what you wanted, we were chosen by Iturri to be the moderators of life and death. It is not about wants. It is about justice. Divine Justice. It is about doing what is right for this world, and giving whatever is required in the process."

"But—"

"We are Harbingers of Death. Whether you like it or not," he continued over her, "we were made to keep the balance between this world and the one beyond. We protect this balance with everything that we are. It is our duty."

"That's not a choice, that's a chain…"

"Call it as you wish, call it a curse, call it anything," he replied, his eyes darkening as he spoke. "But know that it is the truth."

"The curse on the lands…" she mumbled under her breath. Shivers traced the length of her spine as she thought back on all the information she'd been given about the Arima lands. "The transfer of energy requires blood. Your lands are dying. Your people…"

"…were used in the making of these chains—as you so rightly called them."

"But how? If no one else has these powers, how could they—" She froze, reaching for the stone around her neck that had begun to pulse as if calling for acknowledgement. A sudden realisation washed over her, wiping all the warmth from her body. "This…"

"Sacrificed in the name of power, by those who fear our nature. You speak of choices? Well, ask me if they had a choice," he began, murder and redemption glinting in the red glow of his eyes. "Ask me if any of them had a choice in their fates."

"This is wrong," she said, but his rant continued.

"What was wrong was the actions of those who fought against this balance. I know you feel it, the darkness that roams the world beyond. What you don't realise is that I am not this darkness. It was born the day the cage was created. The day the bonds were made."

"I didn't come to help you exact revenge," she whispered fearfully.

"You came because your soul was called, in the same way mine was, to do what it knows is right. To fix what has been broken. To remove the bindings on our powers—on things that were not meant to be bound."

"I can't do this," she replied. "I won't…"

"This is greater than you, Savara."

"I'm sorry," she said, as tears began streaming down her petrified face. There was no use hiding her agitation any longer. Fear filled her heart. She should never have trusted him. She backed away slowly before bursting into a run. She raced back through the palace halls and did not stop running until she was safely behind the doors of her bedroom—and not even that felt safe anymore.

CHAPTER 17

PAST PAINS AND PIANOFORTES

"WHAT DO YOU MEAN, I HAVE TO WAIT?" growled Amon at the surly-looking guard in the sweeping white robes. His white hair and cloudy blue eyes might have hinted at age and lessened agility in anyone else, but this high-class brute was the leader of the Royal Izarian Guard—and a consistent pain in Amon's side.

"She has requested you wait," he replied without remorse, sparing no downward glance at the recently returned Prince of Light.

Amon turned, as if to question the reasons for his queueing outside the doors to the throne room. There were no other guests of the palace that morning. No files of people filling the halls, no visiting dignitaries or alike. Any wait could only have been attributed to a discussion on the appearance of the shadow that he'd heard about around town—a discussion for which he wished to be present.

"I am not a subject looking to harp on about the harvest season," he said, returning his eyes to the captain of the guard. "I am the prince of these lands. You cannot tell me to wait."

"She has requested you wait," the captain of the guard repeated, still no shift in his expression. No acknowledgement either.

"*She* is my *mother*. Or has she forgotten that too?"

"She will not see you now," the captain of the guard clarified, leaving no room for discussion, no room for misinterpretation. Occupied or not, his mother would not see him.

Amon grew restless, realising that he was being placed at the mercy of her mind games. He'd seen them play out enough times to know when he was being subjected to one. But now was not the time for play, especially not with the lives of so many hanging in the balance. Especially not with *her* life hanging in the balance.

Divination Day was upon them, and so, it seemed, was the end of the world.

The questioning voices of the town had reached him through the small window of his private flat. They'd spoke of the shadow that had swept through the streets. The Izar people had never been given reason to worry or fear, but no creature had ever bypassed the force of the Izarian guard with such ease, let alone a creature not of flesh and blood.

The second he'd heard of the strange occurrence, Amon had rushed over to Griffin to confirm it. He'd known instantly what such a visit meant; surely his mother had as well. She must have received the same letter as all the other lands. She was the final target, the final keeper of stones. She was the last person whose blood needed to run to fulfil the ritual. There was no avoiding it. He was coming for her, the Prince of Shadows.

"Orpheus, I am not in the mood. Let me through," Amon demanded.

"Nor am I, princeling. You no longer have the sway here that you once did."

Amon cocked an eyebrow. "And why is that?"

Orpheus rested his gaze on Amon for the first time since their conversation had begun. His expression was unchanged, but his eyes burned with violent amusement. "You have been missing for over a decade. Did you think your absence would go unnoticed?"

"Actually, yes," Amon grumbled.

"You have always been self-centred, Amon. It is no wonder that you would have thought something so ridiculous," replied Orpheus. "Regardless, you have lost any rights you had here as a prince, and you will now wait like the commoner whose actions you mimicked in leaving."

"Orpheus, this is important."

"So were your duties as a prince."

"Being locked in an ivory tower, forced to entertain myself with the loneliest of arts, until such times as my mother needed me paraded around like the latest proclamations from those ridiculous priests who claim to speak to Iturri?" Amon hissed, the vibrant blue of his eyes glimmering with anger and urgency as he fired off each word.

Orpheus turned away, disregarding Amon's rant as he fixed his gaze to the hall beyond the throne room doors.

"You will wait until summoned," the captain of the guard said, his voice soberingly severe as it echoed through the empty hall.

Amon let out a resounding huff as he turned away from the doors. Bougainvillea trees poked through the courtyard, their little flowers falling from the branches like grains of sand in an hourglass. They ticked off the seconds uncomfortably.

We're running out of time, he thought. His eyes dropped to the star-shaped scar in his palm. *She's running out of time…*

Somewhere in the Arima lands, Savara was learning the truth about the ritual—about herself. He'd been avoiding thoughts of her ever since Alexei had taken her away, but such a task was becoming impossible, especially given the circumstances.

The words he'd spoken to Griffin and Jasper were all true, but he'd downplayed their gravity. He hadn't wanted to tell them of the way his heart yearned for her, bond or not. Of how he'd seen her face in the stars long before they'd reunited. Of how the younger him had wished to rebel against fate, knowing of the heartbreak to come, and fighting against the idea that he was without freedom. What he had since learned, and what he'd neglected to tell the others, was that, even in having freedom, his heart, his spirit, always found their way back to her.

He took a deep breath. *She doesn't want me…* Amon told himself, all the while hoping it was a lie. *She doesn't need me…*

In spite of his rational mind's protests, his heart had already made it clear that he was to do everything in his power to keep her safe… Even if it meant getting back into the good graces of his mother. The first thing he had to do was get into the throne room. Standing there arguing was a grand waste of his time—and one he knew his mother had orchestrated for just such a thing. He turned back to Orpheus, decided on his next course of action.

"I'm not going to argue with you over the authoritarian rules of being royalty in Yozora. Let me through, or it will be Iturri to pay."

"One would have thought your time away would quell that arrogance you harbour within, and yet, you come brimming with violence."

"Arrogance? You cannot rightfully use that word with me, working under *her*. You do realise this, no?"

Again, Orpheus ignored the comment.

When Amon was younger, he found the decorated captain of the guard's austere demeanour and regimented nature to be little more than a mild annoyance. An easily avoidable inconvenience. He'd known all the ways to slip past Orpheus unseen, a skill that proved useful during his many escapes from the palace—and for his eventual return.

Upon such return, however, Amon had found himself called to move through the proper channels when addressing his mother, as if still clinging to the hope that he could make her accept him. But this game of hers had eaten up what little time and patience he had left. Getting through was a matter of urgency. Amon found himself tempted to use the light prodding at the edges of his fingertips, but he knew better than to make such a scene. Especially not as news of his sudden return was making the rounds of the town, and not in the friendliest of tones.

"Fine, have it your way…" Amon stifled the darker urges that resided within him and clenched his fists. "Will you at least allow me to peruse my old torture chambers?"

"Of course, your bed chamber has not changed in your absence. I shall summon you an escort…"

"I can find my way perfectly fine," Amon growled. "You already said nothing has changed, then I will have nowhere to get lost."

If Orpheus insisted on being difficult, he'd use the same tactics that allowed for his original escape. There were no corners of this palace that he had not traversed, no secret tunnels or passages that remained hidden from him. He'd find his way into his mother's court, protocols be damned.

Amon retraced the halls of the wretched Palace of Light, following the moonstone and gems that lined the walls towards his chambers. Even on the darkest of nights, in the gloomiest of halls in the land of spirits and shadows, there was more happiness there than between these frigid, open walls. These halls, for all the pretence and purpose they wished to portray, were lined by only cunning and deceit. No place for a child to have grown up, but then, there had never been the intention of having a child grow up here.

He climbed the stone staircase to the isolated tower where his chamber lay waiting. Just as Orpheus had proclaimed, it sat untouched, save for the occasional polishing of the metal finishes on the furniture and wood of his pianoforte. The vast library which covered most of the available wall space had not been so much as breathed upon. Not a speck of dust had lifted from the various leatherbound tomes that comprised it. The chandeliers hanging from the cavernous ceiling held the same half-melted candles that had provided light to the rooms from the time before his divination, before he could create his own light. His princely circlet lay on an aged cushion, on the same pedestal which he'd almost knocked over many times distractedly walking around his room, nose buried in the book of the day.

When he was younger, Amon would've happily seen the blasted circlet fall to the floor, in more ways than one. It was a simple coil of metal that was only as important as the amount of fear that existed within the public. His mother had insisted he wore it at all times when out and about, to distinguish him from the commoners and the riffraff, but he wanted nothing more than to be amongst them, to be treated as equal. He wanted to be seen as a person, not like a polished and pampered pet that she lorded around instead of raising. It crossed his mind more than once that this treatment might have been what had led him to pursue other role models— and seek out other understandings of life. But there would be no explaining the err of her ways to her.

His mother was a terrifying powerhouse of a woman stuffed into a deceptively meek and petite vessel. With a flick of her wrist, she could steal the light from the moon if she so pleased. She could create visions of light with the fullest density that one would mistake them for reality. She was a master of dreams and precognition. She was one of the oldest beings in Visanthe and would easily be a hard opponent to defeat in any other fight.

But the Prince of Shadows was no ordinary opponent either. His powers of darkness easily surpassed hers of light. His experience with the unseen forces struck fear into the hearts of all who crossed his path. And, of course, he had Iturri on his side.

His feelings for his mother aside, Amon feared the outcome of such a battle. But for anything to change such a battle was a necessity, and the outcome a mere formality. They were the product of the old world—a dying world. Both of them would need to meet their ends for a new age to begin.

Amon doubted they'd go quietly.

As he continued his contemplative stroll down memory lane, he crossed towards the beautiful black wooded instrument bathed in ethereal light whose tunes accompanied his almost every waking moment. The glimmering pianoforte sat expectantly, polished to perfection as it had been every day throughout his childhood—as if he'd never left. His relationship with the instrument was tenuous at best. A combination of utter respect and admiration for all that it was as both an idea and an avenue for musical exaltation, and yet simultaneously a symbol of neglect, suppression, and isolation.

"We meet again, old friend…" he said to the instrument as he glided his fingers over the polished wood. Amon lifted the fallboard gently, the act alone bringing back a stream of notes wishing to be played.

He cracked his knuckles and stretched his fingers. With the simple act of sitting at the bench, the sombre tunes of childhood began filtering into his consciousness. They transported him back to a time before the end of the world had become his objective goal, back to a time when the midnight lilies beneath his balcony were the only audience he'd ever cared for and the summer friendships he'd made had gone to their southern homes for the winter. Amon took a deep breath, filling his lungs with the scent of night flowers and melancholy; the same scent he wore when he was far from home to remind him of the world he'd left behind—and why he could never go back. He closed his eyes, letting his hands hover briefly over the keys.

And then, he played.

The notes, sharp and sudden at first. Anger, resentment, pain. They each had their chords. Low, dark. Over and over. He played, unsure that anyone would hear. But then, the softer ones found their way into his melody. Soft and sad and echoing. Like lengthy river channels, they filled the space between the sharper notes. As he played, they blended seamlessly into the tune, pulling his consciousness from the present moment and carrying him to that sacred space between worlds where creatives and passionates alike trade their souls in return for channelled masterpieces. The place that cannot and somehow must exist all at the same time. He played, unsure whether or not time continued to exist around him, for feeling alone remained as the measure, but feelings are known to last from mere instants to entire lifetimes. He played until the sharper notes disappeared entirely, and his heart was left with only the softness and sadness that came before silence.

Finally, he opened his eyes.

If he had expected the world to have changed in whatever time had passed in his playing, he was wrong. The manicured room before him was just as he'd left it before his eyes had closed. There was no sunlight filtering in through his balcony, nor were there rain clouds on the horizon. The storms on the inside were contrasted by the stark stillness of the waiting day outside. And most disappointing of all, there was no woman with doe-like, rainbow-flecked, teary eyes and gentle smile sat before him. Though, in all fairness, he hardly expected her to be after all that had happened.

Suddenly, the scar in his palm began to tremble. He stared at it with a furrowed brow, wondering if the thought of her somehow spurred on a phantom feeling. It burned. No, he was not imagining it. Something was happening to the woman at the other end of that connection. Something that he hadn't planned for. Something that she hadn't either.

Whatever just happened at the other end of his scar was something not even fate could have planned.

Without warning, he crumpled to the floor. A sharp burst of pain appeared in the hollows of his chest which left him trembling and gasping for breath. His vision blurred. Fear filled his heart. Beads of sweat formed at his brow. Nausea swept over him.

What in Iturri's name is going on?

Just as soon as it appeared, the energy rippling through him began to fade. Something was very wrong. Amon pulled himself up using the pedestal, using the weight of it to steady himself as he regained his composure. He caught a glimpse of himself reflected in the mirror on the wall. The sight shocked him. His skin had gone a ghostly white. His breath was laboured. It was as though a bolt of lightning had shot through his heart.

Alexei, he realised. *If the psychopath so much as harmed a hair on her head...*

Then, his worst fears came to light. For a moment, the attachment at the other end of the bond disappeared. The feeling of being connected to someone else in a way that traversed space and time vanished.

Where is she?

He searched the contours of their accidental bond for a sign of life but came up with nothing. The feeling was of something more than loss, more than grief, more than pain. Absence filled the space where part of his soul should've resided. More than emptiness. Worse than a missing limb. It was as if he'd been made to breathe with a single lung. No. As if he'd been sliced down the middle. As if he were half a person—half a soul. For that split second, he was alone. Truly. In a way he hadn't been for years. Anxiety rippled through him, casting doubt on everything he'd done up until that moment. Without her, his world felt off-kilter, his goals seemed insignificant, his longing felt as though it would be forever in vain...

Had it all been for nothing?

But, just as his panic threatened to overwhelm him, a heartbeat appeared at the other end of the bond again. Softly, faintly, nothing more than the shadow of a heartbeat, at first. Amon waited, frozen by the fearful anticipation. Slowly, it grew into the low pulse he'd come to know as the light at the end of his dark tunnel. She was alive—thankfully—and it seemed as though she was unharmed. It was as though she'd disappeared from the world for a moment. A single moment. Whether or not it was true, her 'disappearance'—even for just an instant—gave him pause.

Amon had lost her only for an instant, but in that instant, he'd lost a part of his soul. If he had ever doubted his feelings for her, he did no longer. That instant had shown him what a lifetime of seeking could not. There was something more to the bond between them, an invisible thread that ran deeper than a scar on his hand made by glass and spirit. It was something that had lain dormant for most his life, something of which he was utterly ignorant until that moment. The realisation was both thrilling and terrifying.

Either way, one thing was clear: he wouldn't lose her again.

Time was running out. He couldn't waste another moment trapped in this room of empty memories and hollow lullabies.

Amon sat down again at the piano, but no ballads came from his fingers. He began to play the most inharmonious of chords in sequence, revealing a secret tunnel beneath the instrument that led directly to the throne room. If his mother would not schedule a time to meet, he'd force himself into her schedule. There were things, he began to realise, which were more important than pride.

He took one last look around the chamber, knowing there was little chance he'd be seeing it again, before descending into the dark passage. His time there had come to an end, and he knew better than anyone that the past could not linger anywhere for too long before it became a problem.

L. M. SANGUINETTE

Whatever may come, let it be better than this… he wished to the closing door behind him.

CHAPTER 18

COUNCIL WITH THE QUEEN

THE EERIE SOUNDS OF THE WINDS BEYOND the tunnel walls spoke in tunes of foreboding and fear. As Orpheus had rightly pointed out, it had been years since Amon had graced the halls as anyone of standing and rank. Now, hiding away in the tunnels that had caused his fall from grace, he wondered what might have become of him if he'd been content with his simple understanding of the world before the stars—before the stones. Yet, surrounded by the waiting darkness, he realised that these same tunnels might actually be the key to regaining his honour.

Fate, as he knew her, was nothing if not poetic—just or otherwise.

Reaching the end of the passage, Amon took a steadying breath. On the other side of the stone wall, a beast awaited him. One he hadn't seen in years, but he doubted that time had given him a halo in her eyes. He pushed open the secret door, landing before a great marble column near the throne.

The grand courtroom was empty save for the standard guards, a councilman, and her.

She was a being of stardust, housed in a shell of earth, a grace that hovered rather than walked, with hair that floated in equal gravity. Time had not placed a wrinkle on her skin or crease in her lips. She was as ageless as he'd remembered, looking as though time itself was swallowed whole by the sapphire set of eyes that stared at him from beneath those snow-white brows. Her face, impassive as it gazed upon him, had not changed. Not in the decade he'd vanished, not in all the time since she'd grown on these lands. She retained her youth the way a marble statue would if given a spirit to flow through it.

She, the leader of the Izar, had been awaiting his appearance.

She, his mother, not so much.

"My dearest child," she began, the soft, dulcet tones of her voice a mask for the ageless quality she'd inherited from her possession of the stone of light. "Have you not missed me?" Though they were meant as pleasantries, there was nothing pleasant about her words. Yet, nothing could sully her reputation in the eyes of her adoring people. To them, she was just as good and gracious as any god, if not more so. Therein lay the problem. She'd taken too much of a liking to her position of power, forgetting that such positions come with reckonings of their own.

"Be glad it is my face that graces you, Mother," he replied as he made his way to the centre of the room, keeping his head high as he met her gaze.

The sound of his footsteps echoed in the lofty room, a testament to both the stillness and the tension that filled the air. Flickering lights mapped out in the form of constellations across the ceiling bounced their glow off him. Basins of shimmering water sat between each of the columns, holding in them memories of the meetings in these halls. They glowed still, which meant they were capturing his every move. Amon kept his face stoic, unwilling to unintentionally feed her information through his features.

"Young man, you must address her as—" began a guard, but his mother raised a hand to silence him.

"Calm yourself, Adrastos. He is still the prince, after all," she replied.

"How good of you to remember," Amon murmured.

A vein ticked in his mother's jaw. "How have you fared on your journey of self-discovery, my darling son?"

"Mother, neither of us have the time for this."

"No, you made it perfectly clear with your absence that decorum was not high on your list of admirable qualities—"

"He is coming for you," Amon hissed, interrupting the surely rehearsed speech on how much of a disappointment he was, and how he'd disgraced their royal house, and how she should never have given him so much *freedom*—a thought which existed in her mind alone, for he'd never seen true freedom until leaving her. Past parental squabbles aside, his words had the intended effect. There was no need to explain which 'he' was coming. Only one truly posed a threat to her.

Only one could destroy her, and potentially the world in the process.

The Prince of Shadows.

Her gentle smile dropped. For the first time in his life, his mother had begun to listen.

"Leave us," she said in a voice that rolled low and heavy like thunder. Without hesitation, the guards departed, leaving the two of them alone in the chamber. His mother glided towards him, her hair floating behind her like a ghostly halo. Stripped of her previous mask of serenity, she narrowed her eyes at him, analysing the changes in his face and the marks that time had left on him since his disappearance. She circled him like a wolf on its moonlight hunt, casting her gaze up and down his person, scrutinising his stance and growth, tearing at the seams of his spirit, all without saying a single word. "You are certainly not the child who ran away from this house, nor are you the man whose identity you claim to have."

"Have you officially stopped pretending you care about me?" Amon asked, noticing how much smaller she was in person than in his head. Looking at her now, the image of innocence and purity, with her halo of glowing white hair and expansively galactic sapphire eyes, he almost understood how people had fallen for the charade of docility.

But this was only a façade.

Anyone standing within a few feet of her would feel the crushing weight of her power. Her soul's age, though unknown to all but her, added an extra layer of mystery and caution to her person. His mother, the ruler of the House of Light—and illusions—beholden only to the moon and the stars, could very well have appeared a god to any other mortal. But she was no god—or at least not yet, if her intentions remained unchanged.

"Like me or not, I am still your mother."

"Which is the only reason I have come. I have no obligation to warn you of anything. I could have let him take your head in the middle of the night without losing a moment of sleep," Amon replied.

"Yet here you are, sneaking into my house to speak with me, and I sense that you don't sleep as well as you claim," she said. "So, tell me, Amon. What danger do you think I am in?"

Amon withheld the bitter comments that waited patiently on his tongue. "I've heard of your guest. Know there is another on the way. The Prince of Shadows is coming for you."

Her shoulders softened as she chuckled. "He will destroy himself before he even gets close. I have nothing to worry about."

"You can't believe that," he said. "You've seen the stars. You know what kind of a battle is coming…"

His words had unintentionally piqued her interest. Her previous amusement subsided. "As have you, apparently…" She tilted her head again, contemplating him in light of this revelation. Whatever she saw brought a scowl to her face. "I will not assume you were born with such a gift. You must have found the stone yourself, not so?" A rhetorical question. She gave him no time to reply before she continued her rant. "Yes, I have seen my own death in the stars."

"And you do nothing to protect yourself?"

"Would you have me fight against fate?" Her eyes sparkled with mischief. "Perhaps you and I are not so different after all."

At this Amon snarled. "You and I are nothing alike."

"Oh, my son…" she said as she reached up and cupped his cheek in a disarmingly gentle hand. "We are more alike than you will ever realise."

Amon grabbed hold of her wrist. "Like I said, we don't have time for this."

His mother dropped all pretence of cordiality as she made her way over to one of the many basins around the room. "You ask if I am aware of my impending demise?"

At the wave of her fingers, light from around the room pooled into her palm. Images of smoke and shadow appeared from within. Then, she raised a hand, warping the world around them, turning it from the throne room to a barren, indistinguishable mountain range beneath an open sky full of stars. In her other hand she summoned a staff of light tangible only to her, but which he knew would slice through him as good, if not better, than any man-made blade.

"I know that it comes sometime after this meeting. I also know, however, that, if I kill you now, my darling son, a new path will unfold."

She pointed the staff towards him. For now, she stayed her strike, making no obvious moves against him.

Amon wondered for a moment why she hadn't chosen to execute him then and there. He was, after all, the reason she would soon lose her life, if the stars were to be believed. Throughout his childhood, he had thought his mother's indifference and occasional hatred towards him had stemmed from a lack of maternal instincts. Now, with the opportunity to kill the object of said hatred and the reason for her future demise before her, she paused. It appeared to him that she could not bring herself to do it. Perhaps she was not lacking in them at all. If that were the case, she would have killed him on the spot without so much as displacing a single hair on her head.

No.

This wasn't indifference at all, he realised. It was hesitation.

"I see now," Amon replied, cautious of the threat against his life. His entire body tensed with the proximity to death, but he tried his hardest not to let it show. "This is why you hate me." She raised a brow. "You knew, the moment I was born, that I would have a role to play in your demise. You fear your own mortality, but not quite enough to kill the one person who makes you most mortal… And it is eating at you."

His mother released the staff of light back into the atmosphere. She let her hand fall, causing the manipulated scene around them to revert to the empty throne room.

"Politics and powers aside, you are still my son. It is not too late to come back to me," she said, softening her voice to the sweet, innocent tones she used on the masses. Amon knew better than to take her words as a sign of care. When she appeared to be at her most docile, she was in fact at her most deadly. "To stand by my side, be the heir to my throne, as you were always meant to be…"

Her words made his skin crawl. Pleasant as they were, he knew there was an agenda lurking just behind them. And as for the thought of actually inheriting a throne? His mother would not allow herself to die. She would fight time, fate, and death at every turn…and win. Yet, she had never been as close to death as she was now. He hadn't needed the stars' foreboding message to see it; her act of pandering alone gave away the game.

Amon was about to shrug her off, as he'd so often used to do when she tried to manipulate him in his youth, when a thought occurred to him. His mother had taken the news of her imminent death almost *too* lightly. There had to be something more to it, another game she was playing in the background. Perhaps in this strange pandering state, he might be able to coax out the rest of her plans.

"Say I agreed…" he began, letting a tentative silence fall between them. "Say I decided to stay on and help you keep your throne. Say we somehow managed to defeat the Prince of Shadows. What then?" he continued, wanting to keep the conversation alive enough for her to drop any suspicion. His mother resumed her predatory circling, as if newly sizing him up. "Would you still feel the need to be rid of me?"

"You make me sound so cruel, Amon. Is that truly what you think?"

"I think you are more concerned with infinite life than the nurturing of temporary beings. Even if we do defeat the Prince of Shadows, you would still have to contend with death. Sooner or later, we all do."

At that she smiled. Murder glinted in her eyes as she spoke. "Have you ever wondered how Adrius, our dear Prince of Shadows, cheated death? How his soul lingered on past the expiration of his body?"

Amon held his tongue. This was the story he'd been waiting for: this was the final game.

"I'll tell you," she continued. "It all started before Divinations, before the bindings were placed on Iturri, before there was a separation between the world we know and the world of the humans, and before we came to know the Arima as Blood Daemons. Back then, people were either born with varying degrees of power from their nation of origin or with none at all. It was as if the land itself where a child was conceived imbued said child with its powers. There was an Argia king whose daughter conceived a child in secret away from her lands, such that, when the little prince was born, he developed the powers of the Izar, rather than the Argia. This caused one of the first wars between the nations of Visanthe, for how could an Izar rule the house of the Argia? At first, this child's powers were kept a secret, but as it became time for him to take on the responsibilities of his title, it became impossible to hide.

"At the same time, the prince of the Arima, had become close with this boy. They became the best of friends, in fact. By that time, Adrius, the most powerful Arima to date, had already stepped into his throne. So, when the time came for judgement to be passed on this boy, he fought with the elders of the other nations to keep them from executing him. The decision was finally made to send the young Argia child to the human world and allow him to live out the remainder of his days away from Visanthe, where his existence would cause no further trouble. From thus forth, they would seal the gates to the other world. We, the people of Visanthe, would become the myths and folktales of the human world, and their world would lose all relevance to us."

"But not to Adrius…"

"No."

Suddenly, she shot a hand up to the ceiling again. The room shifted once more. Soon, he found himself in the halls of a different palace, one he'd only visited twice before, and whose memory alone made his inside recoil. The first time he'd set foot in it, he'd met her. The last time, he'd slaughtered her family. Guilt gnawed at him as he remembered his actions. A cold surrounded him, one that felt like sadness incarnate. Alexei was right, possessed or not, they were his hands that committed the atrocity, his feet that fled from the scene.

Before him, his mother stood alongside a younger version of herself who, in all fairness, looked exactly like her present self. She walked in circles around her phantom double and another figure, a yet unchanged Prince of Shadows. He looked agitated, and very much less composed than he'd come to know him. A heated debate played out between the two illusory figures, which ended in the young Prince of Shadows assuring he would find a way to change everything—change the world if that was required. He'd claimed no rule—or ruler—should live forever, a sentiment he'd echoed to Amon during his apprenticeship.

As the phantom version of the Prince of Shadows stormed off, the younger version of his mother watched on with fear in her eyes. The present version of his mother looked upon the scene with a scowl, as though she'd relived it many times before and still had not accepted the outcome.

Amon realised that it was this very moment which had sealed their fates. Adrius, the Prince of Shadows, would do everything in his power to change the world, and she, the Princess of Light, would do everything in hers to maintain it…

Even if it meant caging the spirit of Visanthe itself.

"It was you…" Amon whispered into the illusion. "You trapped the spirit of the lands on Middle Isle. You are the reason we hold Divinations. You are the reason these lands are dying, the reason the people are not receiving powers anymore. It was all you."

"I did what I had to," she replied, unmoved by his realisation.

"You threw off the balance of the world…"

"I protected this world," she growled, her voice echoing something deadly. "He was going to destroy us all. You saw it for yourself. I had no choice."

Amon had never been privy to his mother's past. Any revelations now were only an act of pandering. An attempt at swaying him towards her cause. This act alone was proof of how much she needed him to play along with her scheme. But there would be no swaying him after what he'd witnessed. He hadn't realised the extent of her meddling in the world's affairs until now. She was the reason for all the turmoil in the world, and if it were up to her, he knew it would only get worse.

"You cannot win against fate, Mother. You cannot run from these changes," Amon scoffed.

His mother dropped the illusion around them and glided over to another of the basins around the room. She toyed with the glowing water, as though indifferent to his comment. She pulled the light from it, moulding it into a floating disk in which she contemplated her own reflection. "I will not be giving up my throne because he cannot drop his futile crusade."

"He has Iturri on his side——"

"Iturri is not yet freed," she corrected, the indifference fraying at the edge of her voice. "I am still the most powerful being in this world."

"You cannot believe you are stronger than the master of death himself."

"Perhaps it is time we rid ourselves of that dreaded god once and for all."

"Mother, you can't kill Iturri," Amon hissed. "If you so much as try, the world will lose its power."

She laughed. It was the kind of gentle, feathery laugh that might have hinted at actual amusement if it hadn't also been accompanied by the glinting malice in her eyes. Before he could register what was happening, his mother cast chains of light around him, binding his hands and feet together. She stalked over to him, embodying the aura of a goddess of discord. This was the truth hidden beneath her innocent façade. The beast that feared her own mortality. She mirrored the version of herself that he'd seen in the memory. As she spoke, the same passionate sentiment of wanting control radiated from her.

"I can, and I will. And if you try to stop me, I will kill you too."

CHAPTER 19

IN TIMES OF DESPERATION

IF THE PREVIOUS DAY'S SHADOWY VISITOR hadn't caused enough of a stir within the confines of the Ur kingdom, today's visitor surely made a splash.

The woman in the long, hooded fur cloak had swept past every guard, every soldier, and every barricade without so much as breaking a sweat. She left the tides in a state of hurricane-level agitation, upturning even the most profound of icebergs. One woman, the damage of a century's worth of storms.

Her identity, a mystery to all.

As she neared the old manor house of the queen, the guards scrambled to prepare a blockade which, given her force and trajectory, would do little more than stall her. This woman of exceptional power could have levelled the building with a flick of her wrist, sunk it beneath a shoreline-changing tidal wave. The soldiers from the inner isles had already begun sounding the alarm bells. But, to their surprise, just as easily as the rising tide of her destruction had appeared on their shores, it vanished. Instead, the strange woman halted, floating in the watery courtyard, waiting in the bougainvillaea and mangrove-lined entrance to be acknowledged.

"I need to speak with your leaders," she called out. Her voice, though steady, held all the hallmarks of urgency.

Unsure of how to respond, the guards planted themselves around her, keeping enough distance between them in case things went sour. Trepidation consumed them, standing before the woman who had breezed past their ranks with excessive ease. They exchanged bewildered glances, their training and instincts urging them to act, but uncertainty clouding their judgement in the face of such an unprecedented situation.

"Now," she demanded, tension fraying at the edge of her voice.

One of the guards peeled off from the pack, scrambling to find his leader as instructed. The rest waited, arms and weapons raised, careful not to accidentally renew the woman's lust for chaos.

The noise of the attack beyond the manor house had reached Queen Noor and General Kyara before the guard. By the time he'd arrived to fetch them with news of the stranger, the twin rulers of the Ur Kingdom had already dropped their latest heated debate on how they should fortify the lesser isles and had prepared themselves to face the opponent. They raced out to meet her, arriving just as the waters began to settle.

Much to their surprise, the figure that greeted them was not one of overwhelming power and brutish strength, but one of average stature and build. The sisters exchanged a look of confusion between them. The cloaked figure hovering over the shallow waters of the courtyard was impossible to miss, and judging by the way the guards held their positions around her, this truly was the architect of all the chaos.

How had this one, unsuspecting woman sent their lands into such a fearful frenzy?

Queen Noor shot a hand out and cast a grand cage of ice around her, though, based on the wake the woman had left behind, she knew it would do little to hold her back if she desired a fight.

The woman made no attempts to free herself. In truth, she scarcely moved at all. Her composure both astounded and struck fear in the hearts of the twins. She'd entered with all the force of a tropical storm but now stood in serenity, like the stillness of the eye of the storm.

"Who are you?" Queen Noor called out to her. "And what is it that compels you to this place and demands an audience?"

"I am but a grieving mother, and a messenger of ill tidings…"

The woman encased in ice removed her cloak, revealing short icy locks and a face, though slightly older, that resembled the queen and her twin. Even before she spoke, concern settled in the air around the twins. General Kyara tightened her grip on her spear. Queen Noor ground her teeth. An unspoken history stood before them dressed in the prospect of family reunion.

"I am Aysel, mother to the late heir to the throne of the Ur…"

The warring twins had already put aside their differences in efforts to protect their kingdom from external threats, but they had scarcely imagined that the greatest challenge to their rule might come from within their own borders. This woman held more power in her than the two of them combined and a legitimate claim to the throne…

Aysel, their elder sister, had finally returned. Would she challenge their rule?

Queen Noor released her command on the ice cage, letting the water melt away and return to the seas from whence it came. "Come inside," she said. "We have much to discuss."

"I pose no threat to your rule, Your Majesty," Aysel replied. "Nor do I request your hospitality. I gave up any claim I had to that throne decades ago, and my intentions have not changed."

General Kyara, the more forceful of the two, growled at her like the bears under her command. "That was not a request."

Queen Noor raised a hand to silence her twin. With more decorum and finesse, she added, "Such conversations could have detrimental effects if spoken about freely."

Aysel shook her head. "With all due respect, Your Majesty, that house is no place for me, nor do I intend to stay longer than is required to bring forth this news. My son was murdered by the shadows that have been converging upon these lands for centuries. Before I fled this life, I stole an object from the house of disorienting mists. I believed my taking it would change the outcome of certain predestined events, that my hiding it would render its use impossible by dark forces. I was wrong. No one is above fate, not even the shadows themselves."

The news sent a ripple of fear through the crowd.

Queen Noor and General Kyara turned to each other, eyes filled with an unspoken barrage of questions that only they two could understand. Their sister had confirmed what Griffin had insinuated before leaving. The shadows were back and out to rearrange the world in their favour. The Prince of Shadows had the stone of the Ur. They were on the heels of war and very much unprepared.

Storm clouds gathered overhead. The isle of Solia had never once seen such darkness as that which accompanied their mourning visitor.

"Someone of your great ability would make an asset in the event of war," said Queen Noor, hoping to appeal to the same sense of justice that had caused her estranged elder sister to flee from these lands in the first place.

Again, Aysel shook her head. "I am not a fighter. I have already played my part in this story."

"With powers like yours, you could save lives," General Kyara hissed.

"No choice I make will change the outcome of this war. I have done enough as it is—I have lost enough. I gave up my family, I was robbed of my son… How much more suffering would you inflict upon me?" she replied, her voice filled with the uniquely traumatising grief of a mother who was forced to bury her child. The mention of him seemed to take its toll on whatever barrier she'd put between her task and her emotions. "I wish to take no further part in this. I came simply as a messenger, and request only to be left in peace from hereon in."

"But—" General Kyara began when her twin shot a hand up to silence her.

"What was the name of your child?" asked Queen Noor.

"Elias," Aysel replied.

"Then it is our task to make sure your suffering was not in vain."

"But Noor—"

"Kyara, you and I are in no place to intervene in her grief. One day, this war will be a distant memory, but her sadness will live on infinitely, in the way only grief can."

Understanding washed over General Kyara's face. It was the kind of mercy she'd never shown, but given the circumstances, it would not be the last time, either. She turned away from the courtyard, signalling her acceptance of her elder sister's wishes of solitude.

"Go, Aysel. Mourn in peace. Live out the rest of your days as you choose. You have my word that no one will look for you or disturb you."

"Thank you, Your Majesty," she said, holding back tears of rage and sorrow like the storm clouds above them held back the rain.

As she turned, the surrounding soldiers dropped their weapons. Aysel paid them no mind, for she had known all along that no damage they could inflict would compare to the loss in her heart. She pulled the cloak over her head once more and waded back through the mangroves from whence she came. Her task completed, her warning heeded, there was no need for further disruption.

The grey clouds overhead finally gave out. The dense rain washed over the isle of Solia, encasing it in a tomb of melancholy. For those who believed in omens, such a rain might indicate renewal, a replenishing of hope in a world that had all but lost it. But, as they looked out over the hazy lands, watching as the gloomy skyline blended in with the unsettled waters, the sisters knew it was far from over. There was much darkness still to come before any break in this storm.

CHAPTER 20

A FINAL CROSSING

JASPER HELPED SEBASTIAN LOAD THE LAST of the barrels onto the ship under the watchful eyes of their vibrant captain. Those beautiful blue eyes of hers followed him up and down the deck, urging him with silent pleas to rethink his plans. She knew as well as he did—as well as they all did—that there was no turning back now. Despite her tempting offers of 'hanging up her hat and retiring on a beach in Solia somewhere', Jasper knew Lucy was as invested in the outcome of this war as they all were. She had a good heart buried under all those layers of fur, feathers, and fire.

"That offer still stands, sweetness. You, me, a shack on a beach, and a single bed," Lucy whispered as he passed with more provisions.

"It gets even more tempting every time you say it, Lucy, but you know I can't," he laughed. She had been getting more direct with her advances of late, but he knew that the flirtation and daring were her way of coping with the uncertainty.

"I know," she shrugged, masking her apprehension with humour and a flirtatious wink. It was a ruse. Even as she laughed off the danger, her eyes spoke of fear where her tongue could not. "But I maintain my position, if a good battle is what you want, come tangle with me in the sheets. At least you'll still be alive by the end of it… Can't promise you'll come out unscathed though. Might be a bit battered and bruised…"

She wasn't the only one coping. They had all been in a mood of late.

Tension pervaded the air of the ship, growing more suffocating with each passing day. Griffin had refused to stay on the ship—in great part because he and water mixed about as well as chalk and water did—citing 'space to think, undisturbed' as his primary motive. He opted instead for a room in a quaint, nearby locale. But Jasper was not so easily fooled—nor were the rest of them, for that matter. Between Lance, Amon, and the war, Griffin was two fraying threads away from snapping.

More concerning still was the fact that Jasper knew there were still secrets Griffin kept close to his chest. Although, if hypocrisy were the name of the game, he was as good a player as Griffin himself. Lucy had once told him the sharpest cuts were made by secrets. If so, Jasper knew he held the sharpest of them all.

The sinister songs of the Book of Blood (as he'd come to know it) continued to ring out in his ears at all hours of the day. Jasper had memorised the legend of the stones, repeating parts of it to himself at random in a way that he couldn't rightly call consciously. The rational part of him wished to believe it was simply a force of habit, combined with a morbid sense of curiosity. The growing spiritual part of him disagreed. Especially when it considered the voice ringing through his head was not his own. It was entirely foreign to him, the sound of it muffled as though reaching out from a distance. Yet he'd come to know it intimately, as though it were a long-lost friend.

But then, if Griffin were any example, long-lost friends were questionable things at best.

Lance—the first of such friends—they'd dropped in the port of Osiir. He was supposed to meet with the current head of the Argia mafia to see about reclaiming control over the lands. Between the two of them, Lance and Griffin agreed that he would be of greater use sitting atop a throne rather than a crow's nest. He claimed it was time for him to take his rightful place as leader, but the truth lay closer to home. It was time to make amends.

Lance had been a walking phantom since they rescued him from Idune. Not even he could deny the way guilt coloured his eyes as he wandered aboard the ship, drifting from the bridge to the hull, dressed in the trappings of regal sadness. Somehow, he managed to avoid Griffin's habit of falsely stoic pacing at every turn—though, Jasper imagined there was a good reason their paths never intersected. One that veered far from indifference.

Sebastian's outburst towards Lance had marked the final grain of sand in the hourglass of patient grief. No amount of moping would change the past or erase the suffering. As for the future, they still had a chance, but time was running out. The outburst must have triggered him, for Lance made a promise to see things put right. That promise he made in the captain's quarters was the first sign that life had not completely abandoned him in the fight.

"Leave that crate alone, Sebas. There's nothing in it for you!" Simon called, pulling Jasper's attention from Lucy to the twins momentarily.

"I don't see why you need all this nonsense anyway, you do know what we're going to do…" Sebastian replied, toying around with a vial of something that looked as though it shouldn't be played with.

Sebastian's twin brother Simon had returned. Having them reunited brought back a harmony that had been lacking in everyone's day to day. Sebastian's passionate and erratic outbursts were, once again, neutralised by Simon's quiet and almost invisible nature. The two still managed to bicker as if they'd never left each other's side, but at least the time apart had made them more distinguishable. Simon had gone and dyed his golden curls dark with a plant-based paste, hoping to hide his natural Argia glow with the earthier tones of the Harri territories. If you looked close enough, however, the resemblance between their faces was still as striking as the first day he'd met them. They were perfect reflections of each other.

Though he kept mostly to himself, Simon's keen eyes had already proven useful. Jasper had tried to hide his affliction from everyone, but Simon had detected it almost instantly and began concocting a tonic that would rid him of the pain, even if it couldn't strip the shadows from his blood. Jasper soon realised that he wasn't the only one Simon had come to treat.

At some point, Jasper had managed to walk in on Simon and Storm whispering heatedly about something that left her usually steady hands trembling. She snatched the vial from Simon's hands and walked off, stopping beside Jasper as she left, saying, "If you tell anyone, I'll kill you." Jasper knew her well enough to know she would make good on the threat.

Something about her seemed to have caved in on itself. Aside from that strange encounter, Jasper had found her on more than one occasion staring out at the vast ocean beyond. Each time he'd found her with eyes as red as the dawn sky, and which she masked with curtains of hair. When asked about it, she would shrug and mumble something about fate taking care of its children before abandoning the deck altogether.

Whether they chose to admit it or not, fear ate at all of them. Each one got a different taste but, whether coated in humour or in sadness, there was no mistaking it. They were headed towards death with sails full, hearts heavy, and enough secrets to slaughter an army.

As for the rest of the crew, most of Lucy's gang had taken leave, and she did little to stop them. To be fair, Jasper didn't know how anyone would volunteer to stay aboard upon learning how they were sailing towards death itself. He laughed to himself softly, realising that no one in their right mind would.

What does that say about us? he wondered as he looked around the deck.

Each of them claimed to be fighting for something greater than themselves, for a better world, for an end to darkness. But the time spent with them, watching from the background, had taught him better. Between Griffin's nerves, Storm and Sebastian's stolen glances, and his own nightmares, the real reason was obvious. They were all fighting for a someone they couldn't live without—him included.

I guess sometimes it is just that simple, he thought.

In the end, we all live, we all fight, we all die for the same reason: love.

"I made a promise to someone that I would take care of her. Bond or no bond, I can't break that promise…" Jasper replied as he turned back to Lucy, the sound of the twins' bickering in the background. A soft frown crept over her lips, but she said nothing.

"Besides, he's probably safer at war than he is with you, Lucinda," called Griffin as he emerged unsteadily from the cabin below deck looking every shade of green.

"I won't hear any comments about my love life from someone who keeps running from his own, Griffin," she snapped back at him. "And especially not from someone whose knees wobble at the sight of a little water."

"First of all, this isn't *a little water* we are talking about; it's an ocean, and the very worst of them," Griffin hissed. "And second, my love life is none of your concern."

"Cool it, pretty boy. I had to sit through enough of your pining and whining on the crossing from the Harri territories to Iliso, and every useless stop you had me make in between."

"There was no pining or—" Lucy shot him a knowing glower, silencing any further qualms on his end. He glowered back, engaging in a staring contest that lasted all of a minute before relenting. Lucy smirked at her win. "In any case, Jasper is right. There is no changing the course of these tides."

"Think of that one all on your own, did you?"

"No, but I figure nothing unrelated to the sea would sink into that flamboyantly blockish head of yours."

In a flash that caught them all off-guard, Lucinda drew her sword and aimed it at his throat. "I don't like you enough not to kill you," she whispered down the edge of the blade. The twins' bickering stopped. Even Storm had raced over from the stern to see what had gone wrong. The cast was all present, it seemed, for this unofficial team meeting.

"Lucy—"

"No, don't *Lucy* me," she growled. "With you gone, we could all get on with what little lives we have left apparently."

Storm drew her sword. Flames burst into Sebastian's palms. They all held their breaths, wondering who might make the first move.

"I know you're scared, Lucy," Griffin began.

"I'm scared out of my wits, sure, but I'm also tired of your nonsense. Look around you, Griffin. All these people are looking to you for guidance, and your head has been anywhere but here. As captain, your emotions affect us all. Your tension becomes our tension. They've all put aside their inner demons to be here. It's time you stopped running from yours. And I don't mean your irrational fear of the sea."

"When did this turn into a lecture?"

"When you decided to march us all into a battle we can't even hope to win, over a girl that—from what I understand—might be the death of us all, while you go about pacing holes in my ship because you're scared of telling a man how you feel."

She certainly has a way of making her opinions known, Jasper thought as a grin swept across his face. She'd stopped his heart for a moment there, but he knew killing Griffin was never part of her plan. She liked making statements and being heard. Needless to say, with that little outburst, she'd achieved both.

Sebastian dropped the flames straining against a snorting laugh. Storm lowered her sword and smacked him on the shoulder. Simon bit his lip, but he too was grateful for the diffusion of tensions that Lucy had provided.

"Wonderful," Griffin groaned as he swatted her blade from beneath his chin. "Are we finished here?"

"In the space between our reunion and now, you've let the love of your life slip through your fingers and your childhood best friend walk into certain death alone. You tell me."

Griffin sighed. Whether he chose to admit it or not, Lucy had reached through to him. "By the way, where is that selfish, narcissistic pain in the ass anyway?"

"Careful, Grif, pots and kettles and all," smirked Sebastian as he clapped a heavy hand on Griffin's shoulder.

"Since when did we declare this 'harp on Griffin' day?" he retorted, though his eyes still bounced around the ship for their missing companion.

"You make it too easy," replied Jasper as he leaned up against the mast.

"Not you too," Griffin mumbled. Jasper shrugged. "Get back to what you were doing, everyone. We're leaving soon under the cover of night. Lucinda, knock off the antics."

She took a sweeping, flamboyant bow, as though she were only a performer. A knowing smile beamed on her face. "Alright, you heard him. You, firecracker, I need those muscles over here…"

As the rest of them peeled away in search of tasks that needed completing before departure, Griffin leaned up against the bow, searching the shoreline for any sign of Amon. Jasper pushed himself off the mast and leaned up next to him. Though Griffin tried to keep his frown at bay, Jasper could tell Amon's absence was eating at him. In spite of his denials, and all the pent-up animosity, the cords of their friendship still held strong.

"He was supposed to be back by now…" Griffin whispered, staring out over the town.

"Go find him," Jasper replied. "You know you want to. We'll sort things out here for when you both return."

"I'm not going to put everyone in jeopardy because that idiot insisted on doing it alone."

"Griffin, we have time," he lied. "Plus, we haven't left port yet and you already look like you need to get back on dry land."

Griffin opened his mouth to deny it, but Jasper stopped him with a shake of his head. He sighed and nodded instead. "I'll make sure to be back before sundown. If I'm not, go ahead without me."

"You'll be back in time," Jasper told him as he held his hand out for Griffin to take. "You're too afraid we'll die without you."

Griffin gripped it firmly. "I'll find him, and together we'll find her. You have my word, we will all make it through this alive," he replied, bobbing his chin before catapulting himself from the ship to the dock.

Jasper watched as he weaved through the wooden paths and disappeared between the buildings of the town. He had utter faith that Griffin would return with Amon, but he feared what was to come of them when he did. The book had been adamant in reminding him of the sacrifice that would be required. It was as though the spirit of the book itself sensed it. Its calls for blood had lessened, as though it were waiting. As though it knew something greater was coming.

This was the secret that weighed heavily on his chest. There was no way around it, at least not one he could see. The ritual required death in exchange for life, a sacrifice that could not be avoided.

Someone would have to die, and there were little doubts in his mind as to who.

CHAPTER 21

BURIED HACHETS

SNEAKING AROUND THE ALLEYS OF YOZORA brought back memories that Griffin had all too readily buried when he left the Izarian Guard. Back then, Amon and Alexei would've been at his side, prodding him to do something reckless or illegal. Most likely both.

Alexei had always been a loose cannon, willing to do the more dangerous parts of their scheme. Amon, the mastermind, had a way of coming up with the most terrifyingly thrilling adventures—and most often to irritate his mother. And Griffin, more often than not, was the reason they never got caught.

Now he was alone, sneaking through the streets he used to call home like the common thieves he used to capture. His only consolation was the fact that he himself had planned out all the routes of the current guards, which meant he knew exactly how to avoid them at each turn.

Soldiers dressed in sparkling silver armour perused the streets, lost in their own grandiose sense of importance. None of them even spared him a passing glance as he mingled in with the usual city folk. Griffin knew the best ways to make himself invisible in plain sight and employed them all now. The glamour he used on Jasper in the Ur Kingdom was an example of one of such tactics; though, the soldiers here were better prepared for such tricks. Still, when it came to the domain of light, there was no such thing as being 'too careful'.

Somehow, he managed to arrive at the base of the palace gates successfully unnoticed. The guards seemed to be discussing other matters. He'd overheard a few of them in the main square talking about preparations, but he hadn't managed to catch the rest of the conversation as, if he'd stayed longer, he might have been recognised by some of his old regiment.

Griffin watched the entrance carefully, looking for an opportunity to enter. The problem was that the palace was watched over by their fair lady of starlight herself. The guards, the guests, the stowaways—no one escaped her watch. She was an omniscient presence.

Before he and Amon had found the stone, Griffin had wondered how such a thing was possible. But after encountering it and its special breed of magic, he realised that she too was a beneficiary of its blessings. His and Amon's gift of reading the stars had appeared after a few minutes with the stone. Her longer exposure to its power must have given her skills that others could hardly fathom.

She was going to be his biggest problem.

Suddenly, Griffin caught wind of a sombre tune drifting in the air above his head. He gazed upwards. The melody was soft, sad, and unmistakably dark. Hateful and gentle at the same time. It reminded him of the day he'd got word of his father's death, and how, even after years of disappointment and disapproval, he still longed for such a connection. The notes were woven together in a web of sorrow, catching only the broken hearts the way spiders catch flies. Griffin doubted that anyone who had lived free of suffering would understand the deeper meaning behind the tune.

But he did.

He's at it again, Griffin thought to himself, knowing of only one person capable of creating such haunting melodies. *Not even a day back in the palace and he's back at the piano. Does the past still have such a hold on him?*

When Griffin was younger, he used to stand at his post outside one of the main halls and listen to Amon's tortured playing. The songs always left him in raptures. He never understood how a boy of such affluence could be capable of expressing such suffering. That was before they'd gotten to know one another.

He must really love her, came an intrusive thought. Intrusive thoughts were not his favourites, but he'd grown too wise to ignore them.

Griffin hadn't wanted to believe Amon's change of heart. He was never one to get attached. Even when they were kids, Amon had been the type of person to avoid any potentially romantic associations with the young ladies. Back then, Griffin had chalked it up to them not being his type. Seeing him on the bridge, the night he'd come to warn them about the Prince of Shadows, made him reconsider his preconceptions of Amon.

Amon had never so much as looked emotionally ruffled. That night, he was distraught.

The way he'd said her name too… The urgency that plagued him. Griffin had never seen him act that way about anyone. Savara had single-handedly brought back his heart—and seemingly tore it from his chest as well.

As he listened on to the sorrowful melody, Griffin realised that the intrusive thought had been right all along. The tune spoke not of the house of the past, but of the home of the future. Every trill, every note, every sad interlude spoke only of her. Savara.

When Amon finally stopped playing, Griffin looked around at the crowd that had gathered outside the gates. Murmurings of the prince's return carried on the wind. If Amon had wanted to keep his arrival a secret, he'd failed miserably.

That would be like him to make a scene without intending to… Griffin thought to himself with a smirk. Jokes aside, he knew he would have to work harder at not being seen, and especially at not being caught. Now that the queen was surely aware of her deserter son's return, she would have the guards swarming the grounds, making sure he would never leave again.

A young guard rounded the corner. The armour hung loose on him. The sword at his side was improperly strapped. He looked as though he were fresh out of recruitment.

Perfect.

Griffin pretended not to have noticed the young soldier as he pushed off the wall. He'd made his stature deceptively smaller than usual, hiding his body beneath the billowing cloak as he purposely bumped into the boy. As expected, the loose sword clattered to the ground. Griffin bent down to retrieve it, keeping his hood low, though making no effort to hide either. Nobody asked after the people who seemed like they wanted to be seen. Besides, by the time anyone did, he would already be gone.

"Sorry, sir!" said the boy, too focused on his sword to realise he'd wandered into a trap.

"It was my fault, I wasn't looking," Griffin replied as he handed him the sword.

As the boy's hands wrapped around the hilt, Griffin spun him around and pinned him to the wall. The boy barely had time to react as he was thrust against the stone. Griffin straightened to full height, using the cloak to hide his attack. He pressed his full weight against the soldier, keeping him pinned as he conjured a vision out of the surrounding light.

The boy fell into the vision willingly. The shock of the attack had kept his mind confused enough for Griffin to warp his perception of the event. It was a vision that only he and the boy could see, but one that would keep the boy occupied as Griffin continued his task.

Griffin was not cruel.

The vision was of a lover—one convincing enough for the soldier to strip his armour off willingly. Griffin collected the armour, squeezing his muscles into it before slipping through the palace gates.

By the time the effect of his powers wore off, Griffin would be far enough out of the soldier's reach. Not that the boy was any match for him, but avoiding unnecessary scenes would be ideal for such a situation. Especially as he didn't know whether it would be possible once he found Amon.

Griffin strolled up to the palace unimpeded. He moved with the confidence of someone whose job it was to protect the place—as it had been, in a past life. Wearing both the armour and the confidence, not a single soldier questioned his presence, not even as he waltzed through the main entrance. He wondered whether it was a testament to his own performance, or if Amon's unexpected return had the rest of the guard scurrying about like headless roaches. He hoped such distraction extended to the queen herself, though he highly doubted there was anything that could distract her.

Everything was just as he'd remembered it. The reflection pool extended the length of the reception area, with waters as dark as the night sky and moonstones shimmering like stars beneath its surface. Marble figures dotted the walkways, each trapped in some artistic pose meant to convey appreciation but whose faces spoke only of toiling away. The ceiling was lost against the glow of floating orbs of light stolen from beyond the palace walls.

This had always been his favourite room. It was a solemn place, perfect for contemplation, though few people spent enough time here to ever question more than the time of day.

A shame, for maybe if people had spent more time here, they would've understood how pointless some of the protocols of the guard were. Hence why he left.

Halls branched out from each of the four corners of the room. Some led to other rooms, others to courtyards that bled into entryways. People drifted through them frequently, paying no mind to the disguised intruder in their midst.

Griffin weaved his way through them, making sure to be seen only enough to not raise suspicion. He searched the many dismayed crowds for Amon, knowing he would most likely be found at the centre of the greatest commotion. No luck. He snuck past a pair of chatty guards and climbed the staircase to Amon's chambers. Empty.

Amon was nowhere to be found.

He wouldn't have confronted his mother directly. Only a fool… Griffin stopped his train of thought. His friend was the biggest, most arrogant fool he'd ever met. *Never mind.* That was exactly where he would've gone.

Before departing, Griffin grazed his hand over the polished pianoforte. For some reason, he'd expected the touch of it to feel ethereal. Supernatural. The wood was cold beneath his fingers. He pursed his lips. The instrument he'd admired for the better part of his childhood was just that: an instrument. Nothing magical about it.

Part of him had hoped that the pianoforte held some secret that would explain the composition of such haunting melodies. Like the powers of the land, this instrument was a tool. A channel for the spirit of the musician to flow through. Sadly, this meant all the torment came from within Amon. He felt bad for not realising it sooner. Perhaps if he had, they might have avoided his descent into darker dealings. But Griffin knew better than to linger on past 'what ifs'.

If something was meant to happen, it would. Fate would have it no other way.

He made haste to the throne room, leaving the pianoforte and the memories of the past trapped in the tower—where they belonged.

Griffin dodged another stream of guards and courtiers whispering amongst themselves about the prince's return. Judging by the gossip, his arrival caught many by surprise. By the sounds of it, the queen had cleared out the throne room to speak with him in private. The throng of people exited the halls, disgruntled by their dismissal. At least that meant he was headed in the right direction.

The thought of Amon alone with her set Griffin's nerves on edge. Would she do anything to harm him after half the court had already seen him? Perhaps that was why Amon had chosen to make such a scene, to ensure he remained just out of harm's reach. His friend was a fool but not an idiot. His actions, his choices, were almost always backed by some sort of judgement—good or otherwise.

By the time Griffin arrived at the throne room, he found it eerily quiet. He pressed a hand gently against the door, opening it just wide enough to peek inside. The room was empty. He was confused. Amon was supposed to be here. He began to fear the worst. He decided that if he couldn't find Amon, he'd at least seek out the stone.

He made his way swiftly to the catacombs of the palace. From the outside, the palace was no more than a few stories high. It was a mostly unassuming building. One could easily be fooled into thinking there was little more to it than that. Few people ever learned of the true depths of the palace, let alone descended to them.

Amon had dragged him down here when they were boys. He followed the same path they'd taken to find the stone, but before he arrived, he noticed an exceptional amount of darkness seeping through one of the locked chambers. Such darkness was not naturally occurring. It was the absence of light, the work of serious power.

Griffin tried holding up some conjured light to it, but the darkness wouldn't move. He would've moved on—he should've moved on—but the little voice in his head told him something important was being kept there. No one would charm a room to reject light if there was nothing to be found in it. He took a few deep breaths, allowing the damp air of the catacombs to fill his lungs and clear his mind before entering the eerie chamber.

The darkness that covered him felt colder and deadlier than any Griffin had experienced before. Not only did the room reject the light, he realised, but there would be no way of conjuring light in it either. He was right. These were no ordinary prisons. These prisons were made specifically to house the Izar. The perfect place to hide the criminals—or a newly returned traitorous prince of light.

"Amon?" he whispered, the sound echoing regardless.

"Look out," Amon replied, relief and disappointment filling the phrase.

But before Griffin could ask after the warning, he felt something take hold of his left arm in a bone-crushing grip. Whoever it was hoisted him easily in the air and tossed him to the ground, sending a metallic cacophony through the chamber. The blow knocked the wind out of him momentarily, but Griffin leapt to his feet as quickly as possible, shyly avoiding another attack.

They were not alone.

"You could've given me a better warning!" Griffin growled.

"Don't speak; they'll locate you."

"They?"

"Shut up and listen. Two guards, blind but not deaf. I'm chained to the wall in front of you. Maybe five paces. The one with the ugly face has the keys."

"That means nothing in the dark, you arse," Griffin hissed.

To his surprise, the guard in question had revealed himself by grumbling a pace or two behind him. Thanks to Amon's insult, Griffin narrowly avoided a fatal blow to the head.

"Thank me later," Amon replied.

Amon hadn't warned him of the size or strength of these characters, but he knew better than to underestimate anyone under Aurelia's employ. Their owners, though blind, were trained for such battles. He'd have to revert to his basic training and hope that fate was on his side.

In the pitch-black darkness of the dungeon, Griffin relied on the heightening of his other senses to guide his movements. He managed to sense the tailwind of the guard's attack. He seized the guard's arm in the recoil, redirecting his momentum to send him crashing to the ground with a resounding thud. Judging by the impact, the guard was at least twice his size.

So much for a quick in-and-out mission.

Before he could catch his breath, the second guard emerged from the shadows. A massive arm snaked around his neck, threatening to crush his throat like a cobra to its prey. Panic surged through him as he struggled against the chokehold. Griffin began to feel the cold of the dark and the stillness of suffocation intertwining. Somewhere in front of him, he heard the other guard rising from the floor. He'd have to act quickly; otherwise, he'd have to contend with the two of them—if he didn't suffocate first.

Desperation fuelled him as he pounded furiously at the arm constricting his windpipe. Summoning every remaining ounce of strength and consciousness he had left, Griffin swung his legs out and wrapped them around the back of the first guard's neck. With a swift, calculated motion, he twisted his body, using the first guard as a makeshift anchor and leveraging him to unbalance the second. As the second guard stumbled forward, Griffin broke free from his grip. He landed on the cold stone floor, gasping for air. Around him, the guards quickly regained their composure. Under better circumstances, the guards would've been no match against his powers. In the dark, he was as good as a sitting deer. His stamina would run out eventually. He would have to find some way to outmanoeuvre them before then.

The sound of chains rattling around him gave him pause. Amon was trying to tell him something. *Blind, not deaf,* he remembered. The guards seemed to have paused as well, unable to locate him through the cacophony.

Under the cover of the echoing chains, Griffin crawled into what he imagined was the centre of the room. He proceeded to remove his boots, waiting for the right moment to strike. When Amon stopped, the room fell deathly silent. Griffin held his breath, unwilling to risk a stray wind revealing his location. He tossed one boot to his left, letting the sound guide the guards astray. The next boot fell far to his right, bouncing three times before settling. The guards' footsteps halted, seemingly confused at the distance between the noises. Griffin knelt down with his sword raised, waiting for them to approach.

Eventually, the guards followed the echo of the second boot. Their path put them in direct contact with the blade. By the time the tip of it touched their armour, it was too late. In one sweeping motion, Griffin sliced at their exposed thighs, sending them both in crumpled heaps to the ground. They snarled in pain.

"Not bad," Amon called. "Now, get the keys and get me out."

As they writhed on the floor, Griffin used the distraction to feel his way around the side of each guard until he heard the successful metallic jingle of the keys. The guard reached out for him, but Griffin brought the blade to his neck.

"This fight is over," he hissed.

When the guard didn't immediately give in, Griffin forced the blade into his throat. He was not one for unnecessary violence, but time was of the essence. The other guard, hearing the gurgling of blood rising in his companion's throat, inched away from the fight.

Griffin let out a sigh of relief. He made his way over to Amon with the keys, finally able to catch his breath.

"You should've heard yourself," Amon mocked. "*The fight is over…*"

"I can leave you here if you prefer," Griffin growled, dangling the keys in front of Amon's face, letting him hear how close he was to freedom.

"Lighten up, it was a joke," he laughed.

Griffin rolled his eyes and set to work unlocking the chains. "You sure have a flare for the flamboyant, by the way. Half the town is talking about you."

"What else is new?" Amon replied as he dropped to the ground. He cracked his wrists and clapped a thankful hand on Griffin's shoulder. "I knew you'd come, by the way."

"You had too much faith," Griffin growled. "Did you at least get the stone?"

"Did you think me that stupid?" Amon asked, brandishing the stone. The eerie blue light filled the room, even in spite of the charm. "Don't answer that."

Amon pulled the darkness into himself using the power of the stone, releasing its hold on the room. His control over his powers had grown vastly since their youth, since the last time Griffin had witnessed them. Amon looked like a fallen god with his dishevelled hair and perfectly tailored suit. Between his regal face and the mischievous glint in his eyes, it wasn't hard to see why people used to fawn over him.

"You're in good spirits for someone who's just been dangling from a wall," Griffin said.

"I missed you too," Amon replied with a smirk. "Just like old times, eh? Me getting us into trouble, you getting us out…"

Griffin looked around for the first time, finally able to see the damage he'd done in the chamber. One guard, pale as bone and surly as a beast of burden, huddled in the corner. The other bled out in the centre of the room.

"I hope you don't punish me for killing one of your guards."

Amon waved a hand carelessly. "They're all traitors anyway."

Griffin furrowed his brow. "I wouldn't make statements like that if I were you."

"I see you're as righteous as ever."

"Amon…"

Amon sighed, unwillingly relenting to the gravity of the situation. "Like I said, lighten up, Griffin. We have places to be." He made his way to the edge of the chamber but, realising Griffin had not followed, he turned back. "Out with it."

"What about your bonds?"

"Ah…"

"Ah?"

"If you mean the ones from the Prince of Shadows, I won't be rid of them until I've given him what he asked of me."

"This stone included?" Griffin asked. Amon nodded. "But there is another bond. Isn't there?"

Amon stared down at his palm fondly, angling it in a way that allowed Griffin to see the strange, star-shaped scar in the dim light of the chamber. He didn't remember such a scar from their childhood, and such a thing would be hard to forget.

"Was it before or after that you fell in love with her?" Griffin asked, only now beginning to understand the depths of his friend's affections towards Savara.

Amon closed his fingers over the scar and sighed. "Do you remember the day you woke up and realised the sky was blue?" he asked in reply. Griffin shook his head. "It's like that. Something that was there before you, and something that will persist long after. What I feel for her has existed and will exist for longer than my rational mind can fathom. I don't know what it is, but I know falling isn't the word."

"I never thought I'd live to see you compare anyone to the sky…" Griffin mused.

"She is my sun, my moon, and my sky full of stars—and not even that encompasses what my soul feels for her."

"How eloquent."

"Shut up."

Griffin strode towards him, frown on full display. "You know of the legend better than any. You know what has to happen, don't you?" Amon pursed his lips. Griffin could see the back and forth of it all playing out on his face. "What will you do about the stone?"

"What can I do? I can't hand it in. Otherwise, I play right into the legend."

"But if you don't, you will never be free." It didn't seem to convince him, so Griffin added, "Neither will she." His words seemed to have the desired effect. Amon sighed. "Go to her. Turn in the stone. We will wait for you at Middle Isle."

"But the legend…"

"Life's too short to worry about legends."

Amon blinked. "You've never been one to shirk a higher calling, Griffin."

"You've never been one to fall in love, Amon," Griffin chuckled. "Exceptional circumstances demand exceptional actions."

Amon furrowed his brow as he contemplated Griffin's words. "Are you sure?" he asked. His voice hinted at apprehension, but his eyes burned resolutely beneath his brow.

Griffin knew his friend would not rest easily until he knew that Savara was safe. Being honest with himself, he also knew that Amon was right when he'd said he was the only person who could check in on her unscathed. He could jump to lands no other could, owing to the nature of his bonds. He could continue to play into the Prince of Shadows' hands, using that misplaced trust to get close to her, to make sure she was safe. And that was more important than higher calling right now.

Griffin nodded. "Just make sure to come back this time."

Amon traded the concern for a friendly smile. "You're never going to let me forget that, are you?"

Griffin breezed past Amon in the doorway. He eyed the various halls cautiously, hoping their raucous had not attracted other guards. When he was sure they remained mostly alone, he replied, "Hope we all live long enough to make that possible."

They followed winding tunnels through the catacombs of the palace, coming to a drainage tunnel that led to the ocean a short distance from the docks. There, they parted ways, Amon to the Arima lands, and Griffin to the rest of his friends. As Amon disappeared in a cloud of dust, he bobbed his head. Griffin bobbed his head in reply, knowing his princeling friend would be back, that there was still more to their story.

CHAPTER 22

A MIRROR TO THE PAST

THE PRETENTIOUSLY PERFECT CHAMBER and its air of protection and care were stifling. Savara threw herself onto the bed in a crumpled heap and cried. All the fighting against her nature, the convincing herself she was the master of her fate, all for nothing. A mourning sensation washed over her. She cried into her pillow like she hadn't in years, helpless, hopeless. Whatever shaky foundation she'd laid crumbled as soon as she'd hit the mattress. All this time, she'd practically been bred for this destruction. All this time, her destiny was to become the thing in the dark.

A barrage of intrusive thoughts added to her torment.

They were wrong…

I am a monster…

It was all for nothing…

She pictured all the death and destruction that had always followed her. Camp Saar, Idune, Haizea… She saw all the faces of the deceased reflected on the backs of her eyelids. Watching her. Their lifeless eyes blamed her, the Queen of Daemons. Their screams, their voices, their suffering. They grew louder and louder in her head with each iteration, until she could no longer take it.

She screamed.

A blinding lilac light erupted from her in all directions, bursting through the confines of the manicured room. Showers of glass soon followed. The room grew cold as though it too sobbed. The world fell silent once more, with only the sound of her ragged breaths to fill the emptiness.

With tears still streaming down her cheeks, Savara gathered herself and slid over to the edge of the mattress. Her glistening reddened eyes gazed around at the destruction of the room. In her anguish, she'd shattered all the windows, leaving a sea of broken glass in her wake.

Savara contemplated the glistening fragments on the floors, finding an odd sense of relief in their shattering. Her foundation had crumbled, irreparably this time. There was no more masking, or pretending, or hiding. She finally found herself face-to-face with the destruction she'd kept within…

In that moment she realised the world had been asking for her to grow, to change, and in fighting it, she had only been prolonging her own suffering. Her breathing eased, as though a weight had been lifted from her chest. For the first time in forever, she felt calm. Still. There were no more voices ringing in her head, no more nerves wracking her body. She was present, truly, as she had never been before.

Savara finally came to the understanding that, sometimes, things had to fall, to smash, to break irreparably, for us to realise they no longer serve a purpose in our lives. And that something better arises from the aftermath.

She took a deep breath, accepting all that she had come to know. She accepted her fears, gruesome as they were, and acknowledged their relevance in her life as guides. Even in the worst of worst eventualities, not even death frightened her as it once had.

Light began to pool into the centre of her palms. Savara contemplated it fondly. The hunger she'd once associated with it had vanished. Now, in the aftermath of the chaos, she found that this light was entirely beholden to her. That she was its master.

With another breath, she rose like a phoenix from the bed, using the light to sweep away the shards of glass from beneath her feet. Those shards, her ashes, chained her no longer. The light within was no longer something to be feared, no longer a burden. She was strong, but more importantly, she was free.

As she took a turn about the room, she imagined all the spirits of the house that she could not see but sensed helping her, providing for her. She wished nothing more than to be able to help them, to set them free… But how? Doing so as the Prince of Shadows wished would mean continuing the cycles of hatred and spilt blood, and she knew she needed to put an end to it once and for all.

Her mind reeled with thoughts of this spilt blood. So much had been required to reshape the world. That of the spirits of these halls—these lands. It had been their blood used to keep them bound to this life. Tethered, unable to be released into the one beyond. But not only their lives. Their blood kept the world at a standstill. The entire Arima nation had been sacrificed in the name of restraint. How much more would be required to undo such a thing?

The Prince of Shadows had insisted that energy could neither be created nor destroyed, but that it could be transferred. She'd seen the outcome of such a thing already…

The lands of Haizea were steeped in power, just as much as they were steeped in blood. The soulbonds themselves were deals tied to the lives of the people making them, energy being shared between their owners in more ways than one. The glowing dust of the House of Spirits even was a testament to the indestructible yet powerful nature of this energy, this life, this spirit…

On her previous attempts at healing others, she'd found the energy within her stop just shy of her skin. Now, she realised she hadn't been willing to commit to the transfer. And thankfully so. Losing even a small part of her life, part of her spirit, felt like nothing she'd ever experienced—nor anything she wished to ever again. It was like having the breath stolen from your lungs, the blood coaxed from your veins, and somehow leaving you with an absence that the very essence of you knew would never be filled again.

If one little flower had taken so much from her, how was she expected to release a hold on the entire world?

The Arima stone around her neck pulsed, as if reminding her of its existence.

Savara touched a hand to it, allowing the energy from it to wash over her. Instead of the all-consuming anguish that had erupted from it before, she felt a sense of warmth, of understanding, of love. She closed her eyes, homing in on that sensation, seeking to understand its origin.

"There are seven stones…" she whispered, hoping that verbalising her thoughts would make them easier to understand. "The world was separated using these stones… It would only make sense that they be used to put it back together…"

When she opened her eyes again, she caught a glimpse of her reflection in one of the larger shards. Tendrils of light danced around her, similarly to how the shadows danced around her father.

The Prince of Shadows was a sick and sadistic entity, but, as he'd made clear, it was his blood that ran through her veins. Originally, Savara had hoped any resemblance between them stopped at lineage alone. There was nothing more she wanted from him. Nothing else to tie her to his cruelty. And yet, staring at her reflection in the glass, a feeling of similarity gnawed at her. Something told her they were more alike than she'd previously believed.

The stone around her neck pulsed again, this time as if responding to the questions in her heart. It urged her to move, to not linger in this destruction. There was still more to come, more to do.

With an open mind this time, she thought back to the lessons with him. Why had he taught her about the transference of energy? Of life? What good would ever come of giving up her soul? A little voice inside her whispered an answer that did nothing to soothe her nerves.

Neither good nor bad, only necessary... And though she wished to believe the contrary, part of her recognised the truth in the statement.

Beyond the frames of the shattered windows, the lake glinted in the distance. The first time she'd witnessed it, she'd felt nothing but sorrow. Now, its tranquil waters called to her. Quiet, secluded, and far enough away from the oppressive atmosphere of the House of Spirits, it looked like as good a place as any to do some thinking.

As if sensing her intentions, the house began to conspire in her favour. A long, fur-lined cloak and suitable attire materialised on her bed—a silent offering from the spirits of the house, perhaps. Savara changed out of her dress and slipped into the tunic and pants, accepting the fact that whichever these spirits were that listened to her innermost thoughts seemed to know more than she did. She draped the cloak over her shoulders before sneaking out of the room, feeling confident in her decision to leave.

The rest of the house was still, shook by the awakening of its queen. Even as the doors to her room closed behind her, they left no echo. Her guide materialised briefly at the end of the hall, bowing her head in reverence before disappearing. The shadows of the halls responded differently to her light, slithering along the walls beside her like guard dogs. The dust overhead parted, as if acknowledging her path. All eyes were on her. Whatever secrets lay within these walls were about to be revealed, and the entire house knew it.

As she pushed past the grand palace doors, Savara felt a prickling on her neck beneath the hood of the cloak. She stared up, catching a glimpse of the Prince of Shadows watching from one of the balconies of the palace as she fled his house of gloom. His beady red eyes burned against the greyscale walls, but he made no attempt to stop her. If anything, it was a silent acknowledgement of his role in her awakening. He turned away, drifting back into the palace, leaving her alone to wander the stagnant lands.

They both knew she would come back when she was ready.

When Savara turned to face the path once more, she encountered a creature that looked like a stallion made of sweeping shadows. It waited for her, grazing its front hoof along in the dirt. A gift, she realised, from the man upstairs. If he was trying to make amends, however, he would have to do much more than alone time and a horse. Still, the lake was a decent distance away, and after suffering through the walk to the palace, she figured it was a blessing to not have to make the trek on foot.

Savara reached out to touch the creature, finding it solid beneath her fingers despite the shifting, waterfall-like flow of the shadows that comprised it. As she had done with the panther in the gardens, Savara heard the whisperings of the voices behind the shadows. They hummed her praises. The trappings of hope littered their words. They spoke of healing and freedom, hailed her as though she were a saviour—a queen.

Her heart no longer recoiled as it had before her rupture, but it did not share in the sentiments. Part of her wanted to quell them, to tell them they were misguided and that they needed to find another hero. Instead, she ignored these thoughts and their praises. She pushed her own uncertainty down into the pit of her stomach as she climbed atop the creature and galloped off down the stagnant path.

On one side of the trail, shells of houses—of lives—blurred at the edge of her vision. Not even vines had grown over them, signalling not just the absence of human life, but of all life. It was a graveyard of houses, a memorial of sorts—or would have been if there had been anyone left to acknowledge it. As it stood now, the village was simply a rock in an undiscovered forest, hardly existing at all.

The further she grew from the House of Spirits, the colder the world around her became. Savara was thankful for the fur-lined cloak that trailed behind her, sheltering her shoulders from this biting cold. Soon, the houses became trees surrounding her on both sides. Though their branches were not entirely barren like the ones that led from the gate to the palace, their muted tones were a breath shy of death. A phantom moan roared through the forest. It echoed in the winds that brushed her ears as she raced down the path. The closer she drew to the lake, the louder the moaning grew. Savara began to think there was something more to the sound than just a shifting wind.

After her lessons with the Prince of Shadows, the chokehold on the lands had become more palpable. Tapping into the souls in the gardens seemed to have strengthened the channels of her powers. No longer did she need to focus as hard as she had in the lessons to sense it. The strangling grip of the curse hung around her neck like a noose, ever-present and waiting for an end it could not achieve.

Even after all the time that had passed since the curse was placed upon them, the lands had not recovered. Savara knew the cold that gnawed at her bones came from this same curse, doing so in the morbid way that only death could. The mountains around her were scorched and black, screaming out in anguish for the life that should've covered them but had long since withered in stagnancy. If melancholia could paint landscapes, this one would have been its masterpiece.

The stallion came to a halt on its own at the edge of the lake, as if it had always had this destination in mind. Savara climbed off its back and strode towards the crystalline waters. They were as deep as the night and twice as still, making them an almost perfect mirror. As she drew close, she noticed the haunting winds had stopped entirely. Silence settled around her as if the world were holding its breath.

She peered over the edge, her reflection clearer than any mirror she'd ever gazed in before. The perfection of it haunted her. The stillness, too, haunted her for reasons she could not explain. Savara touched a finger to it, sending ripples across its body.

As the waters shifted, so too did the reflection. She no longer saw herself staring back. Instead, like with the bathwater, she saw a young man with different coloured eyes standing on an obsidian balcony, gazing out into the distance. One eye matched hers, rainbow-flecked and cavernously dark. The other looked to be filling with blood.

It was him. Her father, the Prince of Shadows.

The glowing dust of the past threaded itself through his youthful, unsalted hair. His princely brow furrowed as he contemplated the horizon. The gate that connected his lands to Middle Isle waited in the distance. Tension knotted the muscles in his back, keeping him stiff as a column. He tapped his fingers on the railing, looking as though he held the weight of the world on his shoulders.

Savara wondered what had set him so on edge.

Then, someone appeared at his side. A young woman wearing humble servant's clothes reached a hand out to his shoulder. Instead of taking hold, the girl recoiled, seemingly remembering her position. She kept a respectful distance, but there was an obvious care between them. She twirled the fabric of her skirt between her fingers as she stared up at him. Her innocent eyes and humble beauty reminded Savara of the phantom who guided her through the palace.

The woman began to speak, but Savara could hear nothing. For a moment, she watched as the muted scene played out before her, trying to read the lips of her father and the servant girl. It was no use. She leaned in closer, hoping to hear the whispers of the past, but to no avail. Finally, Savara decided to approach it the way she had accidentally done before.

She stripped off her coat and lowered herself into the deep waters. They were cold against her numbing skin. Savara took a deep breath and submerged herself the way she had in the bath.

The scene transformed in the waters around her. All of a sudden, she could hear the conversation, as though she were a phantom in the room as they spoke.

"*You can't be serious,*" the girl said.

"*As death itself, my dear,*" he replied. "*I will not sit idly by as the world shrivels and my people are blamed for the crimes of others.*"

"*But we have not done anything. Why would they blame us?*"

"*I have chosen to stand against their exile of my friend, not only out of friendship but out of respect for the will of Iturri. As such, they have branded me and my people as traitors to Visanthe.*" His voice, low and firm, teetered on the edge of anger. "*Their ignorance has put fear in their hearts, and it is all my fault.*"

"*You cannot blame yourself, my lord,*" the girl replied.

"*I am the keeper of spirit. I cannot allow them to go through with their plans.*"

It was a memory. Like in the one she'd seen in the bath, the Prince of Shadows appeared young and untouched by shadow. She felt called to reach for his shoulder, rest her hand there as a form of reassurance to a man yet unchanged by the dark. Her hand slipped through it, reminding her it was all an illusion. The lack of sensation landed heavily in her heart. It was only a memory, after all. She was just as invisible to him as he was to her.

Suddenly, his head whipped around in her direction. For a second, they were face to face. His eyes gleamed as they beheld the spot where she might have stood. Savara began to wonder if she'd been wrong. But then, he frowned. He returned his gaze to the horizon, resolution hardening at his jaw. His grip tightened on the railing.

Savara felt the pressure of the water against her chest reminding her that she would need to surface for air soon. She gazed up at the almost glass-like layer above her head. It was still close enough for her to rush up in a moment.

"*What will become of us?*" said the girl, pulling at Savara's attention once more.

Unable to meet her gaze, the Prince of Shadows dipped his head. "*The souls of this kingdom will be trapped in limbo.*"

The girl said nothing. Not even a sigh escaped her lips. She seemed to have resigned to the cruel fate—or else be numb to it.

"*You still have a chance to be free,*" the Prince of Shadows added. "*Take my ship and stow away in the night. With no powers of your own, you will be able to blend into any of the lands you choose. Go and enjoy the life I cannot offer you.*"

"*I already told you I will never leave you,*" was her only response.

"*I will give you gold and riches and—*"

"*What part of never did you not understand?*"

Savara admired the girl for her bravery and steadfastness. Her heart ached for the two of them. Knowing of her father's solitude in his current state and seeing what he'd once had almost endeared her to him. But one moment of pain would not excuse a lifetime of inflicting it—especially not one as long as his.

Her father did not respond to the question. Instead, he gazed down at his palms. "*I would've thought maintaining balance to cost more than a single life.*"

"*I am not sure I understand what you mean, my lord,*" the girl replied.

"*They have chosen to remove a life from this world in order to maintain their rule. I have done the same.*" He clenched his hands into fists. "*You know of my peculiar ability. Where I go, death follows. I have decided to live up to my destiny, to become a Harbinger of Death.*"

It was at this point the girl reached up to his face, cupping his cheek in her hand and directing his gaze towards her. *"Your eye…"*

"Where the other rulers will receive their powers from the distillations of Iturri, I will become its distillation. They will beg of the land their powers, whereas I will be the power that fuels the land. I have offered my life to the divine, made a bond with death itself…"

"No…" she whispered, taking a step back from him. *"No, this is wrong."*

"What was wrong was them *deciding Iturri should be caged,"* he growled. *"They fear the bloodied bruise without, overlooking the disease within."*

In that moment, Savara spied something deranged in him. The blood-red colouring had fully consumed his left eye and began creeping into his right. No doubt the girl had seen it too, for she inched further away from him as he spoke.

"My blood, my body, my soul—I have bound them all. I will keep with me the power of these lands and all others. If they will not listen to reason, they will learn through fear…"

The voice echoing through the pool of memory was not that of the Prince of Shadows—or at least not that with which he'd begun the conversation. It was a voice Savara recognised now, the same one from her nightmares. She'd long attributed it to him, but after seeing the events of that day with her own two eyes, she realised he'd invited it in.

That voice, who or whatever it belonged to, contained no trace of humanity. An ethereal darkness given breath and tongue. A curse all its own.

Savara realised she'd only scratched the surface of the Prince of Shadows. There was so much more for her to learn about him—his life, his motives, his bonds. But her time of reflection had proved more fruitful than she'd originally expected. Already she'd uncovered a truth that no one had been willing to disclose.

Iturri was not just some faceless name to be cast around. It was an entity. A being with presence. A being that could be found—that had been found. Whether it had started that way or had only recently become so, Iturri was no longer just a myth or curse.

Iturri was a god separated from its omniscience.

The rulers of the other lands, it seemed, had convened and decided to capture their creator. Only then would they be free to control their lands as they pleased. All but one who had refused—her father, the Prince of Shadows.

For his outspokenness, he was exiled.

In fear of failure, he bound himself to death.

Realisation hit her like a falling tree trunk. The Prince of Shadows was not only as flawed as any mortal, but he was also more integral to the functioning of this world than any other entity in existence—aside from Iturri itself.

As the world leaders had already proven, he could not be killed. They'd stripped away his body, but his soul lived on, wreaking havoc as fiercely as any creature of flesh and bone.

Savara finally began to understand the ramifications of her father's actions, and the far-reaching effects of the legend she'd been told. It had become clear to her just how tied she was to the past, no matter how far she'd tried to distance herself from it.

Her story, his story, and that of Iturri were all one and the same, bound by the fragile thread of time and power…

And blood.

Suddenly, a wave of power ripped through the memory. It tossed the girl to the ground and cast away whatever trance the Prince of Shadows had been under. His eyes reverted only a moment to their rainbow-flecked innocence as he ran to her. Another wave hit, this one's effects reaching Savara as well, knocking the remaining air from her lungs.

CHAPTER 23

SAVIOUR FROM THE DEEP

SAVARA HADN'T REALISED HOW FAR SHE'D submerged. The muted sun above her seemed to frown as she slipped further and further from its reach. The wave from the memory had knocked whatever bubbles of air she had left from her lungs. So far beneath the surface, the world was quiet. Her frantic mind doubted that even she could make a noise.

As the pressure of the deep threatened to crush her chest, the edges of her vision blurred. She choked as the water poured down her throat. Her lungs burned as they filled. She watched as the last bubbles of her breath drifted away from her, floating up to the safety of the surface world. She, on the contrary, descended deeper and deeper, to be consumed by the dark.

One thing was certain: she'd run out of time.

It can't end this way, she thought, but it was the last one she would have.

Her eyes began to close. The chill of death nipped at her feet as the legend recited to her by the voices of the palace echoed in her mind. Slowly, Savara relented to the overwhelming power of the dark waters.

Suddenly, a splash sounded overhead.

A hand snaked around her waist and dragged her to the surface. Though she lacked full consciousness, the moment she felt the familiar raking of wind across her skin, she knew they'd broken free. Savara felt herself being hoisted onto the bank.

A heavy force came down on her chest, keeping her heart beating against the darkness. Any harder and it might have broken ribs. Still unable to open her eyes, she focused on the sensation alone. It was just enough to keep her tethered to the world of the living. And then, Savara felt the gentle brush of lips against hers. They breathed life back into her, igniting a fire within her soul. She recognised their touch, but her lack of consciousness made it impossible to remember from where or when. The lips disappeared, leaving her longing. The force came down on her chest again.

"Breathe, Savara," a gentle, sultry voice whispered, followed by another life-giving kiss.

That final kiss did the trick. As Savara coughed and sputtered, expelling the water from her lungs, she felt a surge of life coursing through her veins. Her eyes fluttered open, meeting a pair of intense, furious, electric blue ones.

Droplets of lake water hung from his ebony curls. His jaw was clenched. The look in his eyes set her soul ablaze. There was something carnal and possessive about it that she relished in.

Amon.

Savara pushed her saviour away and coughed out the rest of the lake water. After her first gasping breaths, she lay back down to catch herself.

"What are you doing here?" she breathed.

"I could ask you the same question," he replied tersely. Annoyance burned in his words, but there was no use in him denying it. She'd seen the worry in his eyes.

"I'm not in the mood for your games."

"Playtime is over, princess. Spill."

Even after all he'd done to her, the way he called her princess set her skin alight. "I needed a place to think."

"And you thought the best place would be at the bottom of this lake?"

"Fuck off, I was fine."

"You and I have very different definitions of the word fine," he replied, tension lining the sharp cut of his jaw.

"We aren't doing this again."

"What? Me saving your life?"

"No. I'm done playing hot and cold with you."

"Like I said, playtime is done," he growled as he helped her sit up. His hands were gentle and warm on her back despite the biting cold of the air around them. He seemed to be restraining the urge to chastise her, fearing she might leave him as she had before. Worse still, worry lined his features. She realised her near-death experience seemed to have rattled him more than it had her. "Why are you here?" he asked again, a plea clawing its way through his anger.

Savara glowered at him. "You first."

Amon's eyes flashed with a mix of frustration and something Savara couldn't quite decipher. The air between them grew thick with the many unspoken words and unresolved emotions. Tension crackled between their bodies, one they fought desperately against even now.

"You try my every patience, princess."

"Stand up words for someone who does nothing but play games with everyone he encounters."

"After everything you've seen, after everything I've done to protect you—"

"YOU MURDERED MY FAMILY!" she screamed at him. She sounded like a wild animal, her voice echoing across the stillness of the dying lands. The howling monkeys that had almost attacked them in the bamboo forest screeched softer than she did.

"I did what I had to," he replied, unable to deny the part he played in making her an orphan.

She stared at him incredulously. "Is that your excuse?!"

"It's not an excuse."

Savara could no longer contain the rage she felt towards him. She forced herself to her feet, glowering down at him in anger. She felt the shadows curling around her the way she'd seen them do to the Prince of Shadows. She felt like a tyrant. She felt strong. He triggered all the worst parts of her. Now, he would feel her wrath. She would make him suffer the way she had.

Amon bowed his head, as if accepting punishment, and whispered, "I don't wish to excuse the pain I've caused, but know this… I never meant to play games with you."

Savara lashed out, sending tendrils of violet shadow across the broken landscape—slicing every tree around the lake in half before collapsing to her knees.

She couldn't do it.

No matter how much pain he'd caused her, she couldn't kill him. Nothing in her heart could make a move against him, no matter how much agony she felt. Her body shivered, wracked with nerves and the cold of the lake. Waves of shadow convulsed from her person.

"I hate you," she whispered. "I hate you so much…"

Amon raised his head, unscathed by her outburst. If he had feared her, he didn't let on. Instead, he stood, took hold of the fur-lined cloak she'd discarded, and draped it over her shoulders. He held tight as though trying to pull together the broken pieces of her that she'd ignored for far too long. The aftershock of her power came in waves. They crashed into him, threatening to throw him off balance, but he held firm. Unwavering in his offering of solace.

Slowly, realising the innocence of his embrace, Savara nestled her head into the comforting shelter of his neck. Her ragged breaths echoed through the stillness, reverberating through the empty expanse around them. She did hate him. She'd hated him with every fibre of her being, with every drop of blood in her body. She hated how he'd hurt her, but even more how he cared for her.

But even that began to fade in his arms.

Amon held her through each wave, silently waiting for a break in the storm. Then, when her heart had steadied once more, he planted a kiss on the crown of her head.

"You know why I'm here," he admitted softly, as if the words hurt to speak aloud. "You have no idea what it does to me when you put yourself in situations like these…"

"The king said I was torturing you," she mumbled.

Amon gently withdrew her head from his shoulder and cupped her cheek, his touch tender and comforting. As he looked into her eyes, Savara felt a sense of intimacy wash over her, as though they were the only two souls in existence, the rest of the world fading into insignificance as if there had never been anything but them two.

Only their eyes, their hearts, their souls.

It was the kind of moment of tenderness Savara wished she could distil and live in forever.

"You are my torture, my uniquely heart-wrenching torture," he replied, but before she could object, he added, "because my soul yearns for you in every waking moment. Because even when I close my eyes, I will never be free of my desire for you. Because I knew from the moment I'd first laid eyes on you that I could never possibly feel a connection to another soul as deeply as I do with yours. This knowing resides in every breath in my lungs and every drop of blood in my veins. It haunts me like nothing else in this world ever will."

In his eyes, she spied the flame of passion that had existed between them on each of the occasions they'd met. It had grown since last she'd seen it. It wasn't the fleeting flicker it had been then. Now, it was a wildfire claiming dominance over his soul's terrain. Everything within him burned.

"But… you ran?" she sniffled, unwilling to believe the truth before her, the one that had haunted her too in their every encounter.

The bond between them was undeniable—and not the crude, one-sided channel he'd inadvertently made with her that was marked by the star in his palm. No. There was something deeper between them.

A pull.

A magnetism.

An entanglement that resided in the realm of souls.

She'd known it then, from the first moment they'd touched. She'd felt it in the way her body had practically ignited on the dancefloor. The realisation was sudden, but the connection felt as if it spanned lifetimes. As though it had always existed, whispering on the most quiet of nights, hiding in the shadows of the brightest days. As though they had always been destined to unite… As though fate would have it no other way.

"How do you look love in the eye and admit to every sin you've committed in its name?" he whispered, his voice an almost carnal growl as he wiped away the last of her tears. "I ran because I was not worthy of something so pure, not when I was so broken. What I feel for you runs deeper than any soulbond ever could. It is torture—a torture of the acutest kind—and one I will spend my life happily bound to if you will allow such a thing."

"That doesn't sound like love. It sounds like suffering."

"Love is suffering, Savara. But those who have never suffered have also never truly lived," he replied, leaning in close so the words would have nowhere else to fall but onto her lips.

Each word he uttered, each confession of his tortured soul, resonated within her own being, stirring a flame that had long smouldered within her heart.

"Are you saying you love me then?" she asked, her lips grazing his as she spoke.

"I am saying, I have loved you for far longer than our measly lifetimes could ever hope to comprehend, and I will continue to, far beyond my dying breath…"

As Amon whispered those final words, he let his mouth press against hers, softly, fully. His breath was as sweet as his words. His kiss, as innocent as a morning rain. He was as gentle as a falling feather.

Until she kissed him back.

His admission, raw and unfiltered, ignited her deepest desires. It was a declaration of unwavering devotion, a promise of unyielding love. He'd shown her his weakness, confessed his vulnerability. He'd laid bare the depths of his soul for her to see, and in doing so, solidified her feelings towards him.

The air crackled with anticipation, charged with the energy of their unspoken desires. Her reciprocation of the kiss summoned forth the animal within him. He gripped the back of her neck, eliciting a sigh as he pulled her in closer. With their bodies pressed against each other, the world around them faded. Their breathing grew laboured and heavy as they entangled themselves in each other. This kiss was fervent, intoxicating, and truer than any other she'd experienced. She'd gotten a taste of him in the bamboo forest of Haizea, but back then, they'd been fighting against their desires. Now, they kissed like starved animals feasting on their latest meal. It was a kiss to get lost in, yet somehow, it felt like coming home.

But amidst the whirlwind of passion, a voice whispered in the depths of her soul, reminding her of what she'd seen in the lake. The memory prodded at her, urging her to finish what she'd started. Whatever attraction lay between them would have to wait. It would never be safe until they were. The Prince of Shadows' past actions had assured they would see no peace until the legend of the stones had resolved itself.

Happiness was still a world away, possibly even a lifetime.

As much as she hated to do it, Savara pulled away from him. His absence felt like coming off a high and left her trembling. It had to be done; otherwise, there would be no hope for a future.

Amon released her, searching her eyes for a sign of trouble, but Savara simply shook her head. She couldn't hold his gaze any longer, fearing she'd break out in tears again, and she had no more of them to spare.

"What's wrong?" he asked. Despite the lingering strain of passion, his voice was low and filled with concern.

"He's my father," she said softly. "The Prince of Shadows is my father." When he didn't reply, she asked, "Did you know?"

Amon nodded. "I had my suspicions."

"Why did you choose to join him?"

After all she'd seen of her father's past, of the man he once was, and the shadow he'd become, she couldn't help but wonder what had drawn Amon to him.

He leaned back on his hands, as if wanting to put distance between himself and the question. "I felt called in a way I could not deny."

If it had been anyone else he'd said these words to, they might not have understood, but she did. Savara had experienced the very same before returning to Visanthe. Before their time in the Palace of Winds, she might have thought he'd taken pleasure in the torture and suffering he caused. But she'd seen a different side of him then. He wasn't the murderer, but the martyr. And that man was the same one sitting before her now. The words fell from his lips coated in resounding sadness. Though his response did not excuse his sins, she accepted his honesty.

"He bound himself to Iturri..." she added, wishing not to press the issue further.

"Is that possible?" he asked, his voice riddled with intrigue and concern.

Savara reached a hand up to the side of her ear, remembering Alexei's words as she grazed her fingers along the rubied scar. *If anyone could make a deal with death and come out unscathed, it would be you.* Hadn't she already done just that? The threads of this strange tapestry of coincidences appeared to be coming together, the picture they formed, glorious and grim.

All paths seemed to lead to the same destination. There was an end coming. Her father had started it, but it was her turn to finish it. If this was her destiny, if this would ensure that the world lived on, she knew she had no choice in the matter.

Iturri was once a god and twice a prisoner—and might be the only hope this world had of redemption. She would have to set Iturri free, even if it meant losing herself in the process.

She turned back to him, an idea forming in her mind. "Yes…" she replied. "And I think it's my job to set them both free."

CHAPTER 24

THE RETURN TO MIDDLE ISLE

JASPER HAD PERCHED HIMSELF AT THE EDGE of the bow, contemplating the town he'd not gotten to explore when he noticed a single figure appear at the docks below. Griffin returned to the ship alone, tension marking his every movement from the moment he boarded the vessel. Jasper observed him closely, noting the furrowed brow and the subtle signs of worry etched into his features. It was clear that something significant had transpired in Yozora, something that had rattled him to his core. He'd wasted no time in issuing the command for Lucy to way anchor, and soon enough, they'd set sail under the setting sun. Despite his usual apprehension of the sea, Griffin appeared determined to press forward, his focus fixed on the looming horizon of Middle Isle.

Amon's absence did not go unnoticed, but the unspoken understanding between them kept any questions at bay. Jasper worried that Amon had broken Griffin's trust once more, for he looked like a man consumed by worry.

"Will you be okay?" Jasper asked, approaching him hesitantly from behind, unable to shake the unease lingering in the air. Griffin's response was somehow worse than what he'd expected.

"He loves her…" Griffin replied, ignoring the question. "I'm sorry…"

The truth came as a shock to the system, like being doused in ice water. Jasper had known it. He'd seen it in Amon's eyes the day they met, and still, he hadn't internalised it. Hearing it from the mouth of another felt like a curiously harsh form of punishment.

"I know," he sighed.

"You are a better person than him, Jasper. You care beyond reason. You are loyal to a fault. You still have a chance, if you want it that is. Amon is tortured. He's—"

"A better match for her than I ever will be," Jasper admitted, straining against a closing throat. "I saw it when we arrived in Idune. There was a look in her eyes the night of the dinner that I'd never seen before, and it wasn't directed at me…"

The truth was even more cruel somehow. It was almost as if he'd always known they were never meant for each other, but his heart didn't want to listen. It never had, and doubtless ever would. Her presence had always made him feel safer, lighter, accepted. There was a chance he'd conflated a deep friendship with love, or that what he felt was only the effect of long exposure to her powers. Either way, he'd fallen for her. Heart and soul. But she would never feel the same.

"And yet, you're still here. Still fighting for her…"

"Just because she doesn't love me doesn't mean I have to stop caring for her, stop loving her. I can concede to someone better suited to her, but that will never change the way I feel. She is my best friend, my first love. What I want more than anything is her happiness. If Amon is able to give her that, then why would I stand in the way?"

Griffin lowered his head as a smile crept across his face. An innocent laugh escaped his lips. "You're a better man than even me."

Jasper forced a smile in return, though he could not stop a single tear from escaping the corner of his eye in the move. He couldn't hide the depths of his emotions despite his best attempts. The crack in his voice alone betrayed his true feelings. But he couldn't linger in this state forever. One day, it would get better. One day it wouldn't hurt as much. In the meantime, he found solace in masking the heartache with humour, knowing Griffin also formed a part of their broken hearts club.

"That's because you're arrogant, full of yourself, and prefer to bottle up all your suffering," Jasper quipped.

"Watch it, bookworm," Griffin growled, but the tension in his shoulders visibly relaxed, the corners of his lips still upturned in a faint smile. Soft laughter bubbled up between them, a welcome respite from the weight of their conversation.

As the laughter faded, a contemplative silence settled over them like a blanket, each lost in their own thoughts. Griffin's gaze remained fixed on the horizon, his expression thoughtful yet determined. Jasper could see the worry etched into the lines of his face. He could imagine all the thoughts running through Griffin's mind. Were they doing the right thing? Would they be too late to save their friends?

"I'll be okay when we are safe on dry land and this war is over," he admitted, returning to the original question.

Jasper nodded, though he couldn't deny that he too shared the sentiment. "Quite the order," he remarked, acknowledging the magnitude of the task that lay ahead.

"But not impossible," Griffin countered.

"No… Just very dangerous."

"We've been through worse."

"Ever the optimist," Jasper teased lightly, a playful glint in his eye.

"Don't insult me," Griffin retorted with mock severity, though the fondness in his tone was unmistakable.

Jasper lingered in the light-heartedness a moment longer before the thoughts of Savara returned. "Has he gone to find her?" he asked, remembering the conviction he'd seen burning in Amon's eyes.

Griffin inclined his head towards the sky. "If there's one thing about Amon, he knows how to seek out trouble."

Jasper let out a soft chuckle. "That makes the two of them…"

In the quiet moments that followed, they stood together in companionable silence, their gaze fixed on the distant horizon. Somewhere beyond it lay the gate of Middle Isle corresponding to the Izar. The bridge had not appeared, and Griffin's hasty and agitated entrance meant he hadn't planned on waiting for it either.

Upon arriving in Yozora, Griffin received urgent correspondence from the leaders of the Ur and the Argia. The letters detailed the leaders' expected presence at the upcoming Divination ceremony. The other leaders had surely received similar communications. Doubtless, they would all be making their way to Middle Isle sometime throughout the night as well.

Things were beginning to fall into place. The legend which had lurked in the shadows for centuries was finally rearing its head. Never before had it felt so real, so tangible, so suffocating. Never before had the shadows of the past threatened the world so directly.

But the time had come for lessons to be learned and fears to be faced.

The fading light cast long shadows across the deck, reaching out like the outstretched hands of the shadows awaiting them. Soon, night descended upon them, slowly, the way sleep lingers in the eyes before consuming the mind, before giving way to a sky full of waiting stars. They watched over the ship during its passage. For a second, as Jasper gazed upon them in prayer for a better future, he wondered if they already knew the outcome.

* * *

Savara and Amon arrived at the gates of the House of Spirits, still damp from their unintended swim. When she'd told him of her plan to resume lessons with the Prince of Shadows, he'd looked at her as though he'd already known. He kept his opinions guarded, but Savara sensed the energy around him shift. The open display of passion and affection became one of caution and worry. He only frowned, knowing as well as she did the necessity of such actions. They both knew she wasn't fully in control of her powers, and that the Prince of Shadows was the only person who could teach her. But that didn't mean he was pleased about it.

Nor did it take away the inherent danger.

Amon helped her down from the shadowy stallion and pulled her in close, returning briefly to that moment of concern. He held her as though he wasn't sure there was another time he'd get such a chance.

Savara softened into him, listening to the low beating of his heart. Ever since he'd gotten rid of his other bonds, his heartbeat had grown stronger. She felt it pulsing in tune with her own, as if they called to each other—as if they always had. In his arms, she was home.

Suddenly, shadows began curling around their feet. They rose high up in the air, only to snatch at them and rip them apart. Tendrils wrapped around their wrists, keeping them in place. The Prince of Shadows appeared soon after.

"It seems you two have become well acquainted since our last encounter..." he growled, his eyes burning like murderous coals as they fixated on Amon. Savara made to speak, but the Prince of Shadows silenced her with a raised hand. "No, my child, no need for explanations. It is fitting you two should have become...close... Convenient, even."

The shadows slithered like serpents around Amon's body, restraining his every move.

Amon flushed the emotion from his face, embodying stillness even as the shadows bit into his skin. He became as cold and detached as he had been during their encounter in the gardens of Idune. She knew he wanted nothing tying him to her in the eyes of the Prince of Shadows. Nothing that could be used to hurt her.

But the Prince of Shadows saw through his façade.

"Put him down!" Savara screamed, betraying her own feelings as she strained against the shadows binding her wrists.

"I believe you and I have a bond to complete, do we not?" said the Prince of Shadows, ignoring her outburst. His voice grumbled low and loud like thunder, but his body was taut and still, expectant, like the pause between the echo and the lightning strike.

"Release my hand and it is yours," Amon replied, his voice equally as hollow. The shadows loosened their binding on his wrists, allowing him limited mobility. He reached into his pocket and retrieved a glowing blue stone—that of the Izar. But as the Prince of Shadows reached out for it, Amon pulled it back. "I'll hand it over so long as you promise not to hurt her."

"You presume to hold favour with me. Such presumptions are dangerous things." The shadows tightened their grip around Amon, causing him to wince in pain.

"Stop!" Savara cried. "He fulfilled your tasks; he brought you the stones. Let him go!"

Amon's voice betrayed no weakness as he said, "Swear you will not harm her."

"Hmm…" The Prince of Shadows regarded them with a calculating gaze, a sly smirk playing at the corners of his lips. "Seeing as you have met the conditions of your bonds," he conceded, "I shall heed my daughter's plea. I swear she will be taken care of as well. Now, hand over the stone."

Amon released the stone from his grasp, allowing it to fall into the prince's waiting hand. As soon as the stone hit his skin, the shadows that had ensnared Amon dissipated, leaving him free.

But reunion was still a ways away.

"Let it not be said that I am not a generous man," the Prince of Shadows declared as he snapped his fingers.

Amon gasped for breath, as though finally breaching a sea he'd been cast into. Colour flooded back into his skin, hair, and eyes—fully and vibrantly. There was an almost ethereal glow to him that Savara regarded with increased awe. This was the version of him that had been hiding. Trapped. This was the Prince of Light. And there was only one explanation for the sudden shift. Amon reached his hand down the back of his shirt, unsurprised to find it coated in blood.

The Prince of Shadows had removed all remaining bonds.

"Savara, I—" he had started to say when the shadows around his feet grew restless.

"There will be time for reunions soon, apprentice," the Prince of Shadows growled, his voice carrying an undercurrent of warning. With another snap of his fingers, Amon was engulfed in a whirlwind of shadows, disappearing instantly, leaving them alone to private affairs.

"Where have you sent him?!" Savara demanded, her voice tinged with desperation.

"If I were you, I would not grow too attached. Our place in this world does not allow for such sentiments," the Prince of Shadows cautioned. "When you are prepared for our final lesson, you will find me in the garden."

With that, he vanished, leaving Savara alone with her tumultuous thoughts, the weight of uncertainty pressing down upon her like a heavy shroud.

* * *

Brass stepped off the Zerua ship, the wooden planks creaking beneath his limp as he descended onto the landing platform of the misty marble gate. Bismuth—his loyal counsel since the death of the previous king—followed closely at his side, weary of the ominous lack of a bridge between their lands and this one. The journey had taken three days, even with their constant channelling of winds into the sails. The seas were agitated, as if they too warned of the dangerous nature of the coming events.

Brass raised a hand, sending a current of air to cut through the shroud of mists. Their blanketing wafts continued, regardless of the currents. He furrowed his brow, wary of the apparent ethereal nature of the mists. Bismuth was about to begin his attempt at clearing them when Brass raised his cane in blocking. He knew it was no use. Force would change nothing. The mists would not be swayed. They hung in something far beyond the realm of Visanthian elemental power.

A knowing glance passed between them, yet another warning that would go unheeded.

"We continue blind," Brass said, his voice stoic throughout. He knew he needed to maintain his groundedness throughout the present situation. There was no telling what kinds of surprises were waiting for them on the other side.

Neither spoke of the murder-charged air around them, though they were too in tune with the whispers of the winds to ignore it entirely. Together, they surveyed the horizon, where the silhouettes of other ships emerged against the backdrop of the vast expanse of ocean.

Recent events had confirmed to all that change was coming—a change that would call into question everything they'd ever known about their world. The legend long shrouded in mystery—once branded myth alone—was finally at the cusp of becoming history. Returning to Middle Isle after so many years felt like the closing of a loop, a culmination of events set into motion long ago. The roles they played in what was to come—as well as the choices they made from hereon in—would be the foundation of the world that followed.

"As you wish, my king," Bismuth replied as they descended into the mists.

* * *

The dawn broke tentatively over Middle Isle, but not even the light of the sun could clear the sense of foreboding that stretched across the land. One by one, the leaders of the various realms arrived, each accompanied by their entourage of advisors and guards. With each new arrival, the atmosphere darkened, each of the leaders sensing the concerns of the others.

Queen Noor and her sister, General Kyara of the Ur, arrived around the same time as the delegation from the Harri Territories. Lord Andor and Councilman Dhoot, along with a number of soldiers, made their way to the stands of the Harri, exchanging tense glances between the Ur. Standing alongside the queens of the water and their limited guard was General Isaac. Such an alliance sent whispers through the delegation of the Harri, but General Isaac remained stoic throughout. Councilman Dhoot shot him a wicked smile, as if acknowledging the implications such an alliance might have. The warring nations were one stray comment away from descending into violence. But the parties remained quiet for now—civil even, if only out of hesitation at what was yet to come.

This was not the battle they had come to fight.

King Lance of the Argia arrived next with a few reformers from the Argia Mafia. The princeling had blossomed into a full-fledged king, donning regal robes and a gold circlet, highlighting his amber eyes. Despite having not held power for as long as the other rulers, it was clear by his command over his men that he was not to be trifled with.

The delegation from the Zerua—Brass, the new king, and his consul, Bismuth—had been waiting in the shadows, cautious of the gathered parties and their motives for conceding to the ominous request. Griffin and crew made their way from the Izar gate through which they'd arrived to the Zerua stands, reuniting with their old friend.

"It is a shame we do not reunite under better circumstances," Brass said to him as he bowed his head. The conditions of the reunion being what they were, Griffin was glad to see his friend had not only survived but was in relatively good health aside from the limp. Leadership looked good on him. This, Griffin had always known.

"Great are any circumstances in which I may share pleasantries with the king of the Zerua," Griffin replied, bowing at the waist.

Brass allowed a smile to spread across his face. "Your antics have not changed, Griffin. I will admit, part of me wishes to hear you have not filled my position as medic."

"There will never be anyone to fill your place, Brass," assured Griffin, sharing in his friend's smile.

"It seems we are missing only two..." said Brass, hinting with his eyes at the yet unfilled stands around the dais.

He was mistaken.

By stands alone, they were only missing two delegates: the leaders of the Izar, Princess of Light, and the Arima, Prince of Shadows, but there were others who should've already arrived and hadn't. Amon, for one, was nowhere to be seen. He'd assured Griffin upon parting ways that he would be waiting for him on Middle Isle after returning the stone of the Izar to the Arima lands. Had something gone wrong?

And then, of course, amongst the missing was still the guest of honour herself...

CHAPTER 25

THE FINAL LESSON

THE PRINCE OF SHADOWS MEANDERED through his garden of half-life and half-shadow, twirling the same rose he'd sucked the life from between his fingertips. There was no sign of lingering malice from their squabble at the gate. He seemed stable—relaxed even, as he contemplated the flower in his hand.

Savara approached from behind, the sound of her footsteps crunching on the gravel filling the air where his did not. She watched him cautiously, unwilling to accidentally incur his wrath as she had with Amon. His polished, dark, and unbothered figure shined against the still semi-faded gardens. She waited for him to acknowledge her on his own time, not wanting to intrude on his moment of contemplation.

Finally, he stopped.

"Yes?" he asked as her footsteps came to a halt behind him.

"I need you to finish the lesson," she replied, authority weaving its way between her words.

"Hmm…" The Prince of Shadows turned to her. He scanned her person as though her skin were the pages of a book, recounting the events that had transpired since their last encounter. He raised an eyebrow. "Have you decided you are ready to stop being a child?"

"Yes."

He paused for a moment, assessing the sincerity in her words before finally conceding. "Alright."

Together, they traversed the garden in silence until they reached a secluded plaza surrounded by bushes of black roses and willow trees. It was the same plaza she'd encountered in her previous wandering. The same feelings of sorrow and sadness reached out for her. Savara hesitated only momentarily at the entrance, allowing herself to attune to the dark the energy around them as she crossed the threshold.

In the centre of the plaza, a shallow pond filled with lilies and amethyst crystals sat, protecting encroaching grasses and spirits from a singularly featured statue. Atop a pedestal of pure gold was a young girl, frozen in time and encased in stone. Her legs stretched out beneath her. The dress she wore bunched at her knees, as though she'd fallen. She maintained a defensive stance on the ground with her arms raised.

Savara looked around the plaza in awe. The impression it gave was that of a memorial, well-tended and cared for, more so even than the rest of this garden of miracles.

As she drew closer to the statue, Savara noticed the resemblance it bore to her guide in the palace. The same girl she'd seen in the memory at the lake. Savara tried her best to recall what she'd seen before the wave had knocked the air from her lungs. She tilted her head in contemplation, noting that the statue's position mirrored that of the girl after the wave had thrown her off her feet. Perhaps it was her, a depiction of the girl from the memory.

"Who is this?" she inquired.

The Prince of Shadows maintained his silence, allowing her to piece together her conclusions.

Savara rounded the pond, contemplating the statue further. Every detail had been captured to perfection. The ruffled skirts, the raised arms, the fear-lined features. But there was more. Sorrow seemed to ripple outwards from it, as though she were a stone cast upon stilled waters.

No, Savara realised. *It can't be…*

This wasn't just a depiction of the girl. This *was* the girl. Plucked from the day he'd bound himself to Iturri. She felt the girl's soul reaching out for her, sadness clinging steadfastly to the surrounding rock.

She'd been turned to stone.

Savara turned back to him, finding the shadows of regret and remorse lingering in the ruby-red glow of his eyes. In them, she found her confirmation.

"How?" she whispered, her voice trembling as she allowed the sadness to sweep across her.

"These were the consequences," he replied, his tone devoid of warmth, echoing the harshness of the world beyond the garden.

"Are there more?" she pressed, seeking around the plaza for any similar figures.

The Prince of Shadows refused to respond, further confirming her suspicions.

"How do we get them out?" she prodded.

"This, my dear, is your final lesson," he declared solemnly, his gaze lingering on the statue with a mixture of fondness and regret. "The transitioning of souls." He drew near, gazing fondly upon the statue, allowing her a glimpse of the turmoil that had driven him to bind himself to Iturri. "In time, all souls reach a point where they can no longer be saved in this lifetime. They end up in limbo. When that happens, it falls upon us to release them from their earthly bonds."

"You mean you want me to end her life?!" she barked, still connected to the girl's emotions, woefully unprepared for the task at hand.

"She has stood by me faithfully for many years. Her loyalty transcends time itself, but there is no hope of returning her to her former state," he explained, as he waded into the water. He knelt beside the statue with a sense of resignation. "It's time."

As he reached out to touch the statue, Savara sensed a shift in the air around them. Fear and sorrow gave way to something lighter. Something almost dreamlike. She realised the Prince of Shadows had done to the girl's soul what she had to the dying king of Haizea. Somehow, he had stripped away the darker emotions that clouded her soul.

All that was left was love.

"Why hadn't you released her before?" she said, searching his gaze for some sign of mercy. "If she has been like this ever since, why has it taken you so long to release her from this suffering?"

He turned away from her, as though avoiding any perceived connection to his humanity. "I was not capable," he replied, his voice cold and cruel. "Not without the stone around your neck."

The words he spoke may have hinted at the truth, but Savara could sense there were deeper underlying reasons behind his inaction. He'd regained almost all of his abilities. He was strong enough to release the darker emotions plaguing the girl's spirit, but hadn't, not until Savara had come to him willingly to learn about the subject.

The problem wasn't that he couldn't release her, Savara realised. He wouldn't. As if, in doing so, he was losing something so integral to his very being that he would not be able to live without it.

Savara's heart broke as she considered the shift in his demeanour, his frigidity towards the subject. A heaviness settled in her chest. This was a goodbye, she realised. And one he hadn't been ready to give.

Savara waded into the water beside him and gently rested a hand on his shoulder, allowing the warmth from her skin to settle beneath her touch. For a fleeting moment, a shadow of confusion flickered across his features. He furrowed his brow, searching for an explanation for the confusion. Then, confusion shifted to recognition. A moment of déjà vu, as if they had traversed this path before. The act mirrored the one she'd attempted in the lake as she played witness to the fragments of his memories.

"What do I need to do?" she asked, not wishing to prolong the suffering any longer.

In an act of uncharacteristic tenderness, the Prince of Shadows placed his hand over top of hers and sighed. For the first time since she'd met him, Savara knew with absolute certainty that there was a heart in him, somewhere beneath the layers of blood and shadow.

The Prince of Shadows guided her up close to the statue and rested her hand on the girl's heart. "This will ensure the connection to her in limbo."

Savara nodded, noticing how the Prince of Shadows took hold of the girl's outstretched hand and positioned himself behind her protectively, intimately—the way a lover might.

"Now, take a deep breath and close your eyes. The idea is to release your concept of the physical world and allow yourself to be guided in…"

"Into where?" she asked softly.

"Follow the sound of my voice," he began, the sound resonating deep within her spirit. Unlike the rest of the times they'd spoken, his voice held the weight of oceans and the softness of the skies. This beautiful dichotomy brought her defences down easily. With its effectiveness, she almost wondered why he'd never used this voice before. The sound came again, lulling her into a sort of trancelike state. "Imagine yourself in darkness. With each breath, allow the sensations around you in the physical world to fade…"

Savara closed her eyes and relented. As described, the world around her melted away. Sensations disappeared entirely. Any cues of time or temperature were muted. Here, she was alone, in a place tucked away from humanity and its complexities. Existence as she knew it had vanished. Here, she was an entity, weightless, conceptless. Neither entirely physical nor entirely passed on, she knew immediately where she'd landed—if such a term could even be used to describe the void.

And she'd done this before.

She'd been here before.

This place, this limbo, as the Prince of Shadows had called it, felt familiar. Not only had this been the place Alexei had sent her after electrocuting her, but she realised the shadows had brought her here upon her arrival in Visanthe.

Back then, she'd been pulled into limbo by force and fear. Now, drifting alone in the endless expanse of nothingness, she understood that it had only ever been a projection. A warped projection of her fears onto the blank canvas that the void provided. They'd brought her here to show her the truth that she hadn't been ready to understand.

But she'd grown since then.

Without the fears clinging to her on her second visit, after Alexei's unceremonious electrocution, she managed to catch a glimpse of something truly immortal. It had been a fleeting glimpse, a vision that had lingered in her mind long after she had returned to the physical realm. It was a reminder of the interconnectedness of all things, even in the vast emptiness of limbo.

She would never forget the tree and its guardian.

Savara heard the voice of the Prince of Shadows lingering in the back of her mind. She'd let go of the need to follow it, knowing she would be guided by her own intuition. She knew of her task. Now it was a matter of completing it.

She let herself drift for a moment in silence, using her memory of the tree as a touchstone. Soon, the same time-marked trunk glowed before her, the light stretching out like a beacon of hope in the night. She allowed it to pull her forward, being lovingly ensnared in the grasp of the tendril-like branches. This time, the tree allowed her a closer look at the notches and their strange tales.

One in particular glowed brighter than the rest. Curious, she drifted towards it, her senses heightened as she began to hear faint whispers, like distant echoes carried on the wind. As she reached out to touch the glowing notch, the voices grew louder, filling the void with the joyful sounds of laughter. The voices were young, brimming with the carefree innocence of childhood.

Something within her told her to touch the notch, to seek out a deeper connection to it. Savara pressed her hand against the branch, feeling a surge of energy coursing through her as she connected with the tree's essence.

Suddenly, as if conjured by her presence, two children appeared at the base of the tree. A boy with ebony black ringlets of hair and an almost-princely attire chased after a girl with a dusty blonde braid that swung beneath a servant's bonnet. They ran around the tree in a playful game of tag, their laughter echoing through the emptiness of limbo. In their presence, Savara felt a warmth spreading through her, a feeling of love and happiness that seemed to emanate from the very core of their beings.

It was a moment of pure joy amidst the vast emptiness, a fleeting moment which infinity seemed to have caught, kept, and cared for.

As she floated down to watch them play, the little boy halted his chase and stared up at her. Savara gazed into eyes that looked too much like her own. He contemplated her, tilting his head innocently. In their connected gaze, understanding washed over her.

"Are you the Prince of Shadows?" Savara asked.

The little boy nodded. His curious expression faded. An understanding frown appeared in its place. "Is playtime over?" The innocence of his voice pierced something in her heart. Sadness washed over her.

He knew.

"Yes…" she whispered, the words laden with grief and sorrow.

The boy reached out for the girl's arm and pulled her into a tender, knowing embrace. She hugged him back gingerly, unaware that this would be their final one.

But he knew.

This young soul, with wisdom well beyond his years, knew.

As Savara played spectator to the intimate moment, the two souls transformed into the versions of themselves they'd been in the memory—their last mortal encounter. The Prince of Shadows pressed a kiss to her forehead and guided her towards Savara. He'd plastered on a smile for her, but Savara felt the weight of loss and longing clinging to him.

"Selene, this is Savara," he said, his voice as gentle as his hold on her. "She has come to take you home."

"I remember her from your memories," Savara replied, but the Prince of Shadows only furrowed his brow.

Instead, the girl, Selene, smiled. "Those weren't his," she giggled as she stared up at him lovingly. "They were mine. I'd left them there for you to find."

"But why?" Savara asked.

Selene turned back to her with tears in her eyes. "Because I needed you to guide him back to me, one last time." She rested a hand on his heart as she spoke. "I needed one last game of tag before I said goodbye."

Savara nodded, thankful that she was no longer in the physical realm, for she wouldn't have been able to make it through the encounter without bursting into tears.

"What do I do?" she asked, focusing on the soul of the Prince of Shadows, whose appearance had shifted once more to that of the man she knew in her time, the one with the salt and peppered hair and knowing red eyes. As she gazed upon him, she realised how much pain was contained in their ruby glow. The eyes of others had always shown her multitudes of emotions. His showed one in vast and endless quantities: sorrow. Her heart ached for him, but he was stoic throughout, asking for no sympathy or affection. They were not part of his character.

"Hold your hand to her heart, as you did in the physical realm, and say, *Agur.*"

Savara intended to follow his instructions, but before she did, Selene pulled her in for a final embrace.

"It's a shame we never got the chance to meet in person. Perhaps eternity will give us another chance," she said, and as she took hold of Savara's hand and placed it upon her heart, she whispered soft enough for only them two to hear. "Take care of him for now; it'll soon be time for him to come home."

"I will," Savara whispered in reply.

Selene smiled at her for a final time, her ethereal tears dripping down the sides of her face and falling into the unconscious. She nodded, acknowledging that she was ready to go.

"*Agur*," Savara whispered.

As Selene's soul faded, flowing back into the glowing streams of the tree, Savara heard her call back to the two of them in a voice of angelic serenity.

"Thank you."

And then, darkness consumed them all.

CHAPTER 26

THE HOME TO WHICH WE ALL RETURN

"FIVE… FOUR… THREE… TWO… ONE… Open your eyes, Savara," came the voice; the gravity of it brought her back to the present, gently waking her from the stupor. The Prince of Shadows stood before her, hands clasped behind his back, contemplating the lifeless statue of the woman he'd loved.

Savara felt the difference in the air around the statue immediately. No more did fear and loss linger around it like guardians. The gale of torment and emotion had faded, leaving behind the memorial. The statue had become nothing more than a statue, cold and lifeless as the stone that comprised it.

"What happened to her?" Savara asked softly, not wanting to intrude on the intimate moment. As she addressed the Prince of Shadows, her voice barely above a whisper, the weight of her words hung heavy in the air.

"She has returned home," he replied, his words laden with centuries of wisdom and experience. "As we all must, eventually. To source… To Iturri. No candle burns forever."

"Even the stars go out eventually…" she said, repeating the cryptic words of the panther spirit, understanding resting over her shoulders like a warm blanket.

Savara found comfort in his calling it 'returning home', as though it were a 'somewhere nice to return to', rather than the dreaded concept of nothingness that bore a striking resemblance to limbo. She thought back on all the people in her life who must have gone through the same thing—the King of Haizea, Ori of the Harri, Ms. Short, Uncle Hyrum, her mother… She wondered what they'd all experienced, and if it truly felt like a return to somewhere pleasant rather than a cruel goodbye.

"What does that feel like?" she asked, still lost in the memories of the others.

The Prince of Shadows turned to her solemnly. "It is not for us to know before our time…" And then, as if consoling her, he added, "They all, however, even the most damaged of souls, go in peace."

The way Selene's soul had evaporated before them had told her as much. The idea that even the most damaged souls found peace in the end offered her a glimmer of hope in the face of mortality. In that moment, surrounded by shadows and echoes of the past, she felt a profound sense of connection to the Prince of Shadows, more so than ever before. He was her father and the only other person alive with powers like hers, but it was more than that. He'd committed heinous acts in the name of duty, but also in the name of love. That didn't excuse his actions in the slightest, but it did offer insight into the quality of his spirit.

He was a kindred soul—a broken soul, as broken as she had been.

In the end, we all are, Savara realised, *broken souls in need of healing, of love…even if we can't all see it.*

In her moment of introspection, she let her curious gaze wander around the garden. Understanding began to settle in her soul. These lands were not death nor were they limbo. Death was a gateway to something new. Limbo was a holding ground for something old. These lands were different. They were the healing grounds for broken souls.

"Why doesn't everyone else know this?" she asked, returning her attention to him. "Maybe if they did, they wouldn't fear us…"

"It is not for us to make man brave death. Our job is to simply ferry," he replied. "The fear surrounding it, however, keeps man accountable. Now, I believe all parties are officially present. We, my child, have somewhere to be…" he declared, extending a hand towards her.

"Where are we going?"

"To the place where it all began."

Savara took hold. In an instant, the dust from the garden wrapped them in the same whirlwind fashion that the shadows had Amon. The uncomfortable sensation of being ripped apart flooded through her, but now she found comfort in the understanding that all that had ever been torn apart would be put back together eventually—hearts and souls included.

* * *

There were no fireworks in the sky tonight, no throngs of people, no music or fanfare anywhere to be seen. There were no political statements to be made, no celebratory commencements either. The event merited no celebration, of any kind. It was a sobering affair. Apprehension lingered in the air like the bitter taste of death—a sensation that did not go unnoticed.

The bridges had not surfaced this time, of their own volition or otherwise. They had not joined the lands of Visanthe, as though they too feared this strange invitation. The gates around the island stood like solemn sentinels, barring entry to those who served no purpose attending the event. A magnified thrum of power came from them, hungering for the night's outcome. Regardless of how it ended, one thing was certain: they would receive a tribute of blood.

The leaders took their customary places around the dais, a ritual they had performed countless times during Divination Days past. But this was no ordinary Divination Day. They played their parts as expected, but not without hesitation. They exchanged glances—some fraught with worry, others with concern—as they waited to see how the ceremony unfolded. There were still those amongst them who wished to deny the return of the shadows, but they could not deny the sense of dread washing over them all.

As the sun set over the isle, flames appeared, rimming the amphitheatre. Unlike their customary golden glow, these flames burned as black as shadow. Low hummings appeared in the breeze, whisperings of the legend that had gathered them all here tonight.

Then, in a burst of blue light, the leader of the Izar appeared. No delegation accompanied her, nor did she need one. Despite the innocence of her appearance, the other leaders recoiled from her, recognising her as the powerful threat that she was—a goddess among mortals. The energy surrounding her was that of a chained hurricane, palpable by all present. Though she maintained a semblance of order, the chaos brimmed behind her eyes. She narrowed them as she searched the amphitheatre for someone she had yet to find. Soon, like the others, she made her way to her stand and waited for the man who had summoned them all to this most unceremonious of Divination Days.

Suddenly, tendrils of shadow erupted from the floor with a force akin to bamboo shoots sprouting in a dense forest. They spiralled upward, stretching far above the heads of the assembled leaders before coiling downward, forming ominous cages around them. A chorus of terrified screams filled the air, echoing throughout the arena.

And then, materialising from the very shadows themselves, the Prince of Shadows made his grand entrance.

"Welcome, one and all, to the world's final Divination Day," he announced, his voice dripping with satisfaction as he revelled in the shock and disbelief of his captive audience. The sound echoed through the arena, sending shivers down the spines of all present.

The only person who appeared unfazed by his arrival was the leader of the Izar herself. She regarded him like a hawk to its prey, a smirk growing at her lips. "You have grown bold during your imprisonment, but a being like you has no power here…"

The rest of the leaders shifted restlessly in their seats, murmuring about her choice of wording. Imprisonment was not what their history had said of the realm of spirits and blood. None had expected to see the man they had long considered lost to time and legend standing alive and well before them—none but her.

It was clear to them all that they were only supposed to play the part of spectators in today's events. The real battle would take place between these two: a battle of light and shadow, of stars and blood.

"No power, Aurelia?" he replied. Adrius, Prince of Shadows, reminded them all of the power bubbling beneath his skin as he strode over to his own section of the amphitheatre, a sweep of shadows in tow, clearing away the dust and neglect from the stonework. On his face was a look of triumphant satisfaction as he took his seat in the stands.

"What is the meaning of this?" Lord Andor growled, practically foaming at the mouth out of fear. Shadowy tendrils clamped down on his feet and wrists, binding him to his seat.

"Isn't it obvious? You had all gotten too comfortable with shaky foundations, creaking floors, and leaks in the ceiling. I have returned to bring the house down," the Prince of Shadows replied, revelling in his own brilliance. With a flick of his wrist, six shadowy figures, like the ones that had brought the invitations, appeared at the dais, each holding one of the blood-stained stones.

Upon further inspection, people realised they were not simply shadows. The crowd gasped at the collective realisation that these shadows had taken on familiar silhouettes from each nation—Lord Ori of the Harri, Queen Anissa of the Argia, the King of the Zerua, an unknown child for the Ur, and the very same leaders of light and shadow themselves, Aurelia and Adrius.

At this, Aurelia snapped up, fury burning like the hottest flame in her sapphire blue eyes. She flared her nostrils as the snow-white waves of hair floated around her person, tendrils of it flicking violently in the air. "From where have you stolen my blood, you wretched relic of forgotten tombstones?!" she hissed, light pouring into her palms as she readied herself to strike down the replica.

"Tsk, tsk, tsk, Aurelia. Rage is unbecoming of someone your age," Adrius replied as he rose to the challenge. "You didn't think you'd come out unscathed from our last fight, did you?" He grinned, watching her scan the depths of her memories for that of their last battle. Realisation hit her like a slap to the face, summoning more fury from within her, but Adrius remained unbothered. "Regardless," he continued, "we are still one person short…"

The Prince of Shadows waved his hand, signalling for the shadows to proceed. They glided towards the dais, placing the stones into the notches that would hold golden rings on any other Divination Day but today acted as keyholes. Once their task was complete, they disappeared, reverting into shadowy black dust that slithered across the floors, creating a spiral around the dais.

"And now, may I present to you, our guest of honour…" The dust lifted from the floor in the same vortex pattern, the streams of it creating a gale that caused the rest of the spectators to shield their eyes. The wind roared like the wailing of a thousand souls as it whipped around the amphitheatre. And just as soon as it had appeared, it dissipated, revealing a kneeling woman. She was clad in an airy black chiffon dress and an obsidian crown, rimmed with dagger-like points and adorned with glowing rubies. Her eyes glowed with the brilliance of the rainbow, pulling together the colours of the souls of all the other nations in her gaze. "…our beautiful Harbinger of Death."

CHAPTER 27

THE HARBINGER OF DEATH

SAVARA ROSE FROM HER KNEES, the waves of dark hair trailing down her back dancing in the hesitant breeze. She gazed around at the silenced crowd, reminded of a similar scene from almost a decade ago. She was smaller then, and the crowd much larger. This setting was both more intimate and somehow more distant. The sea of faces before her looked as though they'd seen lifetimes since then, and gazing upon her, looked as though they were about to watch them collapse. Back then, she was just a girl receiving her powers, not yet crowned the Queen of Demons.

Not yet the face of the end of the world.

Apprehension glistened in the eyes of all. Not all the leaders that had exiled her were present, most had already met their demise, but the ones that were here remembered as she did. They saw the consequences of their actions staring them down, dressed to kill and crowned in darkness. This time, they would feel as she had.

This time, they would fear.

She had changed much since her last encounter with them all. Few, like the leaders of the Harri, she remembered with more clarity. They had kidnapped her. Tortured her. They, like so many others, had wished to use her powers for destruction and conquest. To advance their own agendas. Others, like the leaders of the Ur and Izar, were only blips in her memory. Faces lost to time whose lives had changed her own forever.

Savara used these memories as fuel, feeding the burning fire inside. Her powers rattled to life, clawing at her skin from within like starving beasts against iron cages.

She hadn't been capable of more back then, for she too had feared her powers. Now, Savara was attuned to the finest flutters of souls for miles. She could feel every hitched breath in the crowd as if they were her own. She could taste the fear on their tongues, sense the tension in their bodies. She could feel their blood calling out to her in a way almost too gruesome to mention.

She hungered for it—for the fear, for the control, for the power—as she stood before those who had so readily stripped her of it. Savara inhaled deeply, steadying herself from the barrage of sensations. She would not let it overwhelm her. She couldn't.

I am stronger now, she reminded herself to keep up her conviction.

Even her friends seemed to have noticed the change in her. Storm had inclined her body towards Sebas, who in turn held his hand at the ready, as if waiting to see if flame was required. Brass watched from a different stand wearing robes that reminded her of those worn by the deceased king of Haizea—a sign he'd taken up the throne. Jasper had called out to her, looking as though he might rush towards her, but Griffin's muscled arm barred his path. He watched her, concern knotting his brows. They—if any at all—might be able to see through the ruse. But she couldn't have that. She needed them to believe like all the rest that she was dangerous.

Savara raised her hands, mirroring the act she'd seen the Prince of Shadows perform on many an occasion. Lavender light burst from her, sending a wave of energy through the crowd that rooted everyone to their seats. She caressed their fears and darker emotions, adding to them in a way that would immobilise them throughout the ceremony—so long as she remained in control of her own.

The display worked.

For a moment, the world was silent. Then, the Prince of Shadows shattered the stillness with a sharp, rhythmic clap, applauding her display of power as though relishing in his teachings. The tendrils of shadow sweeping behind him gave him the impression of a burning king on a throne of black flames as they drank in the energy of all those around—her included.

"Finally," he declared. "We may begin." He snapped his fingers, summoning forth the same spirit-tinged dagger he'd used in Idune to regain his body—or whatever semblance of a body he now had.

Savara watched as the dagger drifted towards her, feeling a rush of goosebumps over her arms. She anchored her focus to it, allowing the rest of the world to drift away in the periphery as if it were all a dream.

The dagger sang to her like the one she'd first encountered in Griffin's tent. It spoke of legends and endings in ethereal whisperings—as if she didn't already know the path ahead.

Her heart sank as she clutched it, knowing what needed to be done and what would be required. What sacrifice lay ahead. The weight of the task consumed her. She wondered if the others noticed the drastic shift in the density of the air or the chill that blanketed the amphitheatre, or if these sensations lay in her mind alone.

Perhaps it was only the approach of Death.

"Sav, don't!" Jasper cried out.

Savara turned her head sharply to face him. Her mind was still hazily lost to the trance, but her heart was acutely aware of the comforting sound of his voice. It tugged at her. Pleading for her to listen.

Griffin had once again restrained him, pulling at arms covered by a network of blackened veins. The sight alone gave her pause. She'd seen something similar the first time she'd gone into limbo. But in that instance, it had been her body ravelled in the web of tainted veins. She knew immediately upon seeing him that he was dying. That something else was taking over.

Somehow, Jasper had managed to get tangled up in limbo—and limbo didn't want to let go.

"What have you done?" she said, her voice echoing throughout the arena in her state of transfixion.

Jasper ignored her question. "It'll kill you..." he added softly. No one else heard his plea. No one else heard the pain in his voice.

But she did.

She heard it over the lingering echo of her own, as if he'd whispered it in her ear. In his voice, she heard the longing of her friend, the loss of the life they'd once led, the heartache of her having rejected him. But she also heard the ominous undertones of a voice that was very much not his own. It was dark in a way that time itself did not dare explain—could not explain. No concept created by man would ever encompass the gravity of such darkness. It was so pure and so broken...and so very much alive.

Savara hesitated.

The final stone lay somewhere in limbo, waiting to be retrieved. Iturri rattled against its cage, sending a bloodthirsty undercurrent through the air around the dais. The dagger in her hand vibrated with the malicious energy of a countdown to a bitter end.

But Jasper stood before her, the captive of a spider's web of darkness beneath his skin that demanded his life.

Savara hesitated, realising that she might be able to save him, but knowing it would mean giving up her life in his place. If she did, there would be no guarantees as to the safety of the rest of her friends, or even the state of the world afterwards, but at least he would be safe. The guilt of his stay here still weighed heavy on her heart. She could at least spare him the wrath of limbo…

But the Prince of Shadows had been watching her carefully. His eyes flicked from her to Jasper, understanding lining the cruel purse of his lip. He'd seen it, the decision in her eyes. Her hesitation was a sign of weakness and a threat to everything he'd worked to achieve—a threat to everything he'd given up.

"It seems, child, you need a bit more leverage," he growled. When he snapped his fingers next, Amon appeared on the ground, strapped down by the same sinister shadows. Their tendrils held up his face so that she would meet his gaze. So that she would see the challenge in his eyes.

This is what he'd done with him, she realised. *Kept him as a hostage… He knew that I'd have reason to doubt…*

Savara's blood ran cold. Was he making her choose? Her power wavered, releasing the hold she'd had on the crowd. "No…" she whispered.

How could she choose between her best friend and the man whose heart and soul were bound to her own? She couldn't. Yet, if she didn't, she would lose them both.

Suddenly, as if by saving grace, a beam of light blasted towards the Prince of Shadows. He blocked the attack with a wall of shadows that easily absorbed it.

"You will not use this child to fight your battles, Adrius," Aurelia, Princess of Light, called from the stands, rage brimming in her voice. "Nor will you use my child as leverage. If it is a fight you want, let us fight."

"Patience, Aurelia, our time to fight draws near," he replied. "But this must be completed, and if my daughter will not perform her task willingly, I will force it."

Aurelia opened her mouth to reply but found the thought cut short by a sudden burst of lightning. She blocked it just barely, but her shock and fury flourished.

Savara snapped her head to the new arrival who had appeared from behind the throne of the Arima. Standing at the side of the Prince of Shadows, Alexei waved a glove lackadaisically in the air as streaks of lingering lightning caressed his knuckles. He winked at her playfully as if to remind her of their secret bond. She didn't need reminding. The stones weighed on her ear and her soul, more palpable now with her advanced abilities.

Then, to hide their complicity, Alexei turned from her to survey the scene. "Hello Auntie," he said with a smirk, his gaze shifted from her to Amon. A shadow of tension appeared in the malicious curl of his lips. "Cousin… Have I missed much?"

"Alexei, remove yourself from this arena this instant, you *monster*."

Murder glinted in his eyes as he turned back to the Princess of Light. "Oh, Auntie, how could I deny you the pleasure of my company after such an affable salutation? I believe, unlike yours, my presence is appreciated by at least one party today."

Savara noted the bitterness in his soul come alive. They'd already spoken about the darkness surrounding his heart, put there by those closest to him. Now, she got a front-row seat to the trauma. Alexei avoided her gaze as he spoke, but she noted a tingle on the cusp of her ear—where their bond lay.

Savara did appreciate his interruption. It selfishly gave her the space to think. She turned to Jasper whose eyes still pleaded with her. They had lived a beautiful life together—even if the memories were slowly slipping from her mind. Certain things she would never forget. There was love between them. Maybe not in the way he'd always wanted, but it was a love that had transcended worlds. One that always had and always would. Be they the fleeting worlds of life, or the immortal world of death. Her time in the holding grounds had taught her that there are some things that not even death can kill.

Love surpassed them all.

She cast her gaze towards Amon, who lay a few feet in front of her, restricted by the shadows. The violent blue of his eyes burned like the hottest of fires as their gaze caressed her skin. After lifting his bonds with the Prince of Shadows, their vibrance had grown. He purposefully stripped all other emotions from them. She knew he didn't want to sway her heart in any way. The serenity she found in them, even in what could be considered 'final moments', was torture.

Griffin glared at her stone-faced from Jasper's side, still tugging at his arm to prevent him from causing trouble. He, like Amon, made no show of emotion. His glower was a simple message of determination. Of decision, without interference. She'd looked to him for guidance, but not even he could make the choice.

Savara wished she had a minute alone, but even a minute was a luxury in this final countdown. Her mind reeled as the world around her erupted into arguments and bitter exchanges. Violence electrified the air. Soon, the words would turn to action. And she needed to have an answer before then.

CHAPTER 28

THE INTERLUDE TO LIMBO I

THE STARS OVERHEAD GLEAMED BRIGHTER, watching safely from a distance as the tensions ran higher and higher. Agitated winds lifted birds from their perches on the various stone monuments across the lands, as if they were conscious of the coming changes. Around them, a cacophony of flapping and cawing filled the air, setting everyone's nerves further on edge.

"My patience wanes, daughter," said the Prince of Shadows. He'd lost any sense of amusement as he spoke. He tightened the shadows' grip on Amon as he glowered at her.

Amon winced in pain, and once again, she was hard-pressed to make a decision. She could almost hear the countdown in her head. The voices of the spirits whispered, eager for blood.

"Leave them alone," she called amidst the back and forth, her head whipping around to meet the stone-cold face of a man who might have been a true father to her had circumstances and destinies not played such a role in their relationship.

"We will not be repeating this cycle, child," he replied, reminding her of the deal they'd struck. "It is time for you to break the bond."

Nothing had changed since then; Amon was still a captive, her friends were still tied up in this battle, Jasper was still dying, and she was no closer to fixing any of it. Savara didn't know how she would do it, but she had to try something—anything. Time was running out.

Before her, the dais and its resting stones gleamed, waiting, mocking her with their glow. *Six stones, six lands, six bonds...* she counted, but that wasn't enough.

Seven bonds were made; seven must be broken.

There was still one missing.

But where?

Savara thought back to the song of the legend. There had to be answers in it somewhere.

Six to broken lands bestowed, a final one soul alone may hold,

Lay in that which no blood may currency, uniting stone borne to eternity,

She sang the words over in her head, trying to make sense of them amidst the yelling. Beads of sweat formed at her brow. Each second felt like a knife inching closer and closer to her heart.

"That which no blood may currency... What does that even mean?" she mumbled.

Then, a voice appeared in her mind as if to answer the question. It was a voice she hadn't heard in time, that of the late king of Haizea. The words he'd spoken to her on his deathbed rang out within her.

It is in death we learn who we truly are, and what we are made of...

Savara contemplated the words spoken by her strange hit of intuition. *It is in death*, she realised, and in confirmation, she found herself repeating the words of the Prince of Shadows.

"Dead is dead... Something which no blood may currency," she whispered, unsure if to smile at or fear the realisation. But there was still one problem. If the stone lay somewhere beyond life, and there was no returning from death, how would she retrieve the stone to complete the ritual?

Savara cast furtive glances around the arena as she tried in vain to calm the rushing beat of her heart. Amon continued to strain against the shadows. The leaders of the other nations fired verbal threats between them and the Prince of Shadows. Griffin held tight to Jasper's arm, keeping him from running towards her. Her eyes fell on Jasper's arms and the web of blackened veins beneath his skin.

That's it, she realised. *Limbo.*

The Prince of Shadows had primed her to dip into the world beyond the veil. She didn't have the luxury of the spiritual energy of the holding grounds to help her. There, not quite all the way beyond the veil, she could breathe, steady her mind, and allow herself to be guided the rest of the way. Here, still in the realm of the living, she would need a different approach.

Savara homed in on that sensation within her that spoke of peace—the one that all souls felt in passing. She would need it to find her way there, and hopefully the way back as well. The last times she'd entered limbo from outside the gardens, she'd been on the brink of death. She'd have to get there again somehow, get close enough to the other side without losing her life completely.

Suddenly it hit her, her way in.

Savara turned towards the throne of the Arima. Her answer had been there all along, cross-armed and dangerous. A cocked bow, waiting to be fired. It was as if he'd known all along.

"Alexei!" she called out to him, taking the world by surprise. "Do it."

Alexei straightened himself, uncrossing his arms as he grinned. "As you wish, Your Majesty," he replied with a knowing wink before releasing a bolt in her direction.

The blinding streak lit up the arena. It took less than a second from when the lightning pierced her chest for her to slump to the ground. There had been no time for anyone to react, let alone stop it. Even the Prince of Shadows had been taken aback by the request. The echo of the strike lingered, silencing the rest of the world.

In an instant, the world she knew was gone, or rather, she was gone from it.

* * *

The entirety of Middle Isle became a battleground. The island itself would be unrecognisable once the battle was through. The full moon beamed overhead the colour of all soulbonds—blood red. Nothing about tonight would be remembered fondly.

CHAPTER 29

THE INTERLUDE TO LIMBO II

THE LIGHT DISSIPATED AS QUICKLY AS IT HAD appeared. The echo died soon after. The shock of seeing Savara's body crumpled on the ground beside the dais had left everyone speechless… And him without a breath in his body.

Amon felt his heart miss a beat the way it had in the palace, but seeing it occur made the pain worse. Time froze then and there. All he could do was watch as her body crumpled over the heaps of black fabric. Lifeless. Once again, their connection had been severed. His world went dark. His heart, his soul, both stilled. For a moment, he heard absolutely nothing.

Then, Jasper's cry of despair cut through the air, startling him back to his senses.

The Prince of Shadows released him, allowing him to rush toward her body. Even in his tortured state, seeing her like this was the worst type of suffering. Amon dropped to his knees beside her, his hand overing tentatively over the scorch marks on her chest. Her skin was cold beneath his touch. Cold in the way of hollow caves that had never seen the light of day. Amon ignored the ringing in his ears as he held her tight, wondering how somebody so full of life and warmth could be so suddenly zapped of both.

The rest of the world crumbled in his periphery. He didn't care. She was the only thing that mattered in that moment—in all moments. And all he had of her now was a corpse.

No… He thought, straining against reddened eyes and bloodlust. He wouldn't lose her—he couldn't lose her. Not again.

"Don't go, princess, don't go…" Amon pleaded with Savara's corpse, hoping to will her back to life.

In all his time in the shadows, he'd never so much as contemplated their curious connection to the afterlife. Especially not after having been saddled with lethal bonds of his own. Now, even knowing of their danger, he prayed to Iturri, to Fate, to Death itself to bring her back, willing to make whichever bond was necessary.

"Relax, cousin, time heals all wounds…" Alexei replied, his gaze darkening as their eyes met. "Truly."

A muscle ticked at his jaw. "Alexei, you're a dead man," Amon growled. He'd clenched it so hard he could've broken through bone. It took every ounce of restraint in him not to lunge at Alexei and rip his heart from his chest.

It was hard to believe the two of them had actually been friends before all of this started. Before the shadows, before the dark.

But things were different now.

They'd had spats before. Spats that could've levelled small villages had they not had the sense to take them elsewhere. Amon had never truly hated Alexei, for he knew, deep down, there was a decent heart beneath the façade of callousness. As deranged as he could be, Alexei had always been loyal to him. It wasn't until their last fight that he'd noticed the change. The hatred that had festered within him…

The cruelty.

But Amon had become someone different as well. He'd finally found something worth fighting for, something he couldn't bear to lose. And that something lay lifeless in his arms. Amon had wanted to murder Alexei for taking her from him in Haizea. Now, he realised murder was too good for a low life like him. Alexei deserved to suffer, to endure every ounce of pain he'd caused tenfold.

"Oh, cousin, you don't know how right you are," Alexei replied, licking his teeth hungrily like the wolf he was.

Amon passed Savara's body off to Jasper and stood. The light poured into his palms, glowing like the brightest of stars in the night sky.

"Really, cousin, you wish to fight over your little loss?"

Instead of replying, Amon fired a beam towards Alexei, who jumped out of the way just in time. The stone behind him exploded in the wake of the attack. Amon fired off another three bursts of light in succession. Alexei dodged them all, making no move to retaliate.

"Fight me, you coward," Amon growled, his eyes burning with the flames of vengeance. He could feel the heat emanating from his skin. The depths of his anger and heartbreak fuelled each blow. "Fight me, so that I may make you suffer as I have."

He heard his friends calling out to him, but the anger blotted out everything that wasn't his target. His cousin, the blackhearted fiend who'd stripped everything from him, waited at the edge of the scorched stand, glowing blue eyes beaming through the plume of dust. Amon fired off another shot, and another, each one primed to kill.

Alexei continued to skirt around the attacks. "It is not yet time for you to unravel, cousin."

"Your violence knows no bounds when it comes to the innocent, but when it is time for an actual fight, you cannot raise a finger," Amon hissed between gritted teeth. Wrath rang in his ears like the hissing of a boiling kettle.

"I will shoot you, cousin, if only to sit you down," Alexei replied, his voice hinting at impatience.

"And yet I see no lightning…"

More shots fired. None of them hit. None of them quelled his rage.

"Patience is a virtue, cousin. Besides…" Alexei said. "I'd like to see which side wins out before I go." His eyes darted to a scene beyond their spat.

Amon clenched his fists, halting his next attack. He turned to see what had caught Alexei's attention. His eyes flicked between the leaders of the Arima and the Izar, who were already poised for battle. His mother had sat back, amusement lining her wicked smile. The Prince of Shadows glowered at her, his shadows curling around his person like a halo of black flames.

His blood ran cold. The rage had not died, only faltered. This was the scene he'd seen in his scrying mirrors, the one he'd been warned about in the stars. This was how the world would end.

Suddenly, he felt Alexei's leathery hand on his shoulder. His cruel voice, cold and lacking any sense of amusement, whispered, "And, since you plan on living out a much longer life than I, dear cousin, I suggest you do the same…"

CHAPTER 30

THE INTERLUDE TO LIMBO III

A MOMENT AFTER THE GIRL DIED, the world erupted into violence. It was as if her presence had quelled the tensions building in them all. After her death, whatever semblance of civility crumbled. The leaders of the other lands scrambled to get their people away from the colliding forces of light and dark that threatened to tear the world apart. The island itself shook.

Madness took over.

General Isaac scanned the fleeing crowd for the traitorous, fox-like face that had orchestrated his capture. He pressed two fists together and stamped his foot to the ground, launching himself into the air with all the grace of a panther. As he hopped from stone pillar to stone pillar, his resolve grew. Stray rocks and waves invaded his path, injury threatened to stop his stride, but nothing would make him falter. Nothing would stop him from reaching his target.

Dhoot would pay for the bloodshed.

How will you be remembered? the old general had once asked him. The words bounced around in his head even now, as if urging him on in his search.

Back then, General Isaac was naïve enough to think he could lead without violence—to be remembered as the general who won without war. Perhaps in another time, a future not so far from this time, such a thing will be possible. But now, as the war waged on around him, he knew he was not the hero he wished to be. Perhaps when the stories were told in the years to come, he might not be a hero at all. But he'd be damned if he didn't take down the villain.

Then, as if by great fortune, General Isaac spied his target. The scoundrel, after having architected at least part of the world's massacres, had hidden himself from the violence. Even during his days as a respected war general, Dhoot had always put his own life ahead of the rest. Tonight was no different. For all his talk of valour and glory, the newly appointed councilman had stalked away from the fight.

The coward, General Isaac thought as he planted himself heavily on the ground beside the councilman, who fell to his knees in the resulting shockwave.

The scoundrel scrambled to his feet, his usually slicked-back hair falling frazzled in front of his eyes. Fury and fear loomed around him as he searched for the perpetrator of his loss of balance. There was something off-kilter about him. About the way his gaze bounced between General Isaac and his escape route. It was the look of a lunatic; a criminal being cornered.

"So… General Isaac," Councilman Dhoot called, his voice filled with vitriol as he righted himself. "Have you finally decided to show your true colours? That of the traitor you are?"

"You and I both know that the only traitor here is you, Dhoot," replied General Isaac. He stomped a foot, blocking the councilman's route of escape.

The councilman narrowed his eyes. "Is that a challenge, you worthless grunt?"

"I am not letting you leave without answering for your crimes. You were the one who let the shadows into Idune. Lord Ori's death is on your hands."

Councilman Dhoot's face twisted with sinister amusement. "Alright, let's have at it."

The councilman thrust a hand out, forcing sharpened spikes of rock from the ground beneath General Isaac's feet.

General Isaac dodged, flipping backwards onto a raised stone just in time for the next attack. He slammed a fist into the stone, conjuring a part of it into a shield in preparation. The councilman shot out his hands again in rapid succession, debris whipping through the air and grazing an uncovered patch of his arm.

He clapped a hand over the scrape, wincing momentarily before his counterstrike. The earth quaked as he slammed his fists to the ground, sending a series of jagged stone pillars speeding toward the councilman.

"Is that all you've got?" snarled the councilman as he swirled his arms, diverting the stone assault with a barrier of compressed earth. Fragments of sharpened stone flew haphazardly, matching the frantic energy of the councilman himself. Fear highlighted the evil green of his irises. It marked each abrupt move of his hands.

He was coming undone.

General Isaac knew it wouldn't take much more to unhinge him completely. He kept up his speed, somersaulting from the pillars forming beneath his feet as he dodged the bombardment.

The councilman's movements were terse and dense, with a tremorlike quality that wasn't made to endure long battles but rather quick spats. He moved with the force and grace of a landslide, destroying everything in his path. General Isaac's movements, in contrast, were swift. Precise. Consequential.

As he'd been taught to be.

"You are no hero, Dhoot," said General Isaac, thrusting his arms forward and causing the ground to rise in a tidal wave of stone.

Councilman Dhoot's knees buckled with the unexpected force, but that did not stop his wildfire. The councilman slammed a fist to the ground, firing off larger chunks of stone that threatened to crush General Isaac.

"I'll tell you a secret," he snarled. "No one really is. We are all demons looking to devour as much of the world's light as we can before death takes hold of our souls. That's what we were made for—you, me, and everyone else in this godforsaken world."

General Isaac leapt into the air, narrowly avoiding the blows.

"You're wrong!" he yelled, forcing his hands down upon landing. Walls of stone sprouted from the floor, blocking the councilman's next few attacks.

The councilman laughed maniacally. "You haven't lived long enough to understand how right I truly am." He summoned a pillar of stone from the ground and began firing off disks of it towards General Isaac, the barrage beginning to break through his shield.

Anticipating the move, General Isaac kicked the stone wall towards the councilman, forcing him to jump out of the way. As the councilman stumbled to right himself, General Isaac seized the moment for a final attack. He raised bars of stone to catch a hold of the councilman's wrists and ankles, rendering him unable to continue.

"Is this it then?" hissed the councilman, struggling against the hold. "Is this where you crush me beneath a boulder?" He flared his nostrils, attempting to goad General Isaac into another attack. "Do it," he growled. "Deep down, you know it's what your heart wants. To see me finally become a victim. Deep down, you know you're more like me than you wish to admit…"

General Isaac held his tongue, his breath, laboured, watching as the councilman squirmed.

"Do it," Councilman Dhoot added, spit flying from his mouth in the frenzy. "Take down a villain and become one yourself…" Anger and fear danced across his face, highlighting the insanity. "Do it!" he yelled.

General Isaac could do nothing but watch. This was the result, he realised. This was the thing his father had cautioned him against. The corrupting influence of ill-begotten power.

As much as he wanted to kill the man before him, General Isaac knew he couldn't. He realised in that moment that, if he gave in to the desire for revenge, the cycle of suffering would only continue.

Besides, that insanity was its own form of torture.

General Isaac turned on his heels. There was no use in spilling more blood tonight. He'd let the rest of the council deal with Dhoot once everything was over. Now, his friends needed him more.

The echoes of madness chased after him, looking to drag him back down to the level of the councilman. What the councilman didn't realise was that the chains of madness could only bind those who lingered in the darkness. Those who sought out conquest over compassion. The world had already seen enough of those people. General Isaac had no intention of becoming another.

CHAPTER 31

THE INTERLUDE TO LIMBO IV

"IT SEEMS, ADRIUS, YOUR DAUGHTER has bested you," Aurelia called out to him, a smug look plastered across her face.

"The night is yet young, Aurelia," Adrius replied, ignoring the spectacle at the dais. He matched her amusement as he stalked down from his stand towards the main floor of the amphitheatre. "Perhaps our time apart has made you forget that I still have the final say in such matters."

Aurelia's eyes glinted with murder. She thrust a hand forward, sending a beam of light towards him, aiming for his heart. Adrius flashed his palm, summoning forth a wall of shadows to block the attack. When dark met light, it sent a shockwave through the amphitheatre, sending everyone flying backwards.

"I suppose we have time for one last fight," he added, his frustration evident in the tension lining his jaw. Tendrils of shadow curled like serpents around him, dancing hungrily in the ominous light of the stars.

"You cannot hope to win this one now, not without your precious Harbinger of Death," she replied, pressing gingerly into the pain of his loss.

"When I die, Aurelia, it'll be alongside your twisted soul. That way, you might finally atone for the suffering you caused."

"This again?" she spat. "You cannot keep clinging to him, Adrius. You did not see the threat he posed. I made the call that was required—"

"He was a child, Aurelia," the Prince of Shadows growled.

"A child who would throw into question our way of rule. Our order. How things have been done for centuries."

"He was a child you feared because he might have challenged you!"

"Enough!" she screamed, the sound echoing like a banshee's cry over the chaos of the warring nations. "This ends here," she replied as she held her palms out in front of her. An orb of blue light began to form between her hands. It burned with the fire of a thousand dying stars, the shadows it cast across her face highlighting centuries of torment.

The orb flew towards him with a force that could've collapsed mountains. Adrius blocked it, shrouding himself in a shield of shadows. The two forces met in a cataclysmic collision, light and dark intermingling in an explosion that echoed for miles. The entire amphitheatre was engulfed in a blinding white light.

CHAPTER 32

THE WORLD BEYOND THE VEIL

CONSCIOUSNESS WAS QUICKER TO ARRIVE this time now that she knew what to expect. No breath reached her lungs. No sensations touched her skin. No sounds hit her ears. And yet, part of her clung to life—or at least the shadow of it. Her plan had worked. Limbo spanned out infinitely before her. Once again, she was alone in the void.

Savara waited for the tree that had appeared on the other occasions, using it as an anchor for her focus so that she would not succumb to insanity. In limbo, she had no manner of tracking time, not even the act of breathing, for there were no breaths to be had. She simply waited. Alone. In the dark.

For a long time, nothing happened.

"Is this how you choose to spend your time here?" called a voice from behind. Again, it was a voice she'd only recently become acquainted with, but it startled her all the same.

Savara turned to find the Prince of Shadows standing behind her, a friendly smile playing at his lips.

"How are you here?" she asked, ignoring his question, remembering how she'd left him in the world of the living, along with the rest of her friends.

The Prince of Shadows' smile dropped. "I am bound to this place. You know this…"

"But…" she began, stopping as she truly contemplated his figure.

He was younger than the version of him that waited outside of limbo. This version of him was yet unchanged but old enough to have already decided on his bond with Iturri. His hair glowed a vibrant black, even against the darkness of the void. His rainbow-flecked eyes sparkled as they beheld her—not a trace of the blood-red colouring in sight.

This isn't the him that I know, she realised. *This is the side of him that got bound to Iturri… This is the mortal part of his soul…*

"That's right," Savara replied, trying to hide the sorrow in her voice as she spoke. "You cannot leave."

"Why have you come?" he asked, resuming his initial line of questioning.

"Actually, you might be able to help me. I am looking for something," she said, not wanting to linger on her shocking realisation. "A stone…"

"Hmmm…" His figure drifted around her as if analysing the intent behind the request. "Why do you assume it is here?" the young prince prodded, confirming to her its existence.

Savara maintained her gaze level on his eyes as he made his rounds. Even though they were not afflicted with the trapping of blood, there was still something haunting about their glow. The man beyond limbo was a force to be reckoned with, but the one before her, despite his mostly mortal appearance, felt similarly charged, if not more so.

"The legend spoke of a place which was the beginning of the end," she replied hesitantly. "That is this place, is it not? The precipice of life and death…" When he made no move to reply, she added, "The stone is here, isn't it?"

Even lacking full form, his ethereal body's demeanour shifted, as if the topic of the stone had triggered his defences.

"Yes," he said briefly, a hint of pain flickering behind his eyes.

"Do you know where it is?" she asked tentatively, not wanting to get her hopes up too high. There was still more work to be done. Even if she found the stone, she would still have to contend with her way back, and what would happen when she got there.

"Yes," he repeated. The glow surrounding him began to shift as well to darker hues.

"Can you give it to me?"

"No."

"Or at least show me where to find it?"

"No."

The brevity of his responses began to gnaw at her. Something felt off about their interaction. He'd gone from the vibrant version of himself that she'd seen in the memories to something even colder than the man in the living world.

"Why not?"

"I cannot give that which I do not have. You cannot find that which you have not lost."

"Then where…" Savara paused, finally realising what he meant. "I have it, don't I?" She interpreted his silence as agreement. "How do I find it?" Again, he was silent. Her patience waned. Time was of the essence. "Are you going to help me or not?" she hissed, knowing she needed to return to the world of the living—while there was still a world to return to.

The young Prince of Shadows let this uncomfortable silence hang between them for a moment longer before making his move. He raised a hand; palm face up in front of him. Then, shadows bled from his body, falling into his open palm.

It took Savara a second to realise what he was doing, but the swirling of the shadows soon made it clear. He had conjured a small orb of shadow that looked a lot like a stone.

"Is that…?" she began, but the prince shook his head.

With his other hand, the prince pressed a solitary jolting finger to her chest, sending a wave of energy through her phantasmal body. It was as if he had taken a match and lit a forgotten wick inside her soul.

Soon, knowledge flooded her mind. Events from a past that didn't belong to her—or anyone concrete, for that matter—rather, a collective of people. A record of memories belonging to faces that time forgot. The experience was similar to what she'd seen in the grooves of the glowing tree, only amplified and somehow more intimate.

There was sadness, fear, longing, and hurt, but there was also happiness, love, faith, and hope—all the things that made up a life. With or without power, these emotions afflicted everyone, spanned worlds, lifetimes. They were integral parts of existence itself. Beneath his touch, she felt them all. Unlike in the House of Spirits, this time, they did not overwhelm her. They were not heavy. As if any weight attributed to them existed in life and life alone.

Amidst the rush of new information, Savara learned truth behind the legend, the stones, and her destiny.

She had been partially right in her previous assumptions. The final stone resided in limbo, but not in the way she expected. The young Prince of Shadows had, in his touch, shown her a glimpse of the moment before her descent.

At first, the view showed the full scene from above, the crowd around her, the pressure mounting. There she stood, the Harbinger of Death, dagger in hand and primed for the end of the world. Then, the omniscience faded, focusing rather on the dais and the stones atop it.

The stones shimmered before her from their slots, their surfaces still spattered with drops of blood. She considered the shadows who had placed them there, suddenly realising there was a reason behind it. A reason each of those figures had been chosen. All of them had intimate connections to the lands of which stone they'd held. The vivid spatterings of blood on each still held traces of their souls that could neither be washed away nor forgotten, as if the force within the stone itself kept these echoes of their souls alive. Pending. The blood undried despite the air and flames around them, as if waiting for something more.

As if the ritual was yet uncompleted.

And then it hit her. The reason no one could ever find the seventh stone became glaringly obvious. It did not exist in this world, or any for that matter, in the same way the others did. Each stone corresponded to an element—water, earth, fire, air, light, and spirit. The final stone was not a rock, a crystal, or anything tangible. The truth of its existence lay in its descriptor. Not stone, but unity.

By breaking Iturri into the sum of its parts, the leaders had severed its connection to the flow of the world—severed it from the freedom to move on, to transform, to renew. As an unintended consequence, she realised, fewer people were being given powers each Divination Day. The souls with powers that were ready to move on simply could not.

The final stone—the uniting stone—was not something to be found, but to be restored. The union of the previous six stones, or at least the ability to reunite them, rested inside this version of her. But it was no stone at all.

What she'd come to know as the seventh stone was something that transcended life itself. It was a catalyst for release, as was the path to finding it. It was the one thing that had been stripped from the world the day Iturri was bound…

Freedom.

Savara sighed, biting down on a sobering laugh that wanted to crawl up her throat. All the things her friends had told her about this world had been true. Visanthe was a world of darkness, beholden to rituals even more deadly than the bonding of souls. The realisation was grim, though part of her had expected as much. She found a certain peace in knowing, even if it meant the countdown looming over her head was not for the sanctity of the world, but her own. Her time was truly drawing to a close.

In its trapping, Iturri had been severed from Death, and the only way to restore the connection was through Death itself.

That final stone was the relinquishing of her freedom, her life that had been untethered to Iturri and its bond. It was her spirit. This was the one sobering truth withheld from her. This was the reason she'd been heralded as the Harbinger of Death.

Armed with the understanding, Savara knew there was little left standing in the way of her fate. The Prince of Shadows had shown her how to summon forth the trappings of her life. Now, all she had to do was return for her final surrender.

"Before I go," Savara added, remembering another surrender taking place beyond the expanse of limbo. The shadows of it still lay claim to Jasper's soul. She needed to see him restored before she made any further moves. "I need one last favour from you. My friend is dying. Something from this world is draining his life. I need to know how to stop it."

The Prince of Shadows contemplated the concern in her eyes. "Spirits from this world cannot survive in the world of the living without being sustained. They must attach themselves to a host. But the lives they take end up stuck here forever, for it was neither the host's time to go nor the spirit's place to stay," he explained, caution contouring his voice. "These are the grounds of infinite mystery and must remain as such. Anything taken from them will cause only ruin. If it is a spirit attached to this world that eats at your friend's life, it can be released as any other, but it must be done from these lands alone."

Savara frowned. If she could bring Jasper to the Arima lands, through to the holding grounds with whatever he had that belonged to limbo, she could release the hold on him. There was still a chance to save him, but it required her to live.

"The last time I was here, I met a different person who told me it wasn't my time…" She'd wanted to ask about whether she would be able to save Jasper, whether the legend could suspend itself long enough for her to free him, but the response caught her off-guard.

"Correct."

"What do you mean?" she asked instead, wondering at the understanding shared between himself and the shadowy figure.

The young Prince of Shadows tilted his head in contemplation, the way one would at a nonsensical question, as if she'd asked if he could see or hear her. "It was not time for you to return."

"And now?" she whispered, fearing the words as they slipped from her.

"You are on the cusp," he replied plainly. "It could be your time, should you wish it."

Savara thought back on her friends in the world beyond. They had all been burned by this legend, this binding placed on Iturri. Some more than others. She knew there was still more she had to do. There was a world that needed healing.

A friend that needed saving. A lover that needed loving. A whole life that needed living—and one she desperately wanted to live.

She shook her head. "I think my job there is incomplete."

"This is true," he replied.

In that moment, a curious thought occurred to her. Had she not noticed the glow in his eyes or the shift in his demeanour, she might have accepted that the figure before her was nothing more than the mortal part of the Prince of Shadows. But this man was not him, or at least not entirely. And his answer had just confirmed her suspicions.

She'd heard the Prince of Shadows in the living world say he'd given up his mortal trappings for the sake of the bond, but she hadn't realised what that meant until now. This figure masquerading as the Prince of Shadows from before the bond with Iturri was not only the echo of his mortality. This was the bonded part of him. Bound to the embodiment of the divine itself.

"It's you, isn't it? You are Iturri…"

An eternity might have passed in his silence. He simply hovered there before her, but there was feeling creeping into her soul akin to the contemplation of a chasm. This spirit, even in masquerade, was grandiose beyond reason. His essence took over the void. When he finally decided to move, Savara knew she was right. He blinked, as if slowly assimilating the knowledge into his being, as if he too had forgotten who or what he was. It was a subtle gesture, but it was proof enough. This was the very same god severed from its omniscience.

"If I bring you back with me, will that end the cycle?" she added, hoping to get a reaction from him. "Will that set you free?"

"Set me free?" he asked finally, in a voice much more ethereal than the one she'd come to know. His voice morphed into one that spoke in echoes of many lives, as if offering more proof of his identity. It was genderless, timeless, and unhurried.

"Yes," she said.

"Yes," he replied.

Savara found a chill creeping into her soul as she lingered in the gravity of the moment. She'd come in search of a simple stone, but instead found her god of chaos instead. She couldn't help but wonder if this was all part of the legend, or if she had somehow found another path. There were things that could not be helped, someone would have to die to break the bond, the shadows still had a hold on Jasper, and there was a war waiting on the other side of the void, but Savara felt as though things were beginning to fall into place... And this time, for the better.

The waiting god before her made no further movements, as if allowing her to reconsider her offer.

"If I bring you back," she began, knowing it dangerous to ask favours of beings like him, but finding it necessary. "Regardless of whether I live or die, I need you to save my friend."

The spirit contemplated her request with a blank stare before giving his cryptic response. "We will see his spirit restored."

"Then..." Savara held a hand out to the spirit.

Iturri stared at it. There was no hunger or greed surrounding his form, simply curiosity. "Are you sure?" he asked. Again, there was no malice in his voice. Nor was there happiness. Nothing that would indicate the desires of the entity itself. "Death is required."

"I know..." she replied. Death was always required. It was the nature of her being. And though she hadn't entirely made peace with it, after her experiences with the almost-afterlife and its creatures, she found solace in the immortal nature of spirits, knowing there was something better out there. Something to look forward to beyond the veil.

"Then, Princess Savara, daughter of flame and shadow," said Iturri, "I accept."

Iturri, in the form of the young Prince of Shadows, took hold of her phantom hand. She hadn't known what to expect then, but as soon as their forms touched, she felt his power flood through her soul. His figure disappeared, fading into the darkness before her, but his power remained. It took up residence within her spirit, the weight of many worlds and many lives. It was a hard energy to contain. It was life, fate, infinity, all ravelled into one being.

Omniscience in its purest form.

No wonder the Prince of Shadows had become so twisted, she thought, though it was hard to cling to any thought over the tempest brewing inside. The overwhelming sensation of so many other souls, trapped in this one form, threatened to consume her right then and there. She struggled against the multitudes of beings that each wished to take control. Their voices, their pleas, their desires. It was suffocating. It felt like she'd once again fallen into the reflective pool and was on the brink of drowning.

But then, she heard a voice calling out to her.

It was softer than the others, but it came through with a clarity that silenced the rest. "Don't go, princess, don't go…" it said. Savara recognised the love in these words. They anchored her through the tempest, as they had done many times before. There was something eternal about this plea, as though she'd heard it in other lifetimes.

And doubtless many to come, she realised.

The realisation gave her the strength to fight. She still had tasks to complete in the living world. Savara found her footing amongst the storm in her soul and counted herself out. In an instant, she was whisked away from limbo. She left behind the brink of death for somewhere with equally grim prospects, but this time, she was not alone.

CHAPTER 33

A MEETING WITH DEATH

RETURNING TO LIFE FELT LIKE A JOLT of lightning to the chest—harsh, sharp, and sudden. It was nothing like the peaceful sensation of falling asleep that characterised the other end of the cycle. Death was soft, sweet, light as air. Life was a full-speed run into a brick wall.

Savara took a sharp intake of breath, noticing immediately the density of the air in her lungs. The overwhelming tempest of Iturri still swarmed inside her, worsened here in the land of the physical. She noticed first the sharp, disorienting ringing in her ears. Then, shivers wracked her body. Her senses were ambushed all at once. There were lights, and sounds, and dizzying winds… She furrowed her brow, still unable to open her eyes. Another breath forced its way into her lungs. She coughed. Then, she noticed the restring grip of muscular arms around her torso.

"I can't breathe..." she mumbled, struggling against the arms. Whoever restrained her pulled her up to his chest. Her chin rested awkwardly in the crook of his neck. A sigh of relief hit her ears before she felt the trickling of warm tears down her back.

"Thank heavens you're alive, Sav," Jasper whispered. "I thought I'd lost you..."

"Jasper..." she sighed, relieved at the sound of his voice.

The echo of the promise Iturri had made to her in limbo rang out in her mind.

Savara took another deep breath before forcing her eyes open. She pressed herself off his chest and stared up into his vibrant brown eyes. She hadn't realised how much she'd missed them, or the mess of sun kissed curls that spilled over them, or the dorky relieved smile he brandished now. But then, her gaze dropped. His neck, his shoulders, his arms... They were all streaked with blackened veins of having meddled with the shadows.

"Jasper, how did you get these?" she asked. He hesitated. She knew he hadn't wanted her to see them, but there was no use in hiding it. Even if she didn't see the veins, she could feel his faded heartbeat. "I know what they're doing to you," she added as she closed a gentle hand over his afflicted forearm. The energy of the shadows swirled around beneath his skin. "I can fix it, I promise."

She pushed herself off him and made to stand. The sensation of being on her feet after a prolonged period in limbo was dizzying. She leaned up against the dais as she composed herself. Around her, the others were still engaged in combat. No one had realised she'd returned.

"What do you mean…?" Jasper asked, following her to stand.

"I—" she began, when a sudden, blinding flash appeared, followed by an echoing crack.

A bolt of lightning broke free into the sky above, lighting up the heavens and echoing over everything for miles. Instantly, all eyes were on her once more. Alexei's sudden outburst quelled the war between light and dark. She felt the renewed force of their gazes burning into her skin.

"It seems," Alexei called over the chaos, "our Lady Death has returned to the land of the living." He looked over at Amon briefly and smirked. "I did tell you, cousin, time heals—"

"I'll deal with you later," Amon growled in response. His eyes, filled with renewed hope, rested heavily on her. They burned with the same passion she'd seen of him in the Arima forests. Savara wished to get lost in them, spend eternity in the stolen glance and silent conversation, but the sudden sound of her father's voice cut their moment short.

"Ah, the final act," called the Prince of Shadows.

Savara turned to face him. The fight had charred his suit and tousled his hair, but the grin on his face made the rest of him look entirely unruffled, as though he'd expected the return. The shadows still curled around him, growing hungry at the sensing of her presence. But there was more to their hunger than just the simple taste of fresh life. Like called to like. She knew as well as he did that the shadows sensed Iturri within her. If she wasn't careful, Iturri would take over.

"No…" screamed the Princess of Light from the other side of the amphitheatre.

Savara's skin prickled, sensing the energy shift around her. Malice festered in the corner around the leader of the Izar. Before she knew it, an attack barrelled her way. Bursts of light that seemed to be distilled from the very stars above and deadly as a thousand suns hurled towards her.

Then, the world around her slowed. She saw the shock spreading across the faces of her friends. Sebas moved to shield Storm. Griffin, Brass, and Amon prepared for their own strikes. Jasper sidestepped in front of the attack.

But Iturri would not let anything jeopardise its freedom. A wall of lavender light erupted from her, sidestepping her friends and swallowing the attack. Another vicious shockwave rippled through the amphitheatre, sending everyone else to their knees except for her, the Prince of Shadows, and the Princess of Light.

In the aftermath, Savara was quick to catch hold of the woman's soul, preventing any further strikes. With the added strength of Iturri coursing through her veins, she felt invincible—even if only for the moment. She raised a hand, caging the rogue leader of the Izar in the chains of her own spirit, and rendering her unable to move.

Unfiltered fear bloomed across her face. If she had ever questioned Savara's power, she realised in that moment the gravity of her mistake.

The rest of the world was quiet. All the chaos faded the moment she'd returned from limbo. Now, after the attack, no one so much as breathed, fearing the immense power rippling from her. Fearing her. Iturri swirling inside her lapped up the feeling, relishing in the recognition of its power.

Once again, Jasper was the only one to find the courage to break the silence. "Sav… Your eyes…" he called out to her, his voice tentative at best.

Savara hardly heard him over the chorus within her that hailed her as it once had in limbo, as the Queen of Daemons, but as she turned to him, the clarity of the concern in his eyes brought her down from the high. He held a blade out towards her, allowing her to see the vibrant lilac glow of her eyes reflected in the metal. She realised instantly what they'd all seen—what they'd all feared… Her eyes were tinged with the tempest of the god she housed.

And that god was not one to sit quietly. It stared back at her through the steel, waiting for her to make good on the words she'd said in limbo. It would pull the shadows from Jasper and send them back from whence they came, among other things, but its patience was waning. Savara knew it was time to keep up her end of the promise.

"Stand back, everyone," she said. The voice that echoed from her lips sounded less like her own and more like the ethereal being that lay within. She picked up the dagger, spurred on by the hunger of the being inside her as it drew closer to freedom. The charged air around her prickled her skin, anticipation filling it.

Savara slit her palm, holding the stream of blood over the dais. Each droplet hissed as it fell upon the stone. She took a deep breath and waited. The god within her knew what was coming, as did her spirit. The bittersweet cold of Death filtered its way into the air. Her blood called to it, and Death was not one to leave a call unheeded.

Suddenly, a plume of ethereal smoke appeared. It drifted up from the stone flooring, picking up speed as it whipped around her. Fire erupted from somewhere in the stands, hurtling towards the ominous smoke. The acute scent of ash flooded over the amphitheatre, along with flashes of light, the crashing of rocks, and the sharp crack of broken ice.

Beyond the vortex, someone screamed her name, the sound filled with the acutest torture.

The elements were at war. The fight for survival was at stake, but she was numb to it all. The world around her might have been filled with noise, but the closer she got to her final moment, the quieter it became. The whole scene reminded her of a silent dream. A nightmare she'd once had…

A sober smile graced her lips as she realised that she would finally learn how it ended.

Darkness swarmed overhead, showering her with something that looked a lot like travelling dust. She prepared herself for the nauseating sensation of vanishing, but instead of disappearing, being whisked away to somewhere else, someone appeared before her.

The figure she'd encountered at the gates to the Arima lands stood expectantly at the edge of the dais. It was exactly as she'd remembered it, faceless and entirely made of something darker than shadow. It watched her, as it had at the edge of the cliff, like the solemn sentinel it was.

The winds whipped around them, roaring louder than any living creature could, barring anyone from approaching. She was locked in with the figure, alone. Beyond the vortex, she could hear the faint voices of the others, calling out for her amidst the chaos. Despite the uproar beyond, the figure spoke with a softness and clarity that made her bones quake.

"Princess Savara, daughter of flame and shadow, you have knocked on the forbidden gates. Have you come to steal its secrets?"

The figure's words gave her pause. An eerie sense of déjà vu caressed her. She'd heard a similar phrase used by the priest in Idune. Back then, the priest had told her of what he'd deemed a prophecy—what she now realised was the legend of the stones. He'd said that death and darkness followed her like intimate companions. She hadn't understood the gravity of such a statement back then. But now, staring at the figure whose question mirrored that of the priest, Savara realised how literal his words had been.

The realisation was sudden but unsurprising. It finally occurred to her, the identity of this mysterious creature, this entity of seemingly infinite knowledge that observed all. It had followed her out of limbo the first time Alexei had sent her here. It watched over her, even in the waking world. Part of it lingered within her—within everyone.

It had been staring her in the face all along. The identity of the mysterious figure was no mystery at all. She saw it in the tilt of its head and the blackness of its form, the intent, the purpose. Its presence filled the air with the scents of bonfire ash and petrichor. The stillness that surrounded it was unrivalled by anything of the mortal realm. The only question she had was why it had taken her so long to realise who this creature was and what role it performed.

It was a guard, but not just any guard. It was *the* guard.

The one that lingered in the shadows and struck fear into the hearts of all. The one that filled the stories of this and all mortal worlds, known by many names but acknowledged for a singular purpose. The one that watched over all souls, laying claim to them when their time had come.

This was Death.

* * *

The sudden gale caught them all by surprise. Even in the midst of the violent clash between the leaders of shadows and light, the plume of smoke commanded the attention of all. As did the creature that appeared inside it.

"Griffin, she's still in there!" cried Storm.

"I know," he replied, straining against the force of oncoming attacks. Griffin held his protective stance, shielding his friends from the shockwave caused by the colliding shadow and light. The force of the blow rippled across his body. The battle between the Prince of Shadows and the leader of the Izar was in full swing. If left to their squabble, these two beings of immense power would tear the island apart. And that said nothing of the two violent cousins engaged in their own war. "Get back to the ship!" he yelled, still catching his breath from the force of the last blow.

Among the fallen, he sought out Jasper, who had been standing next to Savara as the plume appeared, and whose body would not take much more damage, given the shadows already residing within him. He held his breath a beat, searching for his friend's mop of brown curls against the shadowy backdrop.

Shit, Jasper…

Griffin spied him attempting to reach for Savara through the plume. A line of blood streamed from his forehead. The vicious gale ripped at his clothes and his skin, but still he kept at it. Griffin let out a sharp huff, preparing to race towards him when the leader of the Izar sent another slash of light through the arena. He shielded his eyes from the fallout. The resulting blow hit one of the walls instead, sending dust and stones flying in all directions. The Harri troops did their best to catch them in midair and move them from the crowd, but the barrage was never-ending.

When he reopened his eyes, he noticed Lance running towards the dais as well, as if he could do something the rest of them could not. A shifting dark caught his eye this time. He turned briefly, spying the Prince of Shadows' raised hands. Another attack. And Lance was about to get caught in the crossfire.

"Lance!" Griffin called, sending forth a shield of light that protected him from the next blast. The force knocked them both off their feet. "Stay down," he said as he crawled towards Lance.

"Griffin…"

"What in Iturri's name were you thinking?" he growled as he reached his friend.

"I love you."

Griffin glowered at him. "That's what you were thinking? And you chose now of all times—"

"No, I was trying to save my sister," Lance coughed, trying to catch his breath from the fall. "But I'm telling you now what I should've told you years ago, in case I don't get the chance…"

"Don't be an idiot," Griffin replied furiously. But Lance saw through his fury. He'd always seen straight through to his core. "We'll have time."

"You know me," Lance said softly. "Timing was never my strong suit."

Suddenly, the sharp crash of lightning sounded overhead.

The sound halted the battle taking place around them only momentarily. The pair of them looked towards the dais. Amon and Alexei's squabble had ended. Alexei approached Savara, the way no one else could. He carved his way through the plume as if it had no effect on him. Amon was left fighting the gale.

"No!" Lance cried out as he got to his feet. He shot a hand out, firing a blast of flames that would've levelled an entire field, but it did nothing to break through the winds.

"Brass!" Griffin shouted, asking for assistance.

Brass seemed to have read his mind, already looking to calm the winds. He tried directing the winds, manipulating their flow, but to no avail. "It is no use," Brass called over the howling currents. "It is no ordinary gale. Iturri does not want us present."

* * *

Around her, Savara felt a gentle warmth caress her skin. It felt like peace, like spring showers and summer nights. Like slumber and serenity. It felt like home. *The home to which we all return*, she realised. She realised this lingering sensation was the work of the creature. It was the precursor to the inevitable.

Savara allowed herself to succumb to the figure's manipulative powers of relaxation. She took a deep breath before repeating the words she'd spoken to the priest in Idune.

"Only death may hide, only time may steal, only blood bears witness to the truths we conceal."

The delay between her words and the figure's response had her questioning whether her plan would work, but Savara stood her ground.

Finally, the figure spoke again.

"Speak now, let your wishes be heard. What is it you seek?"

"To restore balance," she said, feeling the proddings of Iturri within her waiting for release. "I wish to set Iturri free."

The figure, Death, nodded. "A living soul must be given."

Savara held firm to her decision. "I know…"

"Take mine," Alexei said, strolling easily through the tempest.

"How did you—"

He approached her, hovering intimately over her as he stroked the stones on her outer ear. "We were bound to Death, princess," he replied.

"But…" She cast her gaze between him and the creature, who made no objections to his request. "Why did you do it?" Savara asked, realising he'd known all along the outcome of such a bond. She'd seen the decision in him when they'd first made it. She'd known there was something more to his request. After all, he himself admitted to never doing anything unless it involved payment. There had been no way of knowing that this was his true prize.

Alexei's eyes glittered with something she'd never seen before, something he'd sworn away from.

Hope.

"Freedom," he replied. "Somewhere beyond this cage, there is a world of souls who do not consider me a monster. Somewhere in that world, my mother is waiting, and I figured the best chance I have at finding her is through the master itself."

So, that was it… Savara realised. *You'd wanted to stare Death in the eyes when you went…*

All bonds in Visanthe can be broken into two things. A hold and a release. The hold is established through conditions, in the same way a contract keeps two or more parties accountable. The release is the fulfilment of such agreements, be they through the completion of a task or the inevitable calling of death. These rules had not changed; not since her first bond with Big Tog, and certainly not now in her bond with Alexei. Death had always been the final mediator, just as life had always been the playing ground.

"You were never a monster," Savara said, tears welling in her eyes as she spoke.

"I was what the world needed of me, as were your father and my aunt, as were you…"

Savara couldn't help herself. She threw her arms around his neck and squeezed. "I'm sorry, Alexei," she whispered.

For once he had no complaints. He embraced her fully so that she could hear the heavy beating of his heart beneath his chest.

"One thing, princess," he said as he took her chin between his fingers and raised it to meet his gaze. "My cousin doesn't deserve you. He never will. But make sure he works like the devil to come close." With that, he planted a gentle kiss on her forehead.

Savara could no longer hold back the tears. They flowed freely from her eyes as she rested a hand on his chest. She tapped into the part of Iturri that remained in her for now, calling upon its power in the world of the living. "*Agur*, Alexei," she whispered, releasing them from their bond, and inevitably into the arms of Death.

"The toll is paid, daughter of flame and shadow. The cage will be broken once you will it," Death said as it inclined its head. "Thank you, for freeing my counterpart." As it turned once more towards the walls of the vortex, Savara heard it call out to her in a final goodbye. "We will meet again but once more in the world of the living, princess of flame and shadow," it said. "That next time will be yours."

"I know," she replied.

"Until then, may our paths cross in limbo." Death did not wait for her reply. The gale around them vanished as suddenly as it had appeared, taking Death and Alexei along with it.

CHAPTER 34

THE END OF AN ERA

THE TEMPEST DIED ALMOST INSTANTLY, but the ritual was not yet finished. Savara let her hand hover over the stones of the dais, connecting with the souls they were bound to and the omniscient being within. She remembered a similar sensation on this very same dais on the day she received her divination. The same forces that gave her the magic that day were unceremoniously stripping it from her now, sucking them from the veins beneath her skin.

"*Agur,*" she whispered, willing Iturri from her blood the way her father had taught.

Savara found herself fading with each droplet. She focused on her breath to steady herself as Iturri drained from her body. The wound magically sealed itself, hardening into the usual crystals of soulbonds, ending the ritual—and the imprisonment.

Thank you, a voice whispered in her ear. It was soft and intimate, like a heart flutter. Savara knew instantly where it had come from, and that she was the only one who would've heard it. The only one who could.

Light-headedness took over. She swayed on her feet, falling swiftly into a safe pair of muscled arms. Their touch alone collected the fragments of her soul dispersed by the ritual. She took a deep breath. The sweet scent of night flowers spilled over her, sending gentle shivers down her arms and spine.

"I've got you, princess," Amon said. "You're safe in my arms."

"I know," Savara whispered in reply. She let herself linger in the point before the blackout, relishing in the renewed stillness of her soul. There was something to it she'd never felt before. More than stillness, it was fulfilment, completion… Balance. For the first time in her life, she felt unburdened by the yearning in her heart. For the first time, her soul was at peace.

In the moments in between, there was silence…

Then, a sharp crack echoed from the stone.

Suddenly, a blinding white light erupted from the dais. It beamed up into the night sky, momentarily washing everything it touched in shades of monochrome grey. The fires around the amphitheatre died. The world went dark again, but this time, it wasn't the suffocating dark of the shadows. This darkness held no monsters, no fear. It was a gentle blanket over the resting world, putting to rest the demons of the past, finally, completely. In a few hours, the sun would rise over a world resembling the one from the previous night, but which had somehow been irrevocably changed.

Old cycles had finally closed. Endings gave way to beginnings, the way they always had, and always would, from now until eternity—and even that couldn't encompass the depths of forever.

"No!" screamed the Princess of Light, her voice echoing in the stillness of the night. "No! You wretch! You've ruined everything!" Her eyes burned with the fury of the hottest blue fires. She cast beams of destructive light towards the dais, wanting to destroy it and Savara.

Amon held her close, readying himself to take the brunt of the attack. He raised a shield of light in front of them. However, before it landed, the Prince of Shadows stepped in. Walls of shadow raised around them, narrowing in on the leader of the Izar as they swept across the amphitheatre. Her malicious light disappeared, consumed by the darkness. The crashing sound that came from their impact reverberated throughout.

"Your reign has ended, Aurelia," he said over the booming echo.

Savara looked up at the Prince of Shadows in awe. His form was crisp and solid—a thing of flesh, blood, and bone. The bloodied red colour had drained from his eyes, returning them to their ancestral rainbow-flecked black. He looked once more like the man she'd seen in the memories, the one unchanged by Iturri's corrupting power. And despite having returned to his mortal form, he was still a force to be reckoned with.

She'd done it.

He was free.

"I will not allow it—" the leader of the Izar panicked, but the Prince of Shadows silenced her qualms.

"Your wish holds no power over Iturri," he declared, his voice unwavering in its conviction. In tandem, he and Amon cast beams of sharpened shadow and light in her direction.

The attack was swift, supernaturally fast and unavoidable, as though Iturri itself had guided it. The blow caught her off-guard, piercing her chest with ease. Aurelia looked up at him, terror highlighted in the whites of her eyes. Blood began to pool beneath her shivering form. "Our time has come, Aurelia. This world is ours no longer," said the Prince of Shadows.

She was speechless, gaping as she stared at the wound. The shadows covered her, trapping her in their darkness as they dragged her towards the dais.

The Prince of Shadows then turned to Savara, a look of regret crossing his face. "I was not much of a parent to you," he admitted. His gaze bounced between her, Amon, and the rest of her friends. "But I see you will be left in good hands."

Savara furrowed her brow. "What do you mean?" She felt Amon squeeze her shoulder as an act of comfort.

The Prince of Shadows noticed this too, allowing a gentle smile to cut through the regret. "We come from two different worlds… Mine needed an ending, yours a beginning."

He outstretched a hand towards her, helping her to her feet. As their hands touched, her powers fluttered with an energy of recognition. That of kindred spirits. There was a look of familial duty in his eyes, one that had come about too late, but was appreciated all the same. And he knew it too. His shadows pooled at his feet, resting like sated dogs. The malice in them had faded. They were guardians of the past whose duties had been fulfilled.

"It is the way of the world, my child," he added. "We are bound to cycles. To growth. To change. This is the reason we cannot linger in stagnancy, lest our hearts grow restless and resentful." He shot a sorrowful glance towards the dying leader of the Izar. "The lessons we learn in this life shall carry on to the next, allowing our souls to progress and find our happiness. And until we do, we will repeat these cycles…" He looked back at her, pride gleaming in his eyes.

As Savara stared into them, she noticed the advance of time on his face. The chains of the curse had been lifted. He was free… Free to live, but also to leave. He'd found his happiness in this longest of long lifetimes, and he knew as well as she did that it lay beyond this world. The choice had long been made in his heart. Finally, he could act on it.

"So we may rise and fall and rise again," Savara replied, referencing the legend that had foretold the day's events.

At the time, she hadn't fully understood these words. The cyclical nature of life had escaped her grasp. Now, having been at the mercy of it, she found the thought of such cyclical renewal comforting. Perhaps in another cycle, they might have a better relationship. One in which familiarity and filial duty could flourish. One unmarked by blood. For now, she was content with the knowledge that there had been nothing lost that couldn't be found again. Somewhere, beyond this lifetime, there were other chances at happiness. She made her peace with that fact. It seemed the Prince of Shadows had as well.

Savara wondered if he hadn't known all along that it would come to this, that all the torture he'd put her through was for this singular moment. There was no darkness in his eyes as he spoke. No malice either. As she noted before, he looked once more like the young man in the portrait back at the House of Spirits—the one with the rich heritage of rainbow-flecked eyes and a spirited glow in his skin. It comforted her to know that he would leave this world in this form, rather than the one that had haunted the nightmares of generations.

Reality began to settle in. The grounds had been scorched and stained with blood. The delegations from each nation had dwindled in number. So much had been destroyed in the various battles throughout the night that it was hard to see where they were to go from here, where they would even start to rebuild a world that had been plagued by a fear of the dark for centuries.

"The dais is gone…" she said, her look alluding to the rest of the damage as well. "The Divinations…"

The Prince of Shadows shook his head. "There will no longer be a need for such things. Iturri is free to roam the lands as it pleases, without being bound to rings in a limited capacity." He cast his gaze around the lands. His eyes sparkled with the curiosity of a last glance, in which one finds that the seemingly familiar sights become anything but. "There will be no need for this prison any longer."

"What shall we do with it?"

"Let not these lands wither in melancholia, but let no man claim them for his own, lest the history be forgotten and repeated."

His words fell upon the lands like a prophecy. Perhaps, sometime in the future, they may be. But for now, they were simply words of wisdom, of peace.

"It is time I allow my cycle to close so that a new one may begin," he said as he pressed a gentle kiss to her hand. "It is time for me to go home… For us to go home…"

"Father…" Savara stopped him, holding tight to his hand. She didn't know how she meant to follow the word. It tasted strange on her tongue. Such a simple word, and yet it felt loaded. That word was supposed to talk of a connection, not unlike soulbonds, that ran blood-deep. But when their time together had been fraught with danger and destiny, such definitions held little weight.

Part of her wished they might have properly explored their relationship. The man uncorrupted by Iturri had shown genuine care and compassion to his people. He'd fought for his friend and the love of his life. But that wasn't the man she'd known. The man she'd known was one of shadow, one of nightmares. Only the last part of their relationship resembled anything familial. It would be a lie to say she would miss him, but she also couldn't deny that he had made her into the person she was today. He'd taught her the ways of the world, the truth behind her powers. In his sacrifice, he'd given her freedom.

There was nothing she could say to encompass the complexity of her feelings. And yet, the word alone seemed to suffice.

The Prince of Shadows bobbed his head. He took a step back from her, his eyes sparkling with the same remorse that burdened her mind. His retreat was an offering of solace, removing himself from the situation that might have tethered them to each other, knowing he was not the person she'd needed—nor would he ever be. Instead, he rested one hand on Aurelia's bleeding heart and another on his own. "*Agur*," he whispered.

"Goodbye," Savara whispered in reply as tears streamed down her cheeks.

Amon held her tighter, knowing she needed the comfort. In theory, they would both lose the final remnants of parentage they had left. In practice, however, the souls of their parents had been broken long ago. At least, this way, they would finally be free. As she looked up into his eyes, she noticed the shifting of his ebony black hair to the blinding white colour of starlight. In that moment, she realised everything was going to be okay.

The leader of the Izar screamed as his shadows consumed her. The bursts of light were too strong to look at, so they all shielded their eyes. After a few seconds, both souls vanished. Their bodies crumpled to the ground, lifeless and grey. Looking at them now, one would never have guessed that only moments before, they had been the two most powerful beings in all of Visanthe.

CHAPTER 35

REUNITING

FOR A LONG TIME, NOT A SOUL STIRRED. The silence consoled them like grey clouds at a funeral. Those who had not already fled to the safety of their ships gathered around the corpses. A chill rustled in the twilight breeze.

Savara stared at her father's body, noticing the serenity plastered across his face. *He's gone to be with her…* she realised. Her spirit lifted. There was relief in her laboured breath.

Then, she caught a glimpse of her reflection in the discarded dagger. Something about it had changed since before Iturri's release. She picked it up, holding it at an angle to better see her eyes in the reflective surface of the blade.

Whatever restrictive properties the curse had placed on her were gone. Instead of the muted flecks she'd grown accustomed to, her eyes glowed vibrantly, rimmed with a shifting pearlescent hue whose lilac base matched the colour of her powers. Her body was worse for wear, but her eyes had never looked more alive.

"Is that it then?" Jasper asked, breaking the contemplative silence. "Is it over?"

Savara beamed up at him before wrapping her arms around his neck in a loving embrace. "It is, Jasper. It's finally over." Tears streamed down her cheeks and onto his neck. She knew he felt them, but he made no mention of them.

Instead, he pulled her in closer.

They hadn't held each other in this way in a long time. Being in his arms felt like coming home. He smelled like ash and iron, tinged with the sharp scent of blood—his own and that of others. Jasper carried himself with a confidence that she hadn't seen in him in the human world. His body was larger than she remembered it. In their time apart, she could tell he'd trained...a lot.

But then, she pulled away, remembering the blackened veins tracing the length of his body. It wasn't over. Not yet. Not until he was safe. She'd done her part, she'd freed Iturri. In return, it had left her with the strength to release the shadows from Jasper's body. She felt the extra power coursing through her.

Savara knew she could've used her powers to soften him, but she preferred that the decision be his alone. She caught hold of his wrist, clenching hard to it as he flinched so that he wouldn't try to brush her off. She imagined he knew what she was about to do. What she was about to reveal. She gazed lovingly into his eyes, pleading with him, and hoping he understood her pleas. The ramifications of such a revelation were great, but they weren't worth dying over.

Jasper nodded. He could hide from the world, suppress his pain from anyone else—anyone but her. There had been too much shared past between them for him to even wish to hide from her.

Savara bit her lip as she prepared herself for what lay beneath the cloth. She pulled tentatively at his tunic, opening it to expose the extent of the damage. The darkness trailed up his arms and over his shoulders, reaching for his heart.

Stifled gasps sounded from within the crowd.

She'd caught it. Just in time.

"What did this?" she asked softly.

"A book," Jasper replied, and as if to ease her worries added, "I guess that's why they say reading is a dangerous thing, huh?"

She let out a sigh of relief, disguised within a snorting laugh. "Only you would make jokes on your deathbed."

"Better me than someone else. Although now that you're all good with Death, maybe you should convince it to get a new look. Ditch the solemnity and sobriety. That way, people won't be as put out by it."

"Jasper, I think they'll be put out regardless," she joked, relishing in the renewed intimacy.

Part of her had feared their connection would've changed once the dust had settled. So many things already had. But not them. Never them.

"Fair point. Might have to speak with it myself when I get there…" he mocked.

"You're not going anywhere. I told you I would fix it," she replied.

He smiled, his brown eyes overflowing with love. "And I know you can."

She'd missed him. She'd missed him more than words could ever explain.

"I'm sorry I got you into this mess," Savara said, unable to meet his gaze due to the new set of tears welling in her eyes.

Jasper lifted her chin towards him. "I would do it all over again just to see you like this."

"What do you mean?"

His eyes fell upon Amon, who surveyed them cautiously, and then back to her. "Happy."

Savara smiled. "I love you, Jasper."

"I love you too, Sav," he replied, pulling her in for another hug. She felt him plant a kiss on the crown of her head.

There was something to be said for the undying nature of their friendship. In the time they'd spent apart, they'd grown into the people she knew they were meant to be. But no matter how much had changed, their love for one another had not. Whether or not they'd chosen to be with one another, they'd chosen to love each other, to stand by each other. And this was something no darkness could touch, not that of Visanthe or any other world in this lifetime or beyond.

"When we get back to Arima——"

"Savara!" Storm screamed, her desperate cry ringing over the stillness of the moment. She ran over to them with tears overflowing. Her eyes were consumed with the deepest maddening sense of pain and sorrow. She was frantic. Pleading.

Savara had never seen Storm show so much emotion. It broke her heart. But more than that, it meant something was severely wrong.

"Savara!" Storm cried again, tossing herself onto the floor at her feet.

Savara dropped to her knees to meet her eyes and reached out to steady her trembling shoulders. "Storm, what's wrong?"

"Fix him," she breathed. "Bring him back. Please…" The words came through hoarse between her sobs. "I can't do it alone…" Her hands went to her stomach, but her gaze didn't falter.

"Who?" Savara asked, but the realisation was beginning to hit.

"I can't lose him," Storm begged, her eyes burning with the ache of lost love.

Sebas.

"Where is he?"

Unable to speak, Storm tugged at her arm and dragged her through the throng of people. Fear rippled from her in a way Savara had scarcely seen before.

I hope I'm not too late…

Sebastian was in a sorry state. He'd been battered and bruised in the worst of ways. Streams of dark blood had dried along the sides of his mouth and beneath his ears. His clothes were torn through and burned, as was the flesh beneath them. His usually glowing tanned skin was pale and afflicted with death. Bluish dark splotches encircled his eyes, creeping over his cheeks. His breathing was soft and ragged.

Savara clapped her trembling hands to her mouth to stifle a sob. As she neared, she felt the mountains of pain emanating from him. The sensation was overwhelming, and much worse than it appeared on the exterior. She was sure he'd broken bones and lost more blood than he could bear to lose.

Death was close. After having only just left with one friend, it had returned, waiting for another. It lingered in the air around them, evident but unspoken, hovering over him with a raised blade to sever his spirit from this world.

"You have to do something!" yelled Storm frantically as streams of tears poured over her cheeks.

"I…" Savara stuttered. If there was anything her time with the Prince of Shadows had taught her, it was that dead meant dead. There was no bringing anything back from the world beyond the veil.

But he isn't dead… Not yet… came a voice from within her. She realised that if she could still feel the pain emanating from him, there was a sliver of hope that he could be brought back. If only she could reach for him in time, she might just be able to save him.

The brink of death was a place not unlike limbo. If the will of the dying soul was strong enough, it could be convinced back, though it would come at a heavy price. She'd brought back the rose in the garden of the holding grounds, but that had brought with it a migraine. To bring back an entire being, an entirely complex human soul… Savara knew it might kill her in the process.

"I might be able to bring him back, but it comes with a price. The toll on my life, especially in the state I'm in—"

"Use mine," Storm blurted out before she could even finish the thought.

"But you're in the same, if not worse—"

"Savara," Storm growled. "Use. Mine." Seeing the resolution in her eyes, Savara knew there was no convincing her of the contrary. "I cannot lose him," she added, waiting for Savara to agree. "I will not lose him."

Savara sighed. "Alright, give me your hand," she said, hoping that she was strong enough for the both of them. She carved a slit down the side of Storm's arm before repeating the same act with Sebastian. "Repeat after me, I hereby entangle our lives. From this day forward, our hearts beat as one heart, our breath is one breath, our souls are bound as one soul."

Storm repeated the words without fail, but that was only half the battle. Now came the hard part. Sebastian needed to do the same. Whether in this world or from within the veil.

Savara took a breath and retreated inward, unsure if such a meditation would be sufficient to get her to where she needed to go. The voice in her head reassured her that all she needed was inside her. That it had been all along. She quelled the barrage of doubts flowing through her mind by counting herself down, as her father had taught her to do in the gardens. She released the sensations of the physical world, allowing herself to fall into a trancelike state of stillness, and looking for that world she knew existed within her. The chaos of the living world faded.

A chill washed over her as the familiar sense of omniscient nothingness filled her heart. Soon, she lost track of the world of the living entirely. By the time she opened her eyes, only darkness surrounded her. Tentative happiness pulsed from her spirit. Perhaps this was part of the gift left for her by Iturri, the ability to move in and out of these lands on a whim. Regardless, she'd done it. Once more, she was alone in the void.

"Sebas!" she cried out. "Please be here…" she said when she heard no response.

Then, as always, the tree appeared. The streams of lifetimes glowed through the marks in its branches. Even at the relative distance, she realised she had started to understand them. She noticed the curious connections between the streams. Some were straight, tracing the length of a single branch, others forked out onto multiple branches. Some were cut, others led to flowers at the tips of the tree. Some intertwined with others, and others merged completely in notches. All were connected through the never-ending network of roots beneath it. It was beautiful. It was life.

Suddenly, a flickering figure appeared, seated beneath the tree of time. Savara's spirit lifted.

Sebas.

"Savara? How are you here? Where are we?" he asked, his voice soft and his form fading in and out. "You look worried. Is something wrong?"

Even in the void, fading forms were never a good sign. Her happiness dipped. He was going. There was no time left for quaint conversation.

"Sebas, do you want to come back?" She rushed through the words, unsure when his figure would fade entirely.

"Back?" he replied, his voice unhurried.

"The world of the living," she said.

He furrowed his brow. "Am I dead?"

"Almost."

"Is… Is Anika okay?"

If they had time, she would've smiled at the way that, even in his own death, Sebas still thought of her. "She's seen better days, but she's alive," Savara replied.

The moments between his flickering form grew longer, but his spirit was entirely at ease—a hallmark of the blissfulness of the transition. "If I choose to move on, what happens?"

"I'm not entirely sure, but I get the feeling there are other lives to be lived," she replied, unable to hide the sadness in her tone.

"And if I stay?"

"There's a woman up there willing to give up half her life to make sure you do."

Sebastian smiled. "Well…" He stood up and walked towards her. The closer he got, the less his figure began to fade. "It sounds like I don't have much of a choice, do I?"

Already she could feel his soul clinging faster to that last bit of life his body held within it. Relief flooded through her; there was a chance he would make it after all.

"You always have a choice," she said.

"No, Savara… You don't get it. With her, there has never been a choice at all."

But she did get it. She'd found the same with a curious apprentice whose life had intertwined with hers across both worlds—and doubtless many other lifetimes. There was something underlying what they could see. A tie that only their souls could feel. She realised that one soul was always more attuned to these calls than the other, but eventually, such connections would settle. They could not be outrun forever.

Savara nodded, offering him her hand. "Alright, repeat after me…"

The crowd had been holding its breath the entire time she'd been gone. As she reopened her eyes, she realised just how many people needed this to work, not just as a testament to the strength of her powers, but as one to the strength of true love. Undying love. She hadn't realised it before her descent into the void, but she was anxiously hoping for the same. If there was anything in the world more powerful than death, she hoped it was love.

Savara bit her lip nervously, almost to the point of drawing blood, as she waited for a sign that the bond had worked. Storm's arm continued to bleed—a bad sign. In theory, it should've stopped the moment they'd uttered the words. Sebastian's wound bled soft and slow, with little more than the echo of a heartbeat to force the blood from his veins. Soon, his chest went still. No signs of life, let alone breath.

It's not holding, she feared. *Maybe he was too far gone… Maybe he'd chosen to stay after all… Maybe…*

But before she could finish her thought, something fizzled. Storm's wound seared itself closed, leaving the trademark gash of rubies encrusted in her skin. Sebastian's followed suit. The world went silent, needing to hear the slightest of sounds. Just to be sure.

After an endlessly troubling minute, Sebastian took his first sharp inhale. It was only a matter of seconds before the colour returned to his skin.

Savara sensed his heart working overtime to get him up and moving again.

"It…worked," she whispered, tears streaming down her cheeks.

Storm clapped a hand over the desperate smile that had appeared on her face. Relief flooded through the crowd. As soon as Sebastian opened his eyes, Storm fell upon his body.

"Gentle, please," he said, forcing the soft words through bruised lungs and broken bones.

"Don't ever do that again," Storm hissed.

"Do what?" Sebastian forced the reply.

"Don't ever go about dying again or I swear I'll kill you myself," she replied, shivering against his chest.

"Dying?" he asked as he tried to console her.

"Do you not remember?" Savara asked.

"I thought it was a dream… My parents were there… And then you appeared…"

"It doesn't matter," Savara said, contemplating the pair of them. "What matters now is that you're alive." She looked around at the faces of all her friends who had gathered to see their mission through. They were bruised and battered and had definitely seen better days, but they were all here. They were all standing. "That we are all alive…"

Amon offered her his hand, helping her to rise amongst them. He wrapped her in his arms, his beautiful scent of night flowers spilt over her. Emotions bubbled up within her. A new day began to break over the horizon, burning the sky with the bright purple and pink hues of dawn. It felt like safety, finally. At the end of such a long road, they were finally able to see a light over the horizon.

CHAPTER 36

AN EMPIRE OF STARS AND SPIRITS

IT HAD BEEN MONTHS SINCE THE EVENTS on Middle Isle, and the world was still coming to terms with the renewed power flooding through it. People were cropping up all over the place with different abilities. The lands themselves had been renewed, transforming even the most scorched and desolate outposts into dreamscapes. It was chaos, but everyone agreed the world needed a little chaos.

Things were going to be different. Just how different was yet to be seen.

For one thing, there would be no more Divination Days. Savara had hardly believed it when the strange spirit in the palace at Osiir had told her such a time existed. Now, she understood what *No One* had wished to express. He was from a time before the Divinations... Before the binding of Iturri.

He'd known all along of the role she was meant to play and tried to warn her. She had a lot of questions for him, but in the meantime, there was work to be done.

The leaders returned to their homelands with a newfound respect for both Iturri and the no-longer banished Arima race. Many of them thanked Savara personally, some even apologising for the role they played in her exile. Others simply agreed to maintain open channels of communication during the adjustment period.

Savara and her friends had returned to the lands of the Arima, which were curiously no longer blocked by wicked storm clouds. The change in the atmosphere was impossible to miss. Life abounded. And not just within the gardens. The grey pallor of the grass and skies, the skeletal corpses of the trees, even the deathly chill of the winds had been replaced by vibrant colours, livelier foliage, and softer skies.

They'd gone there with a mission, of course. Jasper's veins had still been afflicted with the thirst of limbo. Savara took him into the holding ground gardens, along with the strange leatherbound tome resembling those in her uncle's study. Once inside, she'd released the spirit of the book, the entirety of it disappearing in the ethereal garden air. Jasper's veins, however, had been marked permanently.

"I can try healing them," she'd said.

"It's fine. I went to war. No use coming out of it without battle scars," he'd joked, a glimmer of his renewed spirits lighting his big brown eyes.

That was so very like him, too, she'd thought at the time. *Anything to make her smile.*

When they discussed where they would each go from there, however, there was no amusement in his voice.

"I've had my fun and my adventure, but I don't belong here," he'd said.

Part of her had wanted to argue with him. To convince him to stay. After all they'd been through, she wished to relish in their friendship forever. But the sparkle of surety in his eyes swayed her otherwise.

"There's nothing I can say to make you change your mind, is there?" she'd asked, just to be sure.

Jasper embraced her, softening her in the way only he could. "You will always be my best friend. No matter how far apart we are. No matter how many worlds we have to jump or lives we have to lead."

All she could do at that point was hold him tighter. Their friendship had meant so much to her, especially throughout their time in Visanthe. It helped them both blossom into the people they were always meant to be. She realised this now. She also realised that, even though there was more to learn, they would have to do so on their own. Their paths were ready to fork. Jasper had caught onto this realisation long before she had. He was always better at seeing the bigger picture than she was. She was going to miss him dearly, but in the end, this was what he wanted. As a good friend, all she could do was wish him the best.

"Do you know... I might get a little lonely over there..." he'd announced to the group as they pulled apart. "There aren't any seas to tame or battles to be fought, but I'm sure there's still some fun to be had..." he directed the comment at Lucy.

The group turned to watch the mischievous smile grow on her face. "Well… I think I've done enough piracy for one lifetime. These seas and these people have seen the worst of me. It's about time someone saw the best."

Savara fiddled with the hem of her dress again. Something about it didn't sit quite right, no matter how gently she'd tried to lay it on the floor. She wanted it to sweep gracefully, and not clump up in the heap it always seemed to end up in. But it was no use. It practically had a mind of its own.

She sighed, letting out a soft laugh. Considering what happened over the past months, it was almost ridiculous to think this was one of her greatest worries.

The world had changed since their encounter with the Prince of Shadows. Lands had crumbled. Nations united. Rulers had been replaced. And the shadows of the past that had terrorised the world for the better part of a millennial had finally been put to rest.

The world could finally enter an age of peace—and it was their job to usher it in.

"So, little sister, are you ready for the coronation?" Lance called from the entrance to her suite. He strode over to her confidently, glowing with all the warmth of the midday sun. His strides across the granite floors made the flecks in it practically sparkle in salute.

"Lance, there's no need for you to treat me like a child. I'm not the little girl you left behind," she replied, staring at his reflection behind her in the mirror.

The similarities between them were few and far between, owing to the half-sibling nature of their connection, but if one looked hard enough, the signs were there. A curve of their ears, an arch of their brows. But the love between them remained, having grown stronger than ever in the past few months.

"I know," he beamed as he took her in his arms and planted a kiss on the crown of her head. "You certainly have grown…" He heaved a heavy sigh. In it, Savara heard the familiar sounds of melancholia for the childhood that had been stolen from them.

Since their reunion, she'd become intimately acquainted with the sound of such a sigh. In the early hours of twilight— when she found herself unable to sleep out of a residual fear of the monsters of the old world—this same sigh would escape her own lips. There was no wishing for the past. Not after all they had been through. But there was a lingering sense of longing that she doubted she would ever be rid of.

His words, though meant as compliments, left her in a state of contemplation. What would have happened had he not left? Had she not been exiled? What would've happened if she'd never left the island? She'd considered these questions more times than she'd wished to admit. Each time they were brought up, she retreated inward.

When it was clear to him that she had no intentions of responding, Lance whispered—the way one might a prayer to a sleeping child—into the waiting silence, "Mother would be proud."

This caught her off-guard.

Her heart gave a little jolt as he spoke. A stream of tears rolled over her cheeks. Their appearance came as a surprise to her. They came from a place deep within, one she hadn't shed light on in years. "Do you think?" Savara replied.

"I know."

Savara hadn't thought about her mother in a long time. After the time she'd spent with her father, she was done holding on to the ghosts of parents' past. She no longer sought the approval of these titled figures. She'd proven to herself that she was—and always would be—more than enough. She'd become the person she was always meant to be. And she'd done it in spite of them. There was still further to go, the world was far from fixed, and she was far from finished growing, but, with her friends and loved ones by her side, she had the strength to keep at it.

"Save your tears, little sister," Lance added as he wiped the tears from her cheeks. "Your future is waiting, and he needs you to be strong."

Savara smiled. Lance was right. Someone was waiting for her out there, and she knew he wouldn't be patient for much longer. "Let's go, then. Can't keep our King of Light waiting."

Amon paced the floors of the refurbished temple, focusing on the cracks in the marble laid down by the masons. Somehow, this felt like his first test of being a ruler. He worried the imperfect flooring would mark his reign. How could he let it start in such a way? He would have each cracked tile redone when he was crowned. A temple to Iturri should be perfect—or as perfect as it could be.

Savara appeared behind him, looking as resplendent as ever. She took his breath away, the way she had the first time he'd seen her, and every time since. She wore a cowlneck dress that hung on the edge of her shoulders and hugged her petite frame until her hips. From there, it flowed down, like a waterfall of night and starlight. The fabric at her chest was the same ebony colour as her hair, the colour of shadows, but it bled softly into the skirt in glitters until it reached the hem. By then, only shining white gems were visible.

She was a vision.

Suddenly, the cracks in the marble seemed insignificant. The worries he'd had about his reign faded, just as the corners of his vision did when looking at her. It had taken him years to realise it, but she'd been his focus all along. Without her, his goals were simply the product of an obsession with understanding the mysteries of life that should've remained just that. Mysteries. For so many years he'd chased this knowledge, living only in search of a guiding light in a sea of never-ending darkness. But now he knew the satisfaction he'd been seeking would never be found in the knowing. No. It was found in her. In the light behind her eyes, in the softness of her touch, in the sweetness of her laugh. Everything else paled in comparison to her. She was his…

His clarity…

His flame…

"You look like you've seen a spectre," she said, a coquettish smile gracing her perfect lips. Her voice summoned him forward, forced his hands to take hold of hers, pull them to his lips, and plant a gentle kiss on them—the way he planned to do every day for the rest of their lives.

"No spectre could haunt me the way your eyes do, or tease me the way your lips do," Amon replied. "But I beg of you, if you are a spectre, take my every waking moment and my every night's slumber. They are yours."

"You're ridiculous," she laughed, the joyous sound of it sending shivers down his spine.

His heart and soul…

"Ouch, princess," he smirked. "Will Her Highness accept a royal jester for a companion?"

Savara raised her brow and pretended to give the idea some thought. The way she countered his smirk sent his heart into a frenzy. If they hadn't had the coronation to attend, he would've taken the grin from her face, the breath from her lungs, and the dress from her body in that very moment.

"Do I have a choice?" she teased.

His reason…

"Not this time, princess. None whatsoever." Amon guided her body into his, stopping just shy of their touching chests.

Savara reached up and wrapped her arms around his neck, pressing her chest against his. "Perfect," she breathed against his lips.

She drove him crazy in the best of ways, and she knew it. She used every one of her womanly charms against him, and he fell at her feet, no magic required. That abuse of power turned him on even more. If she insisted on such tricks, they wouldn't leave the room.

"Do that again and I will ruin all the work of the nice folks who painted your face and tailored your dress," he countered, straining against every urge to be with her, here and now.

"We can't have that," she giggled. "Not yet. Someone still needs to take up the mantle of King of Light."

"Forget the crown, forget the coronation, all I need is you," he purred softly in her ear. Judging by the way she seemed to melt slightly in his arms, he knew he had an effect on her as well. Since the battle, they'd been able to share their emotions more freely. He still had traumas to work through—as did she—but they were doing it together. Something about their shared healing was even more intimate than any actualised carnal desires.

"You may need me, but they need you," she replied, her tone soft and sobering. She was right, after all. Many people were counting on him to usher them into a new age of peace.

"They need *us*," he countered. "A Queen of Darkness and a King of Light."

Savara bit her lip, the idea toying around in her head. "It has a nice ring to it, doesn't it?" she said after a moment's thought. "Can I make one request of you, my jester?" she mocked, a twinge of mischief dancing in the lilac glow of her eyes.

"Anything. Anything at all," he replied, losing himself to her the moment she reached up and twirled a lock of his newly white hair around her gentle fingers.

"Careful with what you agree to, this one is serious." Her voice was low and intimate, a thing born of secret escapades and promises at twilight.

"Should we make a bond of it?" he asked, lowering his to match.

Savara grinned as she traced her fingers down his neck. Taunting him. "No need. Something tells me there is one already in place."

Amon raised an eyebrow. "Oh?"

Savara laughed. "This is serious, hear me out."

"Oh, princess, you keep teasing me this way and I won't be able to hear anything," he joked as he trailed kisses up her arms. She smirked as she cupped his cheek, bringing his focus back to her eyes. "Go on," he growled hungrily.

"When we die, as we both will eventually…"

"Not anytime soon, I hope."

"No," she continued, leaning in closer. He pressed his forehead to hers, letting her words lull him into a willing submission. "Come back for me."

She was his everything.

He would complete a thousand painful lifetimes if only they ended up together.

"We'll come back together again," he replied, taking her hands in his and kissing them. "We always do…" And the tingling in his heart told him that she was right. The bond was already there. It always had been, and always would be, but it was made of something much stronger than blood.

EPILOGUE

JASPER RESTED HIS JOURNAL DOWN on the old oak desk and rubbed at his eyes beneath his glasses. The fading light of the afternoon sun cascaded through the bay windows, bathing the room in a burnt umber monochrome. Their grandchildren were coming in from the gardens, readying themselves for supper. He knew his wife would be up soon to drag him from his books.

He stretched his arms and stood, cracking his aged spine (as she'd cautioned him against many times). He found a cheeky pleasure in it, knowing that it had little effect on his health.

"Sweetness, it's time to get your nose out of the paper, the little ones are ready," she said, tapping lightly on the door.

Her voice was as sweet as the island's signature rum—her personality twice as strong. Jasper had the utmost respect for her and knew he wouldn't be anywhere near happy without her. So, he married her as soon as he could. Nothing would have swayed his conviction. Thankfully, she required little convincing in the matter.

"I'll be down in a moment," he replied, smiling at her bright cheeks beneath the bouncy white ringlets of hair that had changed little since they'd met. Very little about her had changed, and he knew it had less to do with her curious obsession with slathering her entire person with cocoa butter and more to do with the unique blood that flowed through her veins.

She winked a sparkling blue eye at him before closing the study door.

Jasper gazed around at the room that had once belonged to another old man. A guardian of sorts. The walls were lined with old bookcases and older books whose gold-embossed spines sparkled in the setting sun's light. He'd kept the desk—which looked like it had arrived before the house—but got rid of the armchair. No use in keeping anything with such memories attached to it. Especially not when the rest of the house did such a spectacular job of keeping the fairytale alive.

He supported himself as he walked down the creaky stairs using his prized gorilla-head-tipped cane. He enjoyed the rhythmic tic of its point on the wood floors, punctuating his footsteps. The sound of it soothed him, as though counting off the steps of a waltz that would lead two people to fall madly in love—but then, he'd always been a romantic. Such thoughts were too fanciful for the common folk to understand, so he resigned to the simple explanation of needing it to walk.

At the base of the staircase, two eager young children practically bolted into him, tugging at the leg of his pants as they spoke.

"Grandpa, can you tell us that story again?" said his granddaughter.

"Which one, child?"

"The one about your friend who fell for a star," she replied, her eyes glittering with wishful fantasy.

"I'm tired of that one, it's not even true," his grandson said as he stuck out a tongue at his sister. "It's just a stupid story."

Jasper smiled. "Oh really?" he countered as he made his way into the dining hall, cautiously avoiding a dark stain on the floors that he'd yet to remove. As he took a seat at the head of the table, his grandchildren parked themselves in the seats on either side of him.

"Of course! There's no way you really fought shadows and people with magic, Grandpa," said his grandson.

"But Gran-Gran said she met Grandpa while they were in the middle of that fight," his granddaughter replied. For a girl as young as her, the loyalty she felt towards his stories was strong, surprising even him.

"That's right, child," said his beautiful wife as she walked into the dining room carrying a heavy stew pot. Her smile, knowing and vibrant, hit him with a wave of happiness. She rested the pot on the table, stopping briefly to plant a kiss on his head before taking a seat. "Alright, no more chat. Let's eat."

As they ate, the room filled with the bright sounds of the children's laughter. Their grandchildren recounted the day's adventure in the gardens and down by the cove beyond the fence. Jasper listened with rapt attention, feigning surprise as they spoke of the strange treasures they'd found hidden amongst the flowers, and down by the beach. He enjoyed how much they loved the house and its mysteries. Even its creaking and phantasmal breezes.

After dinner, Jasper ushered the children upstairs to prepare for bed as his beloved wife got to clearing up. Their mild protests soon turned to sighs marked by sleep. Yawns and stretches and promises of tomorrows filled the rest of their waking hours.

"Grandpa, can you tell us the story again, please?" his granddaughter whispered as he tucked her in.

"I think your brother might have already tired of it, sweet pea," Jasper replied, kissing her forehead.

"It's okay, I can hear it one more time…" his grandson said mid-yawn. The little one stretched his arms out in the twin bed opposite them.

Jasper chuckled, setting himself down on the edge of the bed. "Alright, where do I begin?"

"Once upon a time, in a world full of elemental magic, a young Princess of Fire waited to receive her powers…" said his grandson, having memorised the story after countless retellings.

It didn't take long for the children to drift off, their heads filled with the fantastical tales of people with elemental magic and creatures science could not explain.

"Goodnight, Savara. Goodnight, Griffin," Jasper whispered as he lifted himself off the bed, taking care not to wake them as he crept towards the door and turned out the light. Beyond the room, he pulled out a small pocket watch, smiling as he saw the hands marking 11:11—a sign he'd come to relate to her. He replaced it promptly and made his way back down the stairs. He found his way into the kitchen, where his lovely wife was finishing up with the dishes.

"Did they ask for a different story this time?" she inquired as she rested another dish on the drying rack, her voice filled with amusement.

"Do they ever?" he replied, taking hold of her from behind and planting a kiss in her nest of tightly coiled white curls. He moved beside her, rolling up his sleeves as he joined her in the washing.

"It's almost done, sweetness," she said, glancing up at him with a playful smile.

Jasper leaned in and nuzzled his nose against hers. "I can handle a few dishes."

As he plunged his hands into the warm, soapy water, the veins beneath his skin caught the light, revealing their unchanged black hue. Memories of a different life flowed through them. Reminders of another world that had seemed almost too dreamlike to be real, but whose ramifications still clung fast to his person.

A curious thing it was to hold a secret so powerful, so life-changing, that it demanded to be remembered. Even after all this time, he remembered it as if it had been only yesterday when the strange man who would become one of his best friends appeared at this very same house. Jasper remembered it all with such vivid clarity that, even in his dreams, he found himself returning to the beautiful isles of Solia and Iliso, where he'd first met his wife.

The sensation was so haunting that, at times, he found himself rummaging through the library in search of a little black pouch. A gift from another one of his old friends—a King of Starlight whom he'd promised to visit but had not yet worked up the courage. In that pouch, a curious, ash-like dust waited.

"Lucy, my love," he said as the last of the dishes returned to its home in the cabinet. "I believe it's time for bed."

Together, they turned off the lights and made their way back upstairs, stopping briefly to ensure their grandchildren were still sound asleep before entering their own bedroom. With the house and the world beyond all at peace, the pair of them prepared for rest. As he lay in bed, Jasper's thoughts drifted once more to the stories he had told his grandchildren, the many misadventures of the world beyond.

Here, in the safety of their home, they were a far cry from the battles and bloodshed. Beneath the mosquito netting and soft cotton sheets, those stories seemed like nothing but distant echoes of a past he was no longer sure he owned. Yet, even with all the time that had past, one thing remained abundantly clear in his mind, reverberating in the beat of his sturdy heart. Something he knew would not leave him, not in this lifetime or the ones to come.

Love.

Enjoyed the Legend of the Stones series? I'm currently working on other books set in Visanthe. The next one coming is called **Of Arrows and Roses**. Here's a sneak peek:

CHAPTER 1

CASPAR WOKE UP TO THE SOUNDS of the waning night. He strapped his bow and quiver onto his back and tucked his hunting knife into his tunic before sneaking out into the early dawn. He rounded the house, taking care to stop by his father's window on his way to the edge of the desert. His father lay sound asleep, curled up in wool blankets, well-protected against the colder desert nights. *Good, still sleeping,* he thought as he peered inside.

Their house was a hovel, large stones slapped together and plastered with painted mud, but it held up enough during the limited rainy season and provided enough protection from both the heat and the cold of the desert. The rain gutters dangled freely from the wooden pagoda, torn off in the last of the sandstorms, and unfixed ever since. They had money once, before his father's injury. Time, too, in his mother's life. Now, they had neither, and each day brought new hardships.

The stars above him began to fade, but the rising sun was still lost below the horizon. It was time to go. Caspar pulled up the cloth at his neck in preparation for the roaring, sand-laced winds and set off down the trail. If he was lucky, he'd find a desert rodent or two in the nearest plateau and be back before the morning markets opened; otherwise, it was going to be another long day.

Caspar followed the dusty trails from his village through the weaving canyons that had long since dried out under the harsh sun. What little life remained was sustained on the few creatures that still deigned to call this wasteland home. On days like today, when the rains were still months away and hunger in the village was at its peak, Caspar cursed the burnt sienna trails and blackened, skeletal tree trunks that spoke of a life that must have once thrived here, as though the lands themselves were scarred and damaged. Still, this was his home. He'd never seen anything but the rising canyons and red sands. He'd never known anything but the scorching days and freezing nights under cloudless skies. He'd never been beyond the desert.

The first hour of his search had been in vain. The morning sun had already crossed the horizon and he had nothing to show for it but a light coating of dust on his clothes and in his hair. But Caspar would not be deterred. He made his way farther across the plains until his home canyon was completely obscured by the horizon. He'd never wandered this far from home before. Off in the distance ahead of him, he spied the rising treetops of the forest, where the desert gave way to the *Harri* territories. His father had warned him never to cross into their lands; they were uncivilized warriors. On a good day, Caspar wouldn't have even considered it, but today was no good day. The sun was already high, burning his forehead and bleaching his auburn locks bright red, and he couldn't come back empty-handed.

Caspar raised his forefinger and thumb to the sky. *Just going on eleven,* he thought. He scanned the length of the empty horizon, searching for some semblance of movement, but found only the rising ripples of heat from the dusty red plateau. *Father will wonder what's taking me so long with today's hunt.* Caspar reasoned the best course of action would be to turn back and see if he could trade one of his knives for some basic ground provisions and, if Mr. Nacim was in a good mood, maybe even a jackalope. Those might last a week if they were careful, and with that, he would have another few days to tend to his own grounds before having to hunt again. But the fire in his stomach had not been put out by the blazing sun above, and the stark contrast of the green trees with his own red soil called to him. His bare feet carried him across the sunburned lands to the place of which he'd only dreamed.

The world seemed to know the contours of each territory better than any man. A harsh line in the ground, marked on one side by barren soils and on the other by damp grass, signalled the end of his own Argia lands and the beginning of those of the Harri—people of earth. *How curious,* he thought as he bent down to touch it. The earth beneath the blades of well-nourished grass was also damp. Perfect for crop-growing and tending livestock—*and wild animals would have plenty to eat, too.* Caspar took a deep breath and crossed, waiting for some sensation or warning that he should turn back now while he still had the chance, but none came. There was no sign of an attack, no strange mists, no tingling in his shoulders. Other than a refreshing shade from the sun, Caspar felt no difference between the two lands. He let out a soft smirk. *Only bedtime stories, then,* he realized as he remembered his father's warnings.

Caspar pulled out his knife and began etching X's into the trees in case he were to get lost and needed something to guide him home. The deeper into the forest he wandered, the more the grass gave way to mud, and the darker the world around him became. The dense canopy above protected the ground below from the sun. Now and again, patches of sunlight shone onto vibrant green grasses, but mostly the ground was filled with strange bulbous plants and the occasional rotting tree trunk. *Just my luck,* he thought as he marked another tree. Caspar was well out of his realm of knowledge in these woods. Some bushes appeared up ahead, filled with large, brightly coloured fruits. He knew better than to pick without knowing, so he scanned the floor for traces that other creatures had been foraging too—discarded seed pods, half-eaten fruits, even the animals themselves would've been a big help—but he found nothing. *Best leave it be.*

Under the darkened canopy, it was hard to tell the time of day. Caspar felt like he'd been walking for hours and knew he should be heading back, but it irked him to do so empty-handed. He dropped onto his hands and knees, scanning the grounds for signs of life. He imagined tracking an animal in the forest was like tracking one in the desert. No matter the terrain, all creatures leave tracks. But, aside from his own heavy footprints, these grounds seemed untouched. Caspar was beginning to wonder if the forest was really inhabited at all, when a large *thud* sent a cacophony of feathers fluttering into the skies.

He prickled.

Another *thud*. And another…

It sounded like the falling rocks in the canyons, but Caspar couldn't imagine where such a noise could be coming from.

Another *thud*.

Caspar crawled through the bushes, keeping as close as possible to the ground, in search of the source of the noise. He hoped it was an animal. Something *that* big would surely keep them fed and might even put money in their pockets. He could even spend time caring for his father's illness rather than going on these hunts. Caspar stood up behind a tree, pulled an arrow from the quiver and nocked it into his bow.

At the sound of the next *thud*, he fired, the arrow finding its home in something most definitely alive, but *not* a creature—or one he could eat. It dropped to the floor with a soft crash and wailed, sending more birds into the skies, before it called out with a teary voice, "Who's there?" It was a woman's voice.

Casper had no clue what to do. He turned back to his stream of Xs, knowing that the only person he might encounter in these woods was a Harri, and that, if he did, he would be in trouble. The ground beneath him trembled.

"Show yourself, you coward!" She continued with more grit. He heard the *snap* of his arrow and the soft clatter it made as it hit the floor. Caspar contemplated her request, hearing his father's chastising voice even as he stepped out of the shadows. At first glance, she looked like a wild creature. Her dark hair was tangled and full of leaves. Her eyes were rimmed with smudged black kohl, her legs, strong and sturdy between the slits of her long green tunic that had muddied at its hem. "At whom do you think you are blindly firing—" She stopped suddenly as if the sight of him set her on edge. She clenched her bloodied arm and growled at him ferociously. "Argia. Stay away from me!"

"I'm sorry," Caspar began, looking around the young woman for the source of the noise. "I thought you were an animal."

"Whatever would've given you that idea?" she hissed, tears framing the side of her face, though she refused to let her strength waver. Judging by the state she was in and the terrified look in her eyes, Caspar thought his assumptions were not too far off, but he knew better than to make the comment.

"I heard loud sounds… too loud to be coming from someone your size. Let me help…" Caspar stepped towards her, but her good hand flew up automatically in defence.

"I said stay away from me!" Stones lifted from the ground and flew towards him violently. He dodged just in time to avoid a large one aimed at his head.

Caspar's jaw dropped. He'd never seen anything like it before. The woman had raised the earth with nothing more than a twitch of her fingers. "You're *kanala*," he called back in disbelief, his own fear causing him to raise his bow again. The *kanala*, or so his father had told him, were the few people in this world blessed with control over the elements. Their legends said that the great spirit of the land, *Iturri*, poured itself into a select few at birth, allowing them to manipulate the element of their homeland. Caspar had only ever seen the Argia *kanala*, the ones of his land who wielded fire. Their powers usually required a fire to be already present, which made him more cautious of the strange, earth-wielding girl, as she was at no loss for prime material. "Don't hurt me…" he gulped, nocking another arrow into place.

"Me? Hurt you?" the girl replied in disbelief. "You're the one going around, shooting blindly at whatever creature has the misfortune of taking a breath in your vicinity." She tried again to sweep up a wave of pebbles, but her good hand shook. She began to sway on her feet, and Caspar realized the blood had begun to pool beneath her.

"You're losing a lot of blood," Caspar remarked, replacing his arrow, and lowering his defence. "What were you doing out here all alone?"

"I'm fine…" she tried to growl, but the sound faded as her voice trailed. "You shouldn't be here."

"Neither should you…" Caspar took a tentative step towards her, but she retreated. Her damaged arm trembled as tears pooled in her vibrant green eyes.

"I'm warning you. Stay away…"

Caspar stared at the trail of blood streaming from the gash he'd left in her arm. She was Harri. Worse still, she was *kanala*. He shouldn't feel sorry for her. How many times had his father told him they were heartless creatures? How many times had he warned Caspar not to stray from the desert? But this girl, though tattered in dress and prickly in person, didn't look as evil as his village had painted her people out to be. On the contrary, she looked more afraid of him, especially masked and holding his bow and arrow. Caspar rested the bow gently on the ground and replaced the arrow into his quiver before taking another cautious step towards her.

"I'm not going to hurt you," he said as he removed the cloth he used to cover his nose and mouth from the harsh desert sands. The next step he took closed the distance between them. Up close, Caspar caught a whiff of the iron-tinged scent of blood, and just beneath it, the scent of lavender. She might have looked a mess, but Caspar now doubted his initial judgement. She was no savage creature of the forest. She came from a somewhere. She was a someone. He made sure to move slowly as he reached over to wrap her arm.

The girl stared incredulously at the cloth. "What are you doing?" she scoffed as she recoiled from his outstretched hand.

"Helping you."

"Why? We aren't friends. Why not just finish me off? I'm *kanala*, remember? Big, bad, scary Harri *kanala* who will attack when provoked and kill you without a second thought… Isn't that what your kind says?"

"Yes," he admitted bluntly. "But you're also a person, and you're bleeding out."

She frowned at the cloth; heavy black brows furrowed over the most vibrant green eyes Caspar had ever seen. They glowed the colour of sun-hit leaves, startlingly different from his own and those of his people.

"It's dirty," she grumbled.

"So are you."

"How dare…" She stared woozily down at her tunic. Whatever she was about to say remained on the tip of her tongue. With a bite of her lip, she relented, shifting nearer to him, and offering her trembling, bloodied arm.

The arrow had only skimmed her arm, but the gash it left was enough to send a waterfall of blood down to her wrists. Thankfully, he'd missed the bone. Caspar wrapped the cloth around her with care. She winced as he pulled it taut and shifted away from him, but Caspar held her firm. "It's got to be tight if you want it to work."

"You didn't need to help," she said as she cleaned the rest of the blood on the draping part of her tunic, leaving a large red patch that would surely stain the green fibres brown permanently.

"I'm not a monster."

"I'm hardly sure of that," she growled with a pointed glance at her blood smear.

"What were you even doing out here anyway?" Caspar asked as he gazed around at the empty forest. "You must be miles away from any kind of civilization…"

"Don't say it too loudly, they might hear you," she said, suddenly changing her tune. She took an unsteady turn around their small clearing. "I was practising," she added bitterly. "But I doubt I'm going to be able to lift anything bigger than a pebble for a while." She slumped down, resting her back on one of the sturdy tree trunks.

"I'm sorry…" Caspar mumbled. His father would've considered it a triumph to have downed a kanala—especially a *Harri* kanala—but Caspar doubted whether his father had ever met a Harri before. This woman—bitter as she was—didn't seem like the life-sucking, sub-human creature that his father and the rest of the village had made them seem. She actually seemed *normal.* "Why weren't you practising closer to home?"

Her eyelids fluttered closed. "Not that it's any of your business, Argia, but people like me aren't allowed to practice."

"Kanala?"

"Women."

"Oh…" He blushed. "I didn't—what are you doing?" he asked, noticing her droop.

"Resting…" she replied finally, letting the tension in her body fade into the tree.

A soft dip in temperature told Caspar it was time to leave. He would return empty-handed and probably have to explain where all the blood came from, but it could've been worse. *He* could've been the one injured. He hoped the vendor's market would still be open to trade in one of his knives for bread, at least, that way they would have something to eat.

Caspar was about to leave when he turned to her again, half slumped against the tree and breathing heavily. If he left her here, she'd soon faint from loss of blood, and then she'd fall prey to whatever beasts truly hid in this wood. Caspar looked around for other signs of humanity, but he imagined they were the only two around for miles. His lips curved into a sorry frown as he contemplated her again. Anyone else from his village would've left her—anyone else from his village wouldn't have come this far, to begin with. But Caspar had never been like his people.

If you enjoyed this book, please feel free to leave a review of it on your favourite sites. These reviews help small-time authors like me reach new audiences and are much appreciated!

Stay up to date on L. M. Sanguinette's new releases and giveaways by signing up for her mailing list or following her on social media. Find all the links on the page below:

https://linktr.ee/lmsanguinette

Be on the lookout for more books from the wonderful world of Visanthe, coming soon!

ACKNOWLEDGMENTS

This is going to be a bit of a teary-eyed sob story, isn't it…
So much has changed in my life since sitting down to write
the first book. Back then, I didn't even believe it was possible
for me to churn out something that would reach the hands
(and hearts) of so many of you. Back then, I was just a little
girl with big dreams and social anxiety (cured, thankfully).
The person who started out on this author journey way back
in 2015 (yes, that's when Visanthe was born) would never
have imagined everything that this journey has become and
what more there is still left to live. She went from taking
seven years to write her first book (with lots of extended
pauses in between) to being able to see a book through to the
end in only a few months. 80,000 words who? Now, as the
author of a completed series (something which I am stoked
to officially say), I know this is only the beginning.

As always, the first person I have to thank in this long list
of acknowledgements is my phenomenal editor and friend,
Cara Flannery. Without you, none of this would have been
possible. You believed in my storytelling abilities even and
especially when I didn't believe in them myself. You are my
hero, my rock, and my absolute champion. Thank you!

Secondly, I'd like to acknowledge the extraordinary work
done on both the hardcover and paperback editions by the
brilliant cover artists at MiblArt. I swear they are witches—
in the best possible way. Every time I see these covers a smile
grows on my face, knowing not only that the ideas in my head
were given life, but that others around the world enjoy them

as much as I do, if not more. I'd also like to thank my incredible cartographer for the wonderful depiction of Visanthe.

Next, I have to thank the girls in my Bookstagram who are always in my corner and pushing me to hone my craft. You girls probably believe in me more than I believe in myself, which is incredible. I got to meet so many of you in real life at various events around the world, and I'm hoping such things will only continue in the future! Thank you for keeping my motivation alive by loving these stories as much as I do (and occasionally reminding me that I need to get off my gremlin butt and keep writing them).

On a different note, I'd like to thank the person that resides in my heart but whom I have yet to meet. This person, this idea of a soulmate brought this final book—and the series itself—to life. Some of the relationships in the series ended up taking inspiration from my ideas of this connection between souls that cannot be broken, no matter the time or distance between them. This true love, this ultimate love, is one that invaded both my mind and my heart while writing this book, and without which, this book would probably not exist—or at least not for another few years, and certainly not in the way it manifested. I am forever grateful for this feeling in my heart. And if this person does exists and ever reads this, know I am grateful for you and love you very much, my sun, moon, and sky full of stars.

Finally, I would be nothing without the love and support of my family. This first thank you goes out to my parents, for letting me be the quirky little witch with too many fairy tales in her head, and for pushing me to be the best version of myself in whatever I choose to do. Thank you for always supporting my passions, even when you didn't understand them. And, of course, thank you to my siblings, for reminding me not to take life so seriously, and for being the reason I want to do better, I love you guys.

OTHER WORKS

Also available in hardcover!

POETRY COLLECTIONS

COMING SOON...

Of Arrows And Roses (A Visanthian Novel)

ABOUT THE AUTHOR

L. M. Sanguinette was born on a small island in the Caribbean, where the palm trees watched over her like giants and the sea crept up to her feet to say hello. Ever since she was little, she surrounded herself with tales of fantasy and magic, hoping that one day, she too would be involved in a story like the ones that captured her imagination.

Years—and many rewatching's of Avatar the Last Airbender—later, she is happily living in the worlds that her mind created, filling her bookshelves with more books than she will ever read, and practising her own version of magic.

When she's not sitting at the computer, she can be found snorkelling near forgotten shores, twisting from silks that hang from the ceilings, or in one of the many hidden coffee shops of Madrid, conversing with the spirits of the old city and dreaming up new adventures.